MRS. Claus
and ThE HalloWEEn
HomiciDE

Books by Liz Ireland

MRS. CLAUS AND THE SANTALAND SLAYINGS
MRS. CLAUS AND THE HALLOWEEN HOMICIDE

Published by Kensington Publishing Corp.

Mrs. Claus and The Halloween Homicide

Liz Ireland

KENSINGTON
PUBLISHING CORP.

www.kensingtonbooks.com

KENSINGTON BOOKS are published by

Kensington Publishing Corp.
119 West 40th Street
New York, NY 10018

ISBN-13: 978-1-4967-2663-6 (ebook)
ISBN-10: 1-4967-2663-4 (ebook)

ISBN-13: 978-1-4967-2661-2
ISBN-10: 1-4967-2661-8

First Kensington Trade Paperback Printing: October 2021

10 9 8 7 6 5 4 3 2 1

Printed in the United States of America

Mrs. Claus and The Halloween Homicide

Chapter 1

"It was a slaughter," Salty said.

He's not wrong, I thought as I surveyed the ruins inside the greenhouse. He'd warned me what to expect during his emergency phone call summoning me, but a slaughter of pumpkins proved more upsetting than I'd prepared myself for. And by "a slaughter of pumpkins" I don't mean a vegetable term of venery like "a murder of crows" or a "flamboyance of flamingoes." This was literal violence against a greenhouse full of gourds that had been carefully planted and tended by Salty, the elf who was Castle Kringle's head gardener and groundskeeper.

I picked my way across broken glass at the threshold of Salty's greenhouse, horrified by the carnage. Jagged chunks of pumpkin flesh and streams of seedy entrails were strewn across the thermally heated soil. Despite the blissful warmth inside the place, I shivered. I think I knew even then that this vandalism augured worse to come.

My husband, Nick—aka Santa Claus—put his gloved hand on my arm. The set of his bearded jaw told me the sight disturbed him, as well. He was dressed in his everyday red wool suit with black belt and accessories, but he'd taken off his hat inside the greenhouse. This was probably out of habit, but his solemn expression made it appear he'd doffed it out of respect for the pumpkins.

Pumpkins were a novelty in Santaland. Most of these had been earmarked for use during Christmastown's upcoming first-ever Halloween festivities, but Salty had also been conducting tours. He'd installed a rustic *Salty's Pumpkin Patch* sign above the entrance and rigged up a sleigh to resemble an old-timey hay wagon to bring young elves up Sugarplum Mountain to visit the greenhouse. Procuring enough hay bales in the North Pole for this display had been an accomplishment in itself.

"Look at that." Salty pointed to a corner where a scarecrow with a pumpkin head had been decapitated. The top of its head had been crushed so that only the crooked rictus grin was left. The groundskeeper buried his fists in the oversized pockets of his quilted tunic overalls. "It was like this when I arrived this morning."

I couldn't help feeling a little responsible for the elf's heartbreak, since I'd set him on this pumpkin path. Back in the spring, I'd mentioned to him that it would be fun to have a pumpkin patch at Halloween. It had been pie-in-the-sky musing more than an actual suggestion, but resourceful Salty had taken the idea and run with it, digging into the project with his small hands and big heart. Over the summer he'd repurposed a greenhouse previously devoted to the raising of turnips. *"Nobody likes turnips anyhow,"* he'd rationalized, and who could argue? By the time Nick and I returned from our four-month respite in Cloudberry Bay, Oregon, where I run the Coast Inn during the summer months, Salty's pumpkin wonderland was already flourishing, the ground covered with extravagant vines and young pumpkins of all colors and sizes.

Now, a month later, someone had decimated his crop.

"Who would do such a thing?" Nick asked.

"I don't know," Salty said. "Hopefully Constable Crinkles'll be able to get to the bottom of this."

I wheeled toward him. "You've contacted the constable?"

"Sent for him before I sent for you." He stubbed his pointy-toed boot against a broken orange shell. "A crime's been committed. I want the evildoer to pay!"

I couldn't argue with the sentiment, although I questioned Constable Crinkles's ability to get to the bottom of anything besides a custard pie. Better not disparage local law enforcement out loud, however. I was still a relative newcomer to the North Pole, and while a year ago I'd solved a murder before Constable Crinkles had even managed to work up a decent list of suspects, I had to admit that finding criminals was not in my job description.

Then again, Mrs. Claus wasn't supposed to concern herself with Halloween celebrations, either. Halloween had never been celebrated in Santaland. Last year, the first year after I'd married and moved here from Oregon, I put up a few decorations and handed out some treats to the young elves in Christmastown. I told them about the night when children in other parts of the world dressed up in scary costumes and took to the streets trick-or-treating.

No matter what corner of the universe you find yourself in, a holiday in which kids extort candy from adults will be popular with the grammar-school set. Elf children—abetted, I suspected, by my friend Juniper, one of Christmastown's librarians—drew up a petition to bring the celebration to Christmastown and delivered it to the castle. After some wheedling on my part, Nick, who is acting as Santa until Christopher, his twelve-year-old nephew, comes of age, agreed that the night of October 31 could be given over to non-Christmas festivities.

I'd brought Halloween to Santaland, which evidently had caused someone to snap and vandalize Salty's pumpkin patch.

"Thank goodness I culled some of the nicer Connecticut Field variety," Salty said. "We'll have enough big ones for jack-o'-lanterns, but look what they did to the rest of them." As he walked among his battered plants, his voice grew more distressed. "They practically wiped out my Queensland Blues and the Long Island Cheeses."

"Your what?"

"Long Island Cheese," he repeated. "That's what the paler ones are." His brow pinched as he stared at me. "I thought you Southerners knew all about pumpkins."

A *Southerner* to a Santalander was anyone who lived below the Arctic Circle. Apparently, everyone south of the sixty-fifth parallel is supposed to be a pumpkin expert.

"I mostly know how to carve them up as decorations," I admitted. "And cook them once they've been canned. I never knew there were a lot of different varieties."

"Golly doodle—there are dozens. Just looking through the seed catalog made my head spin." His eyes filled with pleasure at the memory.

The sound of approaching motors interrupted our discussion—but only temporarily. The moment Constable Crinkles and his nephew-deputy, Ollie, pushed through the door of the greenhouse, they were agog at the sight of all the pumpkins.

Like a threatened puffer fish, Constable Crinkles inflated in surprise—and he was fairly round already. The brass buttons of his blue wool coat had a hard job of restraining his belly, and the chin strap of his old-fashioned policeman's hat dug into his multiple chins. "I'd heard about these pumpkin doojabbers, but I haven't had time to see for myself." He bent over and squinted distrustfully at a large orange one as if it were an alien life-form.

Ollie, a pencil-thin shadow of his uncle, looked equally perplexed. "I only ever saw one in a can before."

It was natural. Elves didn't travel widely, and the North Pole wasn't conducive to growing a wide variety of vegetables. Castle Kringle's greenhouses provided much of the produce, as did little garden greenhouses around the country, but most were dedicated to foods that were staples at elf tables. Pumpkin pie filling had always been imported from the South.

Crinkles frowned as he peered around the glass-walled building. "Say . . . isn't this the turnip house?"

Salty nodded. "Used to be."

The lawman gulped in panic. "What're we going to do for turnips? They're my favorite vegetable."

Salty and I exchanged looks.

"The problem here isn't a potential turnip shortfall," I told Crinkles. "It's that someone vandalized Salty's greenhouse."

The lawman scratched his head. "But this place is right on the castle grounds. Who would do such a thing?"

"Somebody who doesn't like pumpkins, maybe," Ollie piped up. "Or somebody who likes turnips." He laughed. "Hey, maybe it was you, Unc!"

Crinkles swatted his nephew and then turned to Salty. "Are you sure there wasn't some animal that got in?"

Salty sputtered in disbelief. "What kind of animal can crush a pumpkin like that?"

"Neldor!" Ollie's eyes went wide.

"Who?" I asked.

The young elf mirrored my own bafflement. "You've never heard of Neldor?"

Crinkles rolled his eyes. "Never mind. My nitwit nephew is spouting nonsense—some children's story about a diabolical reindeer. It's a myth." He looked at the pumpkins again. "You really like these things better than turnips?"

Salty cleared his throat, impatient to find whoever had committed the depredations against his pumpkins. "Whoever broke in must've used some kind of club, or an ax."

"Lots of elves have axes," Crinkles said. "People, too. Seen anybody lurking about?"

Salty shook his head.

The constable puffed out his cheeks, clearly flummoxed as to what steps he should take next.

Ollie lifted a chunk of pumpkin off the ground and gave it a sniff. "Phew, these things have a weird smell. Not like a pumpkin pie."

Salty's irritation with the lawmen began to show. "Whoever did this needs to pay," he insisted.

"Sure," Crinkles agreed. "But how do we find them?"

"Footprints, maybe?" I suggested. With Crinkles, it never hurt to point out the obvious. It might be autumn in the rest of the world, but in this land of perpetual snowfall, no one could go anywhere without leaving footprints.

The constable snapped his fingers. "Good thinking."

We all tramped back outside into the cold. I pulled my parka around me and rewound my long wool scarf around my neck, while the elves and Nick barely had to make any adjustments at all.

The trouble with Salty's having conducted tours was that there were sleigh tracks and little boot prints all around. It had been a few days since the last snow.

"Here are some footprints all by themselves!" Ollie shouted.

"By gum, you're right!" Crinkles was practically hopping in excitement.

Nick and I exchanged glances. *Who's going to tell them?*

"I believe those are your and Ollie's footprints, Constable," I pointed out. "You'll notice they lead to your snowmobiles."

"Oh." Crinkles deflated. "That's right. They do."

We finally spotted one set of prints that didn't seem to have come from a tour sleigh. These prints were isolated from the others and appeared to have been made by narrow elf street booties, not the more solid kind worn by the grounds-keepers around the castle. One print was in thick powdery snow and bore a clear maker's mark.

I leaned close and read the letters of the brand aloud. "SB."

"The mark of Sparkletoe's Bootery," Ollie told me. "There are only two places elves buy booties in town—Sparkletoe's Bootery and Walnut's Bootie World."

"Craftsmanship's better at Sparkletoe's," Crinkles said.

"Walnut's Bootie World provides good value, though." Ollie lifted his curly-toed black leather boot to show his uncle. "I got these there."

"Leather looks cheap to me," Crinkles said dismissively.

"Yeah, but they were half the price of a pair at Sparkletoe's."

Unbelievable. They were bickering over shoe stores when there was a criminal at large. "Could we leave the comparison shopping for later?" I said.

Crinkles looked abashed at having gotten so distracted. "The point is, the print at least narrows our suspects down to one of Tiny Sparkletoe's customers."

I tried not to show how the name Tiny Sparkletoe affected me.

"I can't believe another elf would do this," Salty said in disgust. "A grown elf, too, by the size of that print. Why would anyone want to ruin the pumpkin patch? They know it's part of Halloween, and everybody's looking forward to that."

Not true. Not everyone was looking forward to this new holiday. Just days before, I'd had words with none other than the same Tiny Sparkletoe who owned Sparkletoe's Bootery, and who was president of the Christmastown Community Guild. He'd made his displeasure with the upcoming festivities abundantly clear.

"It's going to create all sorts of problems for Christmastown," he'd told me. "There will be noise, and decorations that aren't Christmassy, and trash to pick up."

These seemed ridiculous objections to me, but this had been a one-holiday town for hundreds of years. Change was bound to rattle a few elves and people. Still, I wanted to talk to Tiny Sparkletoe myself before pointing fingers. The evidence so far was thin, and Tiny was a force to be reckoned with in Christmastown. Also, trashing a pumpkin patch didn't seem like something an upstanding business elf would do.

Crinkles tilted his head. "Thought of something, Mrs. Claus?"

Nick was eyeing me intently, too.

"Only that I should probably get back to the castle," I said.

Salty appeared wounded that I was abandoning the cause so quickly, but Nick stepped in to reassure him. "We'll get to the bottom of this, Salty. In the meantime, I think you'll find that the damage looks worse than it truly is. I counted hundreds of pumpkins unharmed." He put a hand on the elf's shoulder. "You did a magnificent job growing them. I'll ask Jingles if he can spare a few castle elves to help you clean up."

Jingles was the castle steward, who was in charge of most of the workers there.

Salty looked slightly less upset than he had when we arrived. "Thank you, Santa."

The minute we were on his sleigh and heading back to the castle, out of view of the elves, Nick turned to me. "What are you planning?"

"Nothing."

He laughed. "You can't fool Santa Claus."

"I think it's Mother Nature you can't fool."

"Well, I can't answer for her. But I do know that you're Mrs. Claus, not Nancy Drew. You don't have to solve the Mystery of the Pummeled Pumpkins."

I trained my gaze away from him. It *was* hard to keep secrets from Nick, and not just because he was Santa Claus—that all-seeing business was a myth. But he had penetrating dark eyes to go with his dark hair and beard; it was the eyes that always did me in.

"I know I don't have to solve anything." Just because I didn't have to didn't mean I couldn't, though.

He was giving me a suspicious side-eye and seemed on the verge of asking me more when sleigh bells sounded ahead. Coming at us from the opposite direction, my sister-in-law, Lucia, statuesque and blond, perched at the reins of her peculiar sleigh looking like a figurehead at the prow of a ship. Her sleigh had a special spot in the back for Quasar, her reindeer companion. It was the only sleigh in Santaland that was pulled by reindeer and also carried reindeer. I waved and Lucia slowed before we could pass. Nick asked his reindeer team to stop.

"Are you going into town?" I called to Lucia.

"I'm headed to Tinkertown," she said.

Tinkertown was the village where the elves lived who worked in the many factories that kept Christmas going—the Wrapping Works, the Candy Cane Factory, Santa's Workshop, to name a few. Getting there required driving several miles and crossing a strip of the Christmas Tree Forest—but from the castle that journey led through Christmastown, which was where I needed to go.

"Would you mind dropping me off at the library?"

Nick eyed me suspiciously. "Thought you needed to go back to the castle."

"I just remembered I'm supposed to have coffee with Juniper. I said I'd meet her at the library."

"Sure," Lucia said. "Hop in."

This was a bit of luck. A year into my life in Santaland and I still didn't have a vehicle. Nick wanted to buy me some-

thing of my own to get around in, but I couldn't decide what
I wanted. Snowmobiles were fast and handy, but they lacked
the style that old-fashioned sleighs had. Then again, those traditional sleighs were dependent on reindeer to pull them, and
I had mixed feelings about that. It wasn't like having a horse-
drawn carriage. Reindeer could talk back to you, which could
be unnerving if you weren't used to it. And then there was the
whole flying thing. One wrong command and it was bye-bye,
biosphere; hello, stars.

"You don't mind my abandoning you, do you?" I asked
Nick.

"No, it's all right. I have work to do."

Nick was something of a workaholic, and in the months
leading up to Christmas, a Santa's work was never done. That's
why it had been so gratifying to have him with me when we
visited Oregon this past summer. He'd had a real rest. The
Coast Inn was near the beach, and Nick was able to sun and
swim every day. I'd never seen him look so relaxed—no running Santaland to worry about, no elf disputes to mediate, no
Dear Santa letters to answer. He'd gotten used to leisure and
had even become addicted to a game he'd bought before the
trip. A little too addicted, frankly.

I shot him a look. "Really? Not sneaking off to play Elfcraft?"

He laughed. "No, I reached the second glacier shield. I'm
good for now."

"I have no idea what that means."

"It means I'm up to my ears doing a last pre-holiday in-
ventory before the final push in manufacturing begins next
month. No more time for games."

Starting in November, Santa's workshops would be going
full tilt.

I gave him a quick peck and hopped off, then reached into

the back of the sleigh and took out a lap robe. I was always cold, but Lucia, born and bred at the North Pole, never bothered with niceties like blankets. Half the time, like today, she didn't even bother with a hat or gloves. I'd never seen her so much as shiver. It was freakish.

I climbed up, wrapping the blanket around me serape-style, and thanked her for stopping. Quasar stood behind us in the sleigh, but his antlered head poked between us, his nose glowing in greeting. He had Rudolph blood in him, but his nose wasn't always dependable. It tended to fizzle. He was a misfit, but he was my sister-in-law's constant companion.

Lucia urged the reindeer team forward. "Jingles said you were called away on an emergency. What's going on?"

Jingles made it his business to know the comings and goings of everyone, but Nick and I had dashed over to the greenhouse without telling anyone why. Salty hadn't been too coherent over the phone.

"Someone broke into Salty's greenhouse and trashed it."

Lucia pivoted toward me in shock. "That's terrible!"

"The one with the p-pumpkins?" Quasar asked.

"Unfortunately."

"If you ask me, this Halloween business is a lot of nonsense," Lucia said. "Now it's encouraging people to vandalize property."

"Halloween isn't about property destruction."

"We *never* had an incident like this before now," she said.

For Pete's sake. "Last year Christmastown had two murders. This was only pumpkins." Thank goodness Salty couldn't hear me say that.

Her brow pinched. "I hope the culprits weren't Christopher and his friends. I know I encouraged his mom to get him that sled and dog team, but he and those friends of his are too rambunctious for their own good."

Christopher, Nick and Lucia's nephew, was twelve now but would become the rightful Santa when he reached twenty-one years of age. Nick was already looking forward to the day when he could pass on the suit and sleigh to his young relative and retire. Christopher might be high-spirited, but his heart was in the right place. He and his friends wouldn't have destroyed Salty's greenhouse. The scant evidence didn't point to them, either.

"It was an adult elf, we think," I said. "The footprints around the greenhouse were from elf booties, with a maker's mark from Sparkletoe's Bootery."

She grunted. "That doesn't narrow your search down much."

"It's not *my* search. I'm not investigating."

"Sure you're not," she said.

We drove on down the mountain, which was pure Currier and Ives winter beauty, even though it was still October. Light snow flurries dotted the air. At the mountain's base, we reached the outskirts of the village of Christmastown, where neat cottages lined the streets and cheery lights wound up the decorative lamps and were strung across the streets and boulevards. Darkness stretched ever longer, the closer toward winter we crept, but Christmastown was so well lit that the shortening daylight hours never felt oppressive.

The reindeer pulled up in front of the library, a solid two-story edifice built from gray stone that would have appeared solemn except for the fanciful details the designer had included: columns that had been chiseled to resemble candy canes, gargoyles reading books at the cornices, and an arch over the large door carved with elven legends. The facade was a masterpiece of architectural whimsy. The building was situated by itself in the center of a large flagstone plaza.

Lucia looked over at me, her face tense with worry. "The last time you started investigating, the whole town was turned upside down and inside out. I'd like to know if we should gird our loins for more chaos."

"It was just pumpkins," I assured her. "Nothing to get alarmed about."

I climbed down and went inside the library. Like all elf buildings and houses, the scale was smaller than what I was used to. I stooped automatically, like Gandalf walking into a hobbit house. Juniper sat on a high stool behind the front checkout desk. She was an exceptionally pretty elf, if a little less plump than ideal. Her brown hair was half hidden by a jaunty green elf cap that matched both her eyes and her tunic.

Her normally smiling face collapsed in a mask of concern when she saw me. "Oh, April, I'm so sorry."

"About what?" Alarm spiked through me. Before I'd left on vacation this summer, I'd forgotten to return a library book. It was amazing that my mere presence didn't trip off some kind of bad-borrower alarm.

"I heard about the pumpkin patch," she said.

I exhaled. At least she wasn't going to shred my library card. "How?" News traveled fast.

"Salty's cousin cuts hair at Four Gals A-Trimming down the street."

Elves phoned, texted, and gossiped as never-endingly as people did, if not more so. Santaland might be cold enough to turn any normal warm-blooded creature into a popsicle, but it was a hotbed of gossip.

"It was just pumpkins." If I repeated it enough, I might even convince myself.

"Maybe . . . or maybe not." Juniper cast a furtive glance around the library and lowered her voice. "Someone sent us a message on the library's Elfbook page."

"What kind of message?"

Her gaze made another scan of the room. Whatever was in this message, she clearly didn't want to talk about it here.

3 Liz Ireland

I'd been lying to Lucia earlier about meeting Juniper for coffee, but maybe a chin wag at the coffee shop was called for. From Juniper's expression, the pumpkin patch damage might be the tip of the crime iceberg.

"Do you have time for a break?" I asked.

Her head bobbed. "Meet you at We Three Beans in ten."

Chapter 2

We Three Beans coffee shop occupied the lower level of a half-timbered building that stood flush against the sidewalk of Christmastown's main thoroughfare, Festival Boulevard. Even in a city abounding in cafés, teahouses, and taverns, We Three Beans was a social hub. Like many elf establishments, it kept a toasty fire burning in its hearth and had music piping out of corner speakers every minute the doors were open. When I walked in, half the patrons were treating the morning regulars to a full-throated version of "Jolly Old Saint Nicholas."

Christmas carols. They weren't just for Christmas anymore. Not in my world, at least.

"Hi, April." Trumpet, the owner and barista in chief, greeted me with a crooked grin. "I was hoping you'd show up. I've invented something special for you—a Halloween latte. It's got pumpkin spice!"

I couldn't bring myself to tell him that the world had beaten him to that particular craze by a couple of decades, so I smiled and ordered a large. When he'd first gotten wind of the Halloween plans, Toggle Hollywell, the wily elf who ran the town's biggest supermarket, had mixed up a shed load of pumpkin pie spice. Now it was showing up in everything.

In other words, it seemed just like home.

A few minutes later, Trumpet pushed a steaming mug across the counter toward me. A free table next to the fireplace opened up and I laid claim to it. Settling down, I sipped my latte—and kept my eye on the door.

Killing time, I took out my phone and checked my messages and Facebook. When I left Cloudberry Bay a month before, my best friend there, Claire, had volunteered to look in on the closed-up Coast Inn for me from time to time. I hadn't heard from her in a while. I worried that something was wrong and tapped out a quick direct message to say hello. Then I decided to check out the *Cloudberry Bay Weekly Chronicle*. The news was about what you'd expect for this time of year. Stores were closing up after the tourist season, a corn maze had opened outside town, and my neighbor and nemesis, Damaris Sproat, was in a swivet over her fellow citizens' laxity in sweeping pinecones and other debris from sidewalks.

I scrolled to the editorial page and saw that Damaris was featured there, too. She was the town busybody, so it wasn't surprising that she was all over the paper. Also, a cousin of hers owned the *Weekly Chronicle*. But the title of this piece caught my eye.

Fair-weather Foreigners Changing Our Town Character
While it's natural that foreign tourists would be drawn to Cloudberry Bay's many attractions, such as our main street shops, cloudberry cuisine, and the unique rock formations, local homeowners should hesitate to sell out to any beach bum who spends a few weeks here. Sometimes, of course, a foreigner will marry into ownership of a heritage building, and that's a shame, too. Homeowners who lack the deep roots that some of us as old-timers possess don't see the danger of losing what makes our town special. Without historical memory, the nature of Cloudberry Bay will change . . .

My face was on fire, and it had nothing to do with the blaze in the nearby hearth. Damaris was talking about me! And she was referring to Nick as a beach bum? I was so incensed, I almost tapped out an angry response on my tiny screen. Then I stopped and went back to my texts and fired off another message to Claire.

Can you believe this???

I attached a link to the editorial. Damaris had disliked me ever since I'd bought her uncle's house six years earlier, but I didn't think she'd stoop to insulting my husband in the paper.

The bell above the door tinkled, and Juniper breezed through. I waved, but my accompanying smile froze in place as Chip Pepperbough tagged along after her. The town optician, Chip was also one of the most attentive suitors the world had ever known. After some bad boyfriend heartaches and headaches, Juniper deserved happiness, and I'd been almost as glad as she was when she wrote me over the summer to tell me she and Chip were an item.

I felt less thrilled now, though I tried not to show it. There was no profit in alienating a friend because you didn't like her significant other. Especially when I couldn't find a way to voice why I didn't like Chip that wouldn't sound churlish. *Sorry, he's overly affectionate and too devoted to you*, wasn't a phrase that would make a person think twice about a current love interest.

And who was I to stand in the way of true, albeit slightly nauseating and clingy, love?

"What are we having?" Chip asked after they'd greeted me.

"I'd like an eggnog latte," Juniper said.

Chip's face broke into an expression of unnecessary ecstasy. "That sounds fantastic! You sit down, sweet cheeks, and I'll get one for both of us."

After he'd gone, I couldn't help arching a brow at my friend.

A blush rose in her cheeks. "He likes to come up with cute names for me."

"I've noticed." I tried to tamp down my cynical side, though, and accept that some people in love were gushier than others. "What's this message you mentioned?"

She reached into her purse and brought out her phone. "Something troubling appeared on the library's Elfbook page last night. We deleted it almost immediately, but I grabbed a screenshot of it."

She angled the phone my way so I could see the copy of the message that had been pasted on Santaland's equivalent of Facebook. In tall red and green letters, someone had posted: STOP HALLOWEEN IN CHRISTMASTOWN OR ELSE!!!

That was the entire message. Then the poster's name caught my eye: Pumpkin Slayer. The thumbnail avatar next to the name, instead of a photograph of an elf, was the image of an orange scythe. I stared at the message again. This had to be the same nut who'd attacked Salty's greenhouse.

Incredibly, I heard myself asking, "Have you shown this to Constable Crinkles?"

"It's probably just some crank," Juniper said. "We're not paying it any mind at the library, but after what happened this morning I thought you should know. I was about to email it to you."

"I'd like a copy."

Juniper had a loyalty to Halloween, a holiday she'd never experienced, because bringing it to Christmastown had been my idea. But now that I'd seen Pumpkin Slayer's message, I felt it only fair to warn her, "I was at the greenhouse this morning. That attack on the pumpkins seemed violent. Whoever did it has escalated from written threats."

"If it's the same elf."

"I refuse to believe there could be two psychotic pumpkin haters in Christmastown."

She didn't argue. "They wouldn't attack the library, though."

The words were spoken with such certainty. Despite the events of the previous December—which had proved deadly for two citizens—most of the inhabitants of Santaland retained their innocence when it came to believing the best in their fellow elves and people. I hated to see that change, but I also didn't want harm to come to anyone. Especially not Juniper. "Who would have thought someone would attack a greenhouse?" I pointed out. "You need to be careful."

Chip returned, bearing two mugs and a peppermint scone for Juniper to nibble on during her lunch break. The eggnog lattes baffled me. It was deeply un-Clausian of me, but I couldn't understand my adopted country's mania for eggnog.

"Careful of what?" He scooted his chair close to Juniper's. "A snuggle bug attack?"

He goosed Juniper, and the two of them dissolved into playful whoops. I couldn't tell if all elves in love were this goofy or if this level of nauseating lovey-doveyness was specific to Chip.

Juniper caught my eye and sobered. "This is serious, Chip. April's worried someone might attack the library like they did Salty's pumpkin patch."

His smile evaporated and his expression mirrored hers. "Why would they do that?"

"To undermine Halloween," I said.

For weeks, children had been cutting out paper jack-o'-lanterns, which now decorated the walls of the library's children's section. Maybe that's what set off Pumpkin Slayer.

"I was just telling her that we at the library aren't going to back down," Juniper said. "Not because of a stupid post on Elfbook."

"No, we won't," he agreed, bizarrely including himself in the category *we at the library*. "My next reading is this afternoon, and I'm going through with it."

His words didn't compute. "*Your* reading?" I asked.

"Chip's been reading to children in his free time."

He leaned closer to her. "And in honor of Halloween—my sweetie's friend's special holiday—I'm reading famous scary stories all month."

It seemed odd that an optician was doing dramatic readings, but whatever. It was the Christmastown library, not Broadway. "I heard something about a scary reindeer today." I tried to think of the name. "Nestor?"

"Neldor!" they exclaimed together.

Chip couldn't contain his excitement. "What a coincidence! I'm reading a story about Neldor today—*The Icy Plunge*."

After spending most of a year in Christmastown, I'd yet to meet any terrifying reindeer. "What makes Neldor scary?"

"Everything!" Juniper gaped at me in disbelief. "You've never heard of Neldor?"

"He scoops up naughty children in his shovel-like antlers and flies them over the Farthest Frozen Reaches, where he drops them like stones to the ice below," Chip said.

My jaw dropped. "That's more than scary, that's traumatizing."

"Don't you have scary stories where you come from?" Chip asked.

"Sure. Frankenstein and Dracula, witches and ghosts."

"Franken-who?" Chip asked.

Juniper's coffee break turned into a cultural exchange. As I recounted the story of Frankenstein, my friend's eyes grew wide. When I was done, she asked, "So you're saying a reindeer with weird antlers is more frightening than a man stitched together from dead people?"

Point taken. "It's a very good novel," I assured her. "I'll bring a copy for the library."

"You should come back to the library with us and listen to me read *The Icy Plunge* to the kiddies," Chip said. "I bet you'd get a kick out of it. The children have reacted positively to my performances."

I couldn't think of anything that tempted me less than Chip Pepperbough doing a dramatic reading for children. I got more than enough of Chip from socializing with Juniper and already longed for the day when they took each other for granted and weren't glued at the hip. I felt guilty for thinking that, though. Juniper was happy. I needed to be happier for her.

Then I resented Chip a little more for making me feel guilty.

Luckily, I had a good excuse to wriggle out of *The Icy Plunge*. "Oh, too bad," I said, giving a reasonable imitation of disappointment. "I have an important errand to run this afternoon. Otherwise . . ."

"That's okay," Chip said. "Maybe you can catch my next reading."

Juniper nodded. "He's a regular fixture at the library now."

"Like the front desk, or the photocopier," I observed.

Chip blasted out a laugh and put his arm around Juniper. I gulped down the rest of my coffee and left the two lovebirds to enjoy the rest of their break together.

I was sympathetic to new love. I'd been a newlywed myself the year before. Honestly, though, what kind of guy starts hanging around for hours at his girlfriend's workplace? Wasn't there something almost stalkery about that? Didn't he have his optician business to tend to?

The scolding voice in my head made me feel ashamed. *Juniper's on cloud nine, you skeptical, cranky harpy.*

My thoughts turned away from my friend's love life

soon as my feet turned off Festival Boulevard and onto the smaller but charming Sparkletoe Lane. That the street bore their name showed what a prominent elf clan the Sparkletoes were in Christmastown. Sparkletoe's Bootery was located a half a block down from Sparkletoe's Mercantile, probably my favorite store in Christmastown. Bella Sparkletoe, Tiny's older sister, who ran the mercantile, stocked everything on the old pine shelves of the place, which was always hopping—and not just with shoppers. Bella's battalion of elf clerks zoomed along wheeled ladders attached to the floor-to-ceiling shelves along the walls, grabbing whatever customers wanted that wasn't within easy reach. Going there was quite an experience.

As I passed the front of the mercantile, a tableau of a spooky graveyard in the front window caught my eye. The Halloween display was well done. Granted, there was cotton wool snow on the ground instead of the usual fallen leaves, but Santa-land elves didn't have much experience with deciduous trees. A white face peered out from behind one of the tombstones. Anywhere else, I would have assumed the figure was a ghost, but on closer inspection I noticed it had a flat nose and pointy teeth: a snow monster. I'd never seen one in real life, but I'd heard stories of the formidable giants who lived beyond the Christmas Tree Forest in the Farthest Frozen Reaches.

A sign in glittering orange and black read, *Everything You Need for Trick or Treat!*

It was heartening. The whole town wasn't against Halloween. Evidently not even all the Sparkletoes were.

Half a block away, Sparkletoe's Bootery presented a different attitude toward the upstart holiday. The first thing that greeted me when I came upon the plate-glass picture window by the swinging elf boot that marked the entrance to the cobbler's was a large poster board commanding passersby to *SIGN THE PETITION AGAINST HALLOWEEN!*

Below that, in smaller print, it continued, *Christmastown means Christmas—not something scary! Don't allow outsiders and those too easily influenced by them to change the character of our orderly, peaceful town! Ask inside to add your signature!!!*

It was hard not to take the words and all those exclamation points personally. Back in Oregon, Nick and I were being protested as fair-weather intruders . . . and apparently I was considered an interloper here, too. But *I* wasn't the one menacing the library and vandalizing Salty's greenhouse.

I'd intended to have a calm, reasonable chat with Tiny Sparkletoe, but that petition got my dander up. I pushed through the bootery's door with a force belied by the gentle ring of the tinkle bell attached to it.

Inside the cozy shop, Christmas lights twinkled all year long, and pine boughs over the hearth made the air smell like December 25th 365 days a year. Louie Terntree, Tiny's lone employee, hunched over a long worktable with a piece of uncut leather in front of him. The wall behind him was filled with narrow drawers, each bearing a label with the name of the elf whose shoe pattern was stored inside it. The brass drawer pulls were all in the shape of pointy-toed elf boots. An adjacent wall was dotted with shelves that held examples of the latest slipper and bootie models Tiny and Louie could custom-make for their clientele.

Though he'd been working at the store since his youth, Louie's official title was still cobbler's apprentice. At thirty, his black hair was prematurely flecked with gray, and his large dark eyes showed creases at their corners from squinting at his close work. There was something sweet about Louie. To me, the lines on his face gave it character. He was the elf equivalent of an old, worn pair of slippers—not the best looking, maybe, but the pair so worn in and comfy that you'd never throw them away.

I knew Louie a little from the Santaland Concert Band, in which he played trombone and I was entering my second year of struggling along on percussion. Some days I dreamed of a hobby that didn't involve glockenspiels, slide whistles, and triangles, but getting to spend rehearsals making music with elves like Louie and Juniper made the endeavor seem worthwhile.

"What are *you* doing here?" he asked.

"I came by to talk to Tiny. Is he around?"

"Yes, but . . ." His face registered alarm. "You *really* want to speak to him?"

I understood where his fear came from. Tiny and I were on opposite sides of the Halloween question. No doubt Louie's boss regularly gave him an earful on the topic.

Before I could answer in the affirmative, Tiny himself swaggered in from the back room. He'd obviously heard us speaking; his face bore a contemptuous expression even before he laid eyes on me.

Without his elf cap on, Tiny was as bald as an egg on top, with a few mere tufts of hair left in the vicinity of his ears. These were fashioned not so much as a comb-over as a comb-around. He compensated for the deficit of hair atop his head by going full-on Gilded Age tycoon with his facial hair, sporting muttonchop sideburns and a full mustache curled to points at the corners of his mouth. His clothes befitted a prosperous elf. His brown coat was flecked with purple and yellow, and he wore brown velveteen breeches, purple stockings, and the finest booties his shop could produce.

I couldn't help noticing that, in defiance of his given name, he seemed to have put lifts in his footwear. His bald dome came up to my shoulder, yet he still acted as if he were sneering down at me.

"Well, well!" The timbre of his voice hovered somewhere between the mayor of Munchkin City and Thurston Howell

III. "I was wondering when someone from the castle would come by to pester me."

Pester him? I hadn't said a word yet.

"Why would anyone do that?" I asked. Could it be that he was going to confess to the damage done to Salty's pumpkin patch?

He nodded toward the front window. "My petition."

"Sorry to break it to you, Tiny, but no one at Castle Kringle has heard of your petition. It's not exactly the talk of the town."

Anger flickered in his eyes. Then he drew his shoulders back. "We already have dozens of signatures. Dozens! And there will be more." His voice rose. "Oh, yes. There'll be more."

"I'm curious what you think that petition will achieve."

"It will show that the will of the elves can't be overridden in Christmastown. It'll show that there's a silent majority of us who object to the muddying of our traditions with unnecessary, questionable foreign holidays."

"What October traditions does Christmastown have that Halloween would muddy?"

He trembled with the effort to rein in his temper, but then burst out, "We are Christmastown three hundred sixty-five days a year! *Christmas*town. Another holiday is a waste of time and money. We don't need to distract our people with scary stories and costumes, send our children begging door-to-door, and deplete our supplies of nutmeg and cinnamon to give tasteless gourds a little flavor."

And there it was, the pumpkin resentment I'd been hoping to tease out. Could Tiny Sparkletoe really be Pumpkin Slayer? "What else have you been doing, in addition to getting people to sign petitions?"

The question brought him up short. "Well . . . I've been talking about it." He turned to Louie. "Haven't I?"

Louie, who up to now had looked like he would have been happy to disappear into the cabinetry, colored and bobbed his head in assent. "Oh, yes," he assured me. "Mr. Sparkletoe talks about the issue to everyone who comes in the shop." Under his breath, he added, "Endlessly."

His employer eyed him sharply, but before he could ask for the meaning behind that muttered remark, I couldn't restrain myself from taunting him. "So much talking, yet you've only gathered a dozen or so signatures."

Tiny bristled. "*Two* dozen." He reached behind the counter, unwound a long scroll, and shoved it in my face. "Look. *This* is what the popular voice looks like."

I scanned the paper.

We the undersigned protest the introduction of Halloween to the municipality of Christmastown and hereby demand that the allocation of resources, elf labor, and use of public spaces be denied to those who want to bring this ghoulish, so-called celebration into our peaceful, cheerful town. Signed,

As he said, there were about two dozen signatories to this petulant statement, with his own John Hancock the most prominent at the top. Directly under his name were those of his wife, Pixie, and Louie. As my gaze scanned downward, most notable to me were the names that *weren't* there, especially those of his sister, the owner of the mercantile down the street, or any other of the members of his own family.

"Funny, I don't see Bella's name."

He snatched the paper back. "All my sister cares about is making a little more money. That's what's happening in Christmastown now. People are turning away from craftsmanship and opening shoddy *warehouses* to make a fast buck."

That last lament had to refer to Walnut's Bootie World. No doubt the presence of a rival bootery in town irked Tiny.

"You're the head of the Christmastown Community Guild," I pointed out. "Surely you're not above promoting commerce."

He drew up proudly. "I may be a business elf, but I have principles."

"It must be frustrating that so many of your fellow merchants don't share them." I peered at the petition that he was rolling up into an ever-tighter scroll. "Evidently your supporters are such a silent majority that they don't even want anyone to hear the scratch of a pen as they write their names."

He raised his chin. "I've only just begun to fight!"

"Yet you already feel so thwarted that you're resorting to violence."

"How—" He swallowed, and for a moment it looked as though he'd stopped breathing. "What are you talking about?"

"Anonymous, threatening messages on Elfbook?" When he didn't respond, I added, "Vandalizing a greenhouse on Castle Kringle property?"

He sputtered. "I-I don't know what you're talking about."

"Someone—some Halloween hater—has done both those things."

He made a show of looking perplexed. At least, I assumed it was a show. "Why would I break into a greenhouse?"

"Because Salty was growing hundreds of pumpkins inside it for Halloween, which you hate."

"That's ridiculous! I'm an upstanding business elf, the president of the Christmastown Community Guild, not some thug. You should be talking to Constable Crinkles, not to me."

"Crinkles is on the case." To my credit, I managed to make this pronouncement without doubling over with laughter. "He'll be looking into your anti-Halloween movement, I can assure you."

"That's persecution!" Nevertheless, he quickly shoved the petition underneath the counter. "Expressing our opinions doesn't make us criminals. *We're* the ones decrying the chaos and untidiness Halloween will cause."

"And what better way to prove your point than by sowing chaos yourselves?"

"My supporters are all law-abiding citizens."

His supporters. But what about him?

"I suppose desperation drives both men and elves to act in ways they'd never dream of normally."

"We're not desperate."

I leveled a pitying look on him. "Twenty signatures out of thousands of elves in Christmastown?"

He was practically quaking with irritation now. "No investigation of that greenhouse break-in will show I did it."

We would see about that.

I left the store then, but I hadn't taken ten steps down the sidewalk before I heard the door's bell tinkling again behind me. Louie, still wearing his work apron over his tunic, scurried to catch up with me.

"Please don't think I'm against you, Apr—Mrs. Claus."

"Please, Louie. People who've played 'The Little Drummer Boy' for hours together are like soldiers who've been through the trenches. To you, I'm April."

"I didn't want to sign that cockamamie petition. Tiny made me."

"I suspected as much."

"His wife, too."

"Pixie pressured you?"

He shook his head. "No—I meant he forced her to sign, too. She didn't want to any more than I did. But Tiny—I mean, Mr. Sparkletoe—"

His words broke off.

"I understand." Tiny had probably threatened his job if he didn't sign. It was outrageous.

He threw a glance back toward Sparkletoe's Bootery, as

if he expected his employer to be glaring at him through the plate glass. To be honest, so did I. Even though there was no sign of Tiny at the window, he said, "I'd better get back now."

He scurried back inside, and through the window I watched him resume his place at his workbench. Sadness for his plight filled me. He was a gifted artisan whose skilled hands had probably created over half the elf footwear in Christmastown. Yet Louie was under Tiny's boot, so to speak.

I'd been taken to task the year before because I hadn't kept the constabulary up-to-date on my investigation into the deaths of an elf and a snowman. Mrs. Claus's job, some said, shouldn't be running private investigations. Fine. My nosiness of last December had brought me distressingly close to a grisly and undignified death. I was happy to let Crinkles and Ollie deal with the greenhouse break-in and Pumpkin Slayer.

Still, it wouldn't hurt to give the constable a nudge in Tiny's direction.

Chapter 3

The Christmastown Constabulary was housed in a cozy cottage far down Festival Boulevard at the edge of the old village. It looked like the kind of place Red Riding Hood's grandma would have lived in, and today it smelled like it, too. When I opened the door, the aroma of fresh gingerbread wafted toward me. Ollie, the deputy, greeted me with oven mitts still on. "Hello, Mrs. C! You're just in time for tea."

He ushered me into Crinkles's office, where a table had been set with teacups.

"Delighted to see you again so soon," the constable said.

Almost as soon as I sat down, Ollie came back with a tray bearing another cup and saucer and a plate with gingerbread slices on it. Crinkles poured. Just a typical local law enforcement scene.

When everyone had their tea cream-and-sugared to their taste, I announced, "I've actually come on business."

Crinkles's eyes bulged. "Nothing else has happened, I hope? What a morning!"

Spoken like the constable from a place where months could crawl by without so much as a sleigh-parking violation.

"Last night someone posted a threatening message on the

library's Elfbook page." I brought out my phone and pulled up the screenshot Juniper had forwarded to me.

"Someone from City Hall mentioned getting an angry message about Halloween," Crinkles said. "They just erased it."

"So did Juniper, but after what happened this morning, she thought it might be relevant. Luckily she'd saved a copy of it."

Crinkles squinted at the screen as if trying to decipher a hieroglyph. "Pumpkin Slayer? What kind of a name is that?"

"A made-up name. But it clearly connects the threat to what happened at Salty's pumpkin patch."

The constable shook his head. "I don't believe in all this social media stuff. In my day, elves wrote each other letters and didn't make up tomfool names for themselves." He frowned at his nephew. "I hope you're not on that thing."

Ollie paled. "Everybody is."

"If everybody slathered themselves in clam juice and jumped into a huddle of walruses, would you join them?"

I had to interrupt. "Can we please focus? Social media isn't the problem here."

Crinkles took a sip from his cup. He might be bowling ball shaped, but he was a dainty tea drinker. "How do you like the gingerbread? Tasty, isn't it? Ollie made it himself."

So much for focusing.

"It's delicious," I said honestly. "Very moist."

"Applesauce and mustard," Ollie said. "Those are the secret ingredients."

I tried to resist getting sidetracked by Ollie's cooking tips. "There's something else I need to talk to you about."

Crinkles hopped up. "We have something else, too." He went to the mantel and came back with a wheel of tickets, the kind given out at fun fairs. "The constabulary's holding a raffle. The winner will be announced at the Halloween festival at Peppermint Pond. It's to raise money for new wallpaper for the jail cell."

I began to despair of ever getting Christmastown's crime-fighting duo to concentrate on crime. "Wallpaper," I repeated.

"You probably haven't noticed, but the stuff we have in there now is peeling."

"We're trying to decide between a green wreath pattern or French hens," Ollie said.

"Maybe you could help us." Crinkles went to a cabinet and came back lugging a decorator's sample book. "For weeks I've been trying to get it through Ollie's skull that the hens would be entirely inappropriate."

He flipped open the sample book to a bird pattern, then showed me the wreaths. I was partial to the hens myself. "What's wrong with birds?"

"For prisoners? It would be like taunting them for being jailbirds." He seemed perplexed that I didn't readily agree. "We don't want to offend our prisoners."

"I don't remember the old wallpaper," I said.

This time they both hopped to their feet. "Come on, we'll show you."

"But—"

It was no use arguing. They were halfway to the jail cell already.

I use the word *cell* loosely. The room of the cottage where prisoners stay was a bedroom with two single beds with matching quilts done in a star pattern, with emphasis on red and green in the color scheme. There were a dresser and mirror, an en suite bath, and framed paintings of winter scenes on the walls. Nothing indicated that this was a place of detention. There weren't even bars on the windows, although Crinkles had once assured me that they were painted shut.

While the constable pointed out the spotted and peeling

wallpaper, a mistletoe sprig print, I was distracted by a young elf seated on one of the beds. He was dressed in a black tunic, with black skinny jeans tucked into no-frills black booties. Even his loose-knit elf cap had a black pom-pom dangling off the end of it. The cap covered all but a few locks of his blond hair, and I wondered if he was covering it on purpose because it didn't go with his all-black image. He seemed young to be sitting in the constabulary's jail cell.

"Who are you?" I asked.

Before the youngster could answer, Crinkles glanced at him dismissively. "That's just Quince. He's from the orphanage."

"Sorry, Quince," Ollie said, "I forgot to bring you some gingerbread." He skittered out to remedy that omission.

Crinkles held the sample books up against the wall, but Quince distracted me again. He said nothing but calmly observed us with curious brown eyes. "Why is an orphan sitting in the jail cell?" I wondered aloud.

"He was caught doing something illegal, and I called the orphanage director, Miss Gladgoose. She thought we ought to leave him here, as a lesson. Quince is seventeen—pretty soon he'll be out on his own. Next time he's caught, we'll have to charge him officially."

"Caught doing what?"

"Illegal vending of forbidden materials," Crinkles said, his tone making me imagine everything from illegal drugs to smuggled uranium. He lowered his voice and added, "Bad movies."

Quince was finally moved to speak. "They're not bad. *I* like them. Other elves do, too."

"No decent elf watches the kind of trash you've been peddling," Crinkles said. "Keep doing it, son, and you're going to find yourself in a penal colony in the Farthest Frozen Reaches."

Quince's lips twisted as Ollie came in and handed him a plate with a generous slice of gingerbread on it. The prisoner took it with mumbled thanks, then said in his defense, "I don't see what's so wrong with them. In some places, they're considered classics."

"Then I feel sorry for people in those depraved places." Crinkles shook his head.

"What kind of movies are we talking about?" I asked.

Quince said, *"Santa's Slay. Silent Night, Deadly Night. Black Christmas."*

I laughed. *"Black Christmas* is great." My friend Claire and I had watched it a few Christmases earlier.

Crinkles and Ollie gaped at me.

I was a depraved Mrs. Claus, apparently. "It's not shown in Santaland?"

"Of course not!" Crinkles said. "And now this young miscreant's gotten his hands on some Halloween movies that would make your blood run cold."

"That's kind of the point," Quince grumbled through a mouthful of gingerbread.

"Quiet, you." Crinkles turned to his nephew. "Go get some of those things to show Mrs. C."

"Mrs. C?" Quince sat up straight and eyed me with interest. "Are you Mrs. Claus?"

I nodded.

"And *you've* seen *Black Christmas?"*

I slid an anxious glance at the constable, wondering if Quince and I would soon be cellmates. "It's pretty well known where I come from."

Ollie returned with an armful of Halloween movies and began going through them. *"Halloween, Scream, Nightmare on Elm Street, Halloween Two* and *Five, Neldor: The Plunge of Terror . . ."*

I laughed. "There are Neldor movies?"

"Three's definitely not the best of the Neldor franchise,"

Ollie said. Then his eyes widened. "I had to research them to see how bad they were, didn't I?"

"No, you did not," Crinkles said. "This is Santaland. We are not in the business of scaring ourselves to death, especially not about Christmas. That's blasphemy. And if we're going to adopt this new Halloween holiday, we can't have it desecrated by all these scary things, either."

"You know Halloween's *supposed* to be frightening, don't you?" I asked. "They're telling scary stories at the library."

"Well, sure," Crinkles allowed. "*Stories*. That's okay. These movies'll scare the stockings off you."

Quince sent me a doleful look. *Thanks for sticking up for me, but don't waste your time,* his expression said. Frustration filled me. The idea that a young elf—an orphan—would be sitting in a jail cell for selling movies seemed insane. Of course, as punishments went, this jail cell wasn't exactly San Quentin. Unless you considered peeling wallpaper cruel and unusual punishment.

"You shouldn't be keeping him here," I told Crinkles. "He ought to be back at the orphanage."

"I don't want to go there, either," Quince said.

I looked at him. "Where do you want to go, then?"

"Somewhere I can be with my friend Pocket."

"Where does Pocket live?"

"On the street."

"You see?" Crinkles asked. "That's the young elf of to-day. Everything's handed to him on a silver platter, but is that good enough? No, he'd rather live with some snowman."

"Pocket's *my* snowman," Quince said. "I made him when I was eight. He's better company than most elves I know."

The constable shook his head, at the end of his mental rope. Which, I couldn't help thinking, did not take long to reach. "Just eat your gingerbread, son." Crinkles nodded for Ollie and me to follow him back to his office.

"Did you decide which pattern worked best?" Ollie asked. I'd forgotten about the wallpaper decision. "They'll both look fine."

"Would you like to buy some tickets?" Crinkles asked. "We're going to draw the winner at the Halloween carnival."

"What's the prize?"

"A subscription to Ollie's bread-of-the-month club. You can tell he's an excellent baker. He gets that talent from my sister. And the tickets are only five bucks apiece."

I frowned and dug into my purse. It wouldn't do for Mrs. Claus to be stingy.

And Ollie did bake well.

After Crinkles had pocketed my money and thanked me for dropping by, I cleared my throat. "There's something else I wanted to talk to you about." I had to remind myself to tread lightly. I was still a relative newcomer in Santaland, while the people I was speaking about—and to—had lived here all their lives. Constable Crinkles and Tiny Sparkletoe were about the same age. They probably grew up together, attended the same school. "If you're looking for a pumpkin patch vandal, speak to Tiny Sparkletoe. He's violently opposed to Halloween."

"You mean the petition?" Crinkles chuckled. "Tiny's always got a petition going about something. That's what he does. He'd be against any change to Christmastown. You should have heard him a few years ago when someone suggested adding blue lights to the street decorations. He was bent out of shape then, too. And what color lights do you see in Christmastown now? Red, green, white . . ."

"And blue." I shook my head. "Maybe he's decided this isn't a battle he's going to lose."

"He's lost it already," Ollie said. "My little nieces and nephews have been talking about nothing else but costumes and candy for days."

"Don't think Ollie and I aren't taking this seriously,"

Crinkles said. "We measured those bootie prints we found by the greenhouse. I'm thinking we could ask Tiny for a list of the elves he's made boots for in that size."

"While you're at it, ask him his own size," I said.

"I intend to," Crinkles said.

That plan of his sounded so logical, so correct, I found myself breathing more easily. *Maybe he isn't as incompetent as I thought.*

The conversation calmed my nerves. Or maybe it was Ollie's gingerbread that did that trick. I split a second piece with Crinkles and rolled out of the constabulary on a sugar-and-butter high.

They were right, I decided. A few destroyed pumpkins, a childish social media post, and a petulant petition were nothing to panic over. In a place the size of Santaland, elves were bound to disagree on all sorts of things. Halloween was new, and change was unsettling to some. Once everyone grasped what a harmless night of fun it actually was, tempers would simmer down.

Surely.

Chapter 4

The next morning after I'd finished dressing, I was kneeling by the entertainment center Nick and I had set up in the corner of the bedroom. A sofa sat in front of a television we used too rarely. I'd brought some DVDs of classics from home, and I was fairly certain somewhere in the pile . . .

I scanned the shelf. Eureka! I pulled out a copy of the original *Frankenstein* by James Whale. I intended to take this to the library to show Juniper, in case she couldn't hunt down the book.

A knock sounded on the bedchamber door. Expecting it to be Jingles, I called out, "Come in." Jingles and I always had a morning chat to go over the day's schedule and exchange whatever tidbits of gossip were floating around the castle. He'd become my confederate last year when I was looking into the murders. I'm not sure I would have survived my first year in Christmastown without him.

When the door opened, however, the servant bearing my morning coffee tray wasn't Jingles but one of the footmen.

"Good morning, Waldo. I hope Jingles isn't under the weather."

"No, ma'am." In his shaky hands, the tray rattled like an

old Ford Pinto. Waldo suffered from bad nerves. "Jingles had another matter to attend to."

He put the tray down on the table nearest the sofa and stepped back, hands folded across the little pot belly that pressed against his black-and-white tunic. With his bug eyes and oversized elf ears, he reminded me of an anxious, slightly lumpy harlequin. His gaze zeroed in on the picture on the package in my hand. It was Boris Karloff as the monster.

"What is that!" he said, almost as if the monster were alive.

"Frankenstein." I offered the box to him, but he stepped back, making it clear that he would no more touch it than he would touch a tarantula. "It's just a story," I said. "You'll probably see Frankensteins all over pretty soon. It's a common Halloween image in the US."

"It's a very peculiar holiday, isn't it?"

"I suppose so." I put the DVD face-down on the table. Waldo didn't need more reasons to be nervous.

"Jingles told me to remind you of your fitting for something called"—his brow creased—"the orphan dress?"

His confusion was understandable. "The Order of Elven Seamstresses is making me a new dress for the ribbon-cutting ceremony of the elf orphan home tomorrow."

"I see."

"Thank you for the reminder. I'd forgotten all about it." Social obligations tended to slip my mind when I was preoccupied with mysteries like the greenhouse vandalism and Pumpkin Slayer's threatening Elfbook posts.

Waldo didn't reply.

I didn't know what else to say. I filled the ensuing awkward silence by stirring milk into my coffee while he watched. I took a sip and nodded, assuming he was waiting for affirmation that the beverage met with my approval.

Evidently that wasn't it. He hitched his throat and held up a clipboard he'd been carrying under the tray. "Jingles also said it's your custom to double-check the rest of your schedule. I'm happy to do that, too."

"Of course." As he looked down at the clipboard, I rattled off what I remembered of my obligations for the day. "After the dress fitting this morning, I'm having lunch with Tiffany at her tea shop, and then later I'm attending a rehearsal of the Santaland Concert Band from three to five."

He nodded.

"Have I forgotten anything?" I asked.

His face reddened a fraction. "I beg your pardon?"

"Jingles usually knows my schedule better than I do. He tells me if something slipped my mind."

He studied the clipboard, tapping his pen against it. "No . . . that's everything."

Nothing too taxing, then. Compared with the routine I'd left in Oregon—running an inn twenty-four/seven—this was a life of luxury and leisure. "Thank you, Waldo."

After he'd gone, I realized I should have pressed harder to find out what Jingles was up to this morning. I worried my mother-in-law was running him ragged. Or, even worse, that Lucia was. Nothing put Jingles in a fouler temper than tending to reindeer business, which was what Lucia, the Clauses' unofficial liaison with the reindeer herds, was usually knee-deep in.

Mostly I was disappointed that there was no one to rehash the events of yesterday with. Though I'd vowed not to do any investigating, that didn't mean I wouldn't enjoy talking about what was going on. Of course no one, not even Jingles, could obsess as much as I did over pumpkin-patch desecrations and Elfbook posts. When I'd mentioned Pumpkin Slayer to Nick, he'd looked at me anxiously, as if I were about to ride this crime wave into another dangerous investigation. His concern was sweet but ridiculous. Pumpkin Slayer was nothing but an anonymous social media troll. The pumpkins weren't murder victims. It wasn't as if Christmastown had another killer on the loose.

The Order of Elven Seamstresses performed their sartorial magic in a sprawling chateau near the base of Sugarplum Mountain. Seamstresses toiled away on the top floor and in the basement, but I, a VIP client, was whisked right into the main-floor showroom, where clothes were tried on and fussed over by the head of the order, Madame Neige. I wasn't sure if that was the name she'd been born with, married into, or simply was made up for business. I doubt anyone had ever asked her. She was the Edith Head of the elf world, the Chanel of Christmastown, and when she made a pronouncement, that was simply the way things were.

She was sparing with her appearances in the salon, however, and for most of my appointment, I was attended by Minty, who plucked and tugged at me in the changing room until I was ready to sweep out into the showroom and face the full-length mirrors that lined three walls.

For the orphan home ribbon cutting, Madam Neige had designed a dress and matching cape in sumptuous crushed velvet in a deep burnt orange. This was not a color I usually sought out. With my auburn hair, too much red and orange could make me resemble a lava lamp. But this color had a rich, depthless quality to it. It was a deep autumn hue that didn't make you think of clowns or peanut butter cups. It was gorgeous. The dress was cut on the bias and fitted, with long sleeves and a low neckline. I couldn't help preening a little as the matching cape swirled around me.

A movement in the mirror caught my eye. I twisted to see someone in a jack-o'-lantern costume crossing the room. Legs encased in green tights protruded from a bulbous pumpkin body, which had been fashioned from stretching orange fabric over a round wire frame. There was a grinning, gap-toothed face done in black mesh so the person inside could see out, but apparently they couldn't see well. The pumpkin bumbled right into a clothes rack. The rack, the clothes, and the pumpkin all spilled to the floor.

"Oh, crud!" the jack-o'-lantern exclaimed.

I knew that voice, so I wasn't at all surprised when the pumpkin hopped back to its feet before I could get halfway across the room to help. My sister-in-law Tiffany, a former competitive ice skater, was used to taking spills and leaping back up onto boot blades on the ice, as if her legs were spring loaded.

But the pumpkin frame was clearly frustrating her. She turned in a circle. "Will someone get me out of this thing?"

I and several elven seamstresses scrambled to help her. When they finally pulled the pumpkin body off her petite frame, mine was the first face Tiffany saw, but she wasn't looking at my face. "What a gorgeous dress!" she exclaimed. "What's it for?"

"The orphan home ribbon cutting." Tiffany would be there, too, but she was going to be on the ice with some of the orphans, helping them show off their skating skills. "Aren't we meeting for lunch at your place in just a little while?" I asked her.

"We are, but I had an appointment here first. I wish I'd known you were going to be coming here, too—we could have ridden together and saved a sleigh."

"I took the funicular down and walked the rest of the way," I said.

The cable-drawn funicular that traveled up and down Sugarplum Mountain wasn't as convenient as a sleigh or snowmobile, but it was reliable and had great views. There was only one car, so there was usually a wait. The top stop where

I picked it up was at the edge of the Castle Kringle grounds, down a long, winding pathway. The funicular's bottom drop-off was just a few blocks from the heart of town. I usually took it to and from town on band-rehearsal afternoons.

"What's the jack-o'-lantern costume for?" I asked.

"The Halloween Festival Ice Show." She shook her head at Minty. "But I can't take to the ice in that thing. The net-ting for the eyes needs to be much more transparent."

Minty nodded. "It will be done, ma'am."

"All the other costumes are awesome. I can't wait to see my Tiny Glider class in them. Tell Madame Neige how pleased I am."

"Madame Neige knows," declared a voice behind us.

Madame Neige always startled me a little. She created such glorious outfits, yet her own style was dark and no-nonsense. Today her diminutive, stocky body was encased in a black tunic over a below-the-knee pencil skirt. The one exception to plainness was her shoe choice, red booties with a significant heel as well as an elaborate swirl at the toe. For a necklace, she wore a tape measure looped around her neck. As she in-spected the pumpkin cage, she pushed her chunky cat-eye frames up her nose.

"The problem will be fixed," she proclaimed in a husky voice that bore a trace of an accent of unknown origin. Was she French? *Do they even have elves in France?* "I will send Minty up to the castle with it tomorrow so you can try it there. Or if you want to try it on skates, I can have someone meet you at Peppermint Pond."

Peppermint Pond, perpetually frozen, was open to skaters all year long. It was where Tiffany gave her skate lessons, and it was also where the Halloween festival would take place in a few days' time.

"Thanks," Tiffany said. "I'd like to try it out on the ice."

The designer turned her attention to my dress. "That

looks good on you. I'm working on the same silhouette for your costume."

Tiffany's eyes gleamed. "What are you going to be, April?"

"It's a secret."

My sister-in-law pouted in disappointment. "Everybody's costume is a secret, even Pamela's."

Pamela Claus was our mother-in-law. She was very pro-status quo—I assumed she'd hate Halloween like Tiny did, and Lucia.

"Pamela's going to dress up for Halloween?" I asked.

"I am designing Mrs. Claus's costume myself," Madame Neige said. "The dowager Mrs. Claus's costume, that is. Her specifications were very particular."

I couldn't wait to see what Pamela wanted to be, but I was equally excited to see how my own costume, which Madame Neige's elven seamstresses were working on, would turn out.

"Normally we would not be running so close to the event," Madame continued. "We have been busy ever since Bella Sparkletoe sent out the invitations for her Halloween party."

"Bella Sparkletoe is having a party?"

Tiffany arched a brow at me. "Were you expecting an invitation?"

"No . . ." But I couldn't help thinking of Tiny Sparkletoe, and how annoyed he would be that his sister was pulling out all the stops to celebrate this upstart holiday.

While Madame Neige and Tiffany figured out a time for her workout-fitting, I changed back into my own clothes and arranged for the dress and cape to be delivered to the castle. Tiffany and I left together and walked to her business, Tiffany's Tea-piphany, a small, bright tea shop right on Festival Boulevard. The interior was intimate, with a welcoming tiled fireplace and coved ceilings. The walls were warm gold, while the two- and four-person tables were draped with crimson tablecloths.

"Let's sit in the back." Tiffany showed me to a table in the corner near the fireplace. Usually the mantel was covered in greenery; now it was decorated with fall colors—mostly man made. The most natural thing on display were a few of Salty's smaller pumpkins. I spotted a couple of Long Island Cheeses he'd told me about. Tiffany must have requisitioned a few before the greenhouse massacre.

She left me while she prepared tea and sandwiches for us—she never wanted her waitresses to waste time waiting on the boss. I looked around at the other tables, most of which were filled. Business was brisk, which made me happy for Tiffany. After her husband, Nick's brother, died, she'd sunk into a deep depression, made worse by her suspicions that Chris's death hadn't been an accident. After her fears were proved correct and the murderer was caught, some of the heaviness of her grief lifted. Opening this place had been another step in pulling herself out of the abyss of sorrow. Now she was busier than ever running the tea shop, giving figure-skating lessons, and raising Christopher.

And the town now had a place to eat the best cucumber sandwiches ever. I couldn't help beaming when she placed a three-tiered tower of goodies in the center of our table before sitting down herself. We loaded down our plates with selections of sandwiches, scones, and sweets, then poured our tea.

"I'm curious about this party of Bella Sparkletoe's," I said.

"Me, too." Tiffany nibbled at a scone. She was probably the only soul in Santaland who counted calories. "I hope it doesn't prevent too many people from coming to my ice show."

"The private parties will be after the festival," I said. "You'll have a huge crowd."

"I hope so. For your sake, too—you'll also be taking part, don't forget."

As if I could. The Santaland Concert Band would be backing up most of the skating acts at the festival and performing a few numbers on our own, as well.

I sipped my tea and thought again about Tiny and Pumpkin Slayer. "You haven't had any pushback on your ice show, have you?" I asked.

She poured cream into her tea. "What kind of pushback?"

"Messages from someone who doesn't want you to go ahead with the show? Threats?"

She paused mid-stir. "What's going on, April?"

I was considering how best to answer that when a shadow fell across our table. Pamela, Nick's mother, loomed over us. It's hard to describe how someone so short and round could appear so formidable. Especially a woman wearing a cranberry-red suit and matching hat with holly and berries festooned around its brim. She was smiling, but it was the kind of steely smile that signaled that I'd transgressed decorum in some way.

"I would also like to know what's going on, April," she announced.

What have I done now? I swallowed. "I'm not sure what you mean."

"The Kringle Heights Ladies' Guild had our monthly breakfast this morning. You missed it."

"Oh." I'd forgotten all about it. "It slipped my mind."

Pamela commandeered a chair from a nearby table and dragged it to ours. She sat down, her posture perfect. "I made excuses for you—said you were under the weather. But why I should have had to is beyond me." She sighed. "And you've been doing *so* much better lately at remembering your social obligations."

Only because Jingles had been doing a good job of

reminding me of them. But Jingles hadn't been there this morning, and he evidently hadn't written anything down about the Ladies' Guild meeting so Waldo would remind me.

Waldo also hadn't told me Tiffany would be meeting Madame Neige, either. Jingles would have. I tried not to jump to conclusions, but I was concerned. "Has anyone seen Jingles this morning?"

"What has Jingles to do with your current state of distraction?" Pamela asked. "It's all this business with Halloween, I'll wager. It's got everyone in a tizzy."

"We were just talking about that." Tiffany attempted to inject a little brightness in the conversation. "So many people are making plans. Madame Neige said they're busy sewing costumes all the time now."

Pamela shook her head. "It's not right."

"Madame Neige is making you a costume, too," I reminded her. "From that, I assumed you *liked* Halloween."

"For the castle folk." Pamela made a clear distinction between the people who lived in vaunted Kringle Heights at the top of Sugarplum Mountain and everyone else in Santaland. "For children like Christopher and his little friends, naturally I think it's an amusing tradition. I grew up in the States, too. Why, some of my favorite memories are Halloween blowouts at the Kappa sorority house in college."

Tiffany and I had a hard time not laughing at the idea of our proper mother-in-law at any kind of "blowout."

"The point is," Pamela continued, "we are all from the South, so Halloween's nostalgic fun for us. But for Santaland natives—especially the elves—this is all new. When you introduce new ideas into a place where tradition is as venerated as it is here, heaven only knows what might happen."

"You mean elves shouldn't have fun," I said.

"Think of the time and resources being committed,"

Pamela said. "Nick was telling me that the factory is making Halloween candy instead of Christmas candy. And what if Christmas candy runs short in two months? What then?"

Tiffany blew out a breath. "Good grief. There are enough candy canes in the Strategic Sweets Reserves to keep the world geeked up till doomsday. A few less peppermint sticks won't ruin Christmas."

At that bit of Santaland heresy, Pamela's mouth flattened into a stern line.

"Halloween's only for one night," I piped up quickly, "and the elves seem to be enjoying it. Especially the children. Why shouldn't they have a night of fun and sugar overload? We'll all get back to Christmas business on November first."

Pamela almost visibly shuddered. "Your cavalier attitude alarms me, April."

Tiffany laughed. "April isn't cavalier about anything. Before you came in, she was hinting that there were controversies surrounding Halloween, and we all know what happened to poor Salty's greenhouse."

"That shows how much trouble this could bring down on all our heads," Pamela said.

I usually tried to see all sides, but I had a difficult time understanding what the harm could be in one night of fun. "Does it matter what we think? The bobsled's left the chute—it's not as if we can reverse course. People are making plans, and chances are the night will pass without incident."

Pamela plucked a sandwich off the tray and chewed. I could tell she wasn't convinced.

Later, standing at the back of the band hall of the Santaland Community Center, I wondered how much fun I'd be having at the Halloween festival. Our conductor, Luther Partridge, had chosen every piece of eerie music he could find for us to play. *Danse Macabre* had quite a few cymbal crashes.

Those always put me on edge. Nothing more jarring than crashing a cymbal at the wrong moment, as I was prone to do.

Smudge, the drummer and leader of our two-person percussion section, always tossed annoyed looks at me when I couldn't keep up. That afternoon, his gaze was pinned on me almost as often as it was on Juniper, who sat a row ahead of us with her euphonium. Those two had been having an on-again, off-again romance for years. Now, because of Chip Pepperbough, it was decidedly off.

After rehearsal, Smudge sidled up to me. "You and Juniper going out for coffee?"

"Maybe. We didn't talk about it."

"I was thinking I might head over to We Three Beans myself," he said in a casual way that wasn't fooling anybody.

As much as the moody Smudge got on my nerves, I found myself longing for the days when he and Juniper had been an item. I considered playing cupid and trying to bring about a reconciliation, but stifled the impulse. My matchmaking instincts hadn't always been the best, and meddling in someone's relationship was always risky.

Still, if Smudge just happened to walk with us, and he and Juniper just happened to reignite a temporarily extinguished flame . . .

"Sure," I said. "You should come with us."

We gathered our stuff and turned toward the door in time to see Chip poke his head through and wave at Juniper. A long sigh built in my chest. The last thing I wanted right now was to tag along with the lovebirds.

"On second thought . . ." Smudge grumbled.

I nodded in sympathy. "I need to get back to the castle anyway."

I repeated the excuse to Juniper, who was disappointed. "No We Three Beans?"

"Maybe next week," I said.

Chip tutted and drew Juniper in for a hug. "The sugar-plum and I were hoping you could join us."

I heard a rumbling, which turned out to be the grinding of Smudge's teeth as he passed by us. I understood the feeling.

"I do need to get home," I said, slinging my bag over my shoulder.

"We'll walk you to your sleigh, at least," Chip said.

"I'm taking the funicular."

"Even better," he said, grinning. "Nothing more relaxing than an evening stroll!" He gave Juniper another squeeze.

There was no shaking him.

He's being gentlemanly, for Pete's sake. "Great." I forced a smile.

All the way across town to the funicular station, Juniper and Chip chatted about the library and how much the kids had all enjoyed his reading of the Neldor story. I'd noticed that Chip's conversations often centered on how much people appreciated Chip. Occasionally I thought I caught Juniper's eyelids drooping in boredom, but that might have been wishful thinking on my part. A devil inside me wanted to mention Smudge and see how she reacted. But I held my tongue.

The lights of the funicular stop up ahead were a welcome sight. I felt like running toward the station, arms outstretched. In the distance, I glimpsed a lone figure leaning against a wall. At our approach, the elf straightened, turned, and scurried away. My eyes narrowed. Was that Waldo?

Juniper and Chip were chattering away and didn't notice him.

"I still wish you could come with us," Juniper said as we reached the funicular. "A little coffee would warm you up."

"Sure would," said Chip. "Or, even better, warm eggnog with marshmallows."

"April doesn't like sweet drinks," Juniper told him.

He nudged her. "Then it's lucky she's not dating you, 'cause you're the sweetest little cup of eggnog that ever was."

Juniper laughed self-consciously.

"Oh, look—the funicular car's waiting!" I was so relieved to get away, I almost singsonged the words. "Thanks for walking with me."

"Our pleasure," Chip said.

"Have a good evening," Juniper called after my fleeing figure.

I waved, then pushed through the door and stepped onto the funicular. At this time of evening—technically rush hour—the workers from Christmastown were heading back to their homes in Tinkertown. It was mostly Clauses who lived in Kringle Heights, and all of them had sleighs, so I was the only person going up the mountain at this time.

The car whirred to life and started pulling me up the mountain. I looked out the back window, hoping I hadn't seemed rude in the way I'd run off. Juniper and Chip were still standing arm in arm. They waved up at me, and as the car climbed, I lifted a hand in return, watching as they became smaller and smaller.

Just as I was about to turn away and sit on one of the benches along the wall, I felt a forceful pop beneath my feet, like something snapping. The car lurched, and before I could brace myself properly, it was plunging back down the mountain. I stumbled backward, hitting a pole, which I grabbed onto for dear life.

It all happened so fast. *The car's out of control*, I realized with a sickening flip in my stomach. The cable must have broken.

Out the window, the frozen figures of Juniper and Chip were rushing closer. An earsplitting shriek filled the car, and at first I wondered if I'd screamed. But it was the sound of metal against metal as the car streaked back down the mountain, surfing along the pulley track below. Without the cable, and slightly off-kilter, it was just sliding, metal against metal, gravity tugging the car ever faster. It was going to crash, and there was nowhere for me to go, no way to brace myself.

The car jerked, and I was thrown against the side of the car. I huddled against the wall, watching the window. The crash came swiftly, but it felt like a lifetime in that windowed coffin of a car thrashing its way down in the wrong direction. I glimpsed the whites of Juniper's eyes as what was happening dawned on her. She was as unmoving as a statue. I waved my hands frantically. *Get away! Get away!* I'm not sure if I yelled the words or not, but the last thing I saw before the car overturned and everything went black was Chip yanking Juniper out of the path of the oncoming disaster.

Chapter 5

In the distance I saw lights, faint at first. It was as if I'd fallen asleep outside and was waking up to starlight. And then a faint series of electronic *blurps* reached my ears. It dawned on me that I was lying in my own bed, staring at the small white lights strung across our room at Castle Kringle, and that Nick had just gulped a line of mollusks in Elfcraft.

I turned my head.

He snapped his phone cover closed and leaned forward, hovering next to me in a chair he'd pulled up so close that his knees were hitting the mattress. He tucked the phone away in his pocket.

"Like an addict hiding the crack pipe," I said.

"April." His sheepish smile and dark hair flopping forward over his forehead didn't conceal the worry in his eyes. "I'm so relieved you woke up."

Had he thought I wouldn't? Maybe so. I was a little astonished myself. The last thing I remembered was being rattled around that funicular car like dice in a cup.

A new face loomed over me. Old Doc Honeytree was the most revered medical elf in Santaland, and his long experience showed in his deeply wrinkled face, perpetual stoop, and eyes magnified by Coke-bottle glasses. "How are you feeling?"

I took stock. All my fingers and toes moved correctly, but from those slight movements I could tell that I'd collected a few bruises during that crash. "Like I went over Niagara Falls in a barrel."

"Amazing you didn't break your neck." He shook his head, almost as if I'd brought the accident upon myself.

The corners of my mouth turned down in a frown. "What caused the funicular to go haywire?"

"The cable broke," Nick said. "I've asked the Christmastown engineers to investigate why."

A vague recollection scratched at the back of my mind. I'd seen something . . . or someone. At the moment, all I could recall was Juniper's round, shocked eyes focused on me as I barreled toward her in that runaway box. "Is Juniper all right?"

"Fine," Nick said. "She's right outside. Jingles has been guarding the door."

I pushed myself up to sitting, but a clanging inside my head made me collapse against the pillow again. "I'd like to talk to her."

Doc Honeytree raised a hand. "Wait just a moment. Before allowing a whole herd of visitors in, we need to make sure you're not suffering from head trauma." He bent down and shined a light into my eyes. "You know your name and what country we're in?"

"Of course. I'm Mrs. Claus, and I live in Castle Kringle, in Santaland."

In any other setting, saying those words to a medical professional would have been a prelude to being hauled off to a rubber room. Here, they brought a satisfied nod by the medical professional. "She'll be sharp as an icicle once she's had some rest." As a warning, though, Doc Honeytree leveled a stern look at me. "Stay put for a while. No hopping about like a yearling reindeer. You're fortunate nothing was broken and that you don't have a concussion. Amazing you're alive, frankly." He snapped his black doctor's bag closed. "Lucky thing no one else was on that contraption."

Amen to that. "I'm usually alone on the funicular that time of day."

As the words left my mouth, a cold thread of suspicion snaked through me. I'd made so many uneventful trips up that mountain after rehearsals, alone in that car in the early dark of the winter evenings. Anyone who'd been following my movements for even a short time would have known that.

But why would anyone bother to follow me, much less target me for a vicious attack?

It was an accident. Why think otherwise? My brain wasn't firing on all cylinders.

Doc Honeytree left, and at my request, Juniper was allowed in. Her eyes were red as she climbed up onto the chair Nick had vacated for her, but her warm smile raised my spirits. "I'm so glad you're okay," she said.

"I was worried about you," I told her. "It looked like the funicular car would run right over you."

"Chip pulled me out of the way just in time." Her eyes blinked back tears. "He saved my life."

"I sure did," a familiar voice chirped from the foot of my bed. Chip. He bobbed on his heels, only his head and shoulders visible above the high mattress. "Lucky thing I was there."

"Isn't that wonderful?" Juniper asked. "I owe him my life."

Oh, God. My gratitude for his heroism lasted about half a second, supplanted by dread. *Now she'll never be rid of him.*

I gave myself a swift mental kick. This was my friend! I was a horrible person.

I determined to do better.

Unfortunately, Chip seemed determined to be his Chippiest. "You should've seen the way that car was rushing down the mountain." He spoke as if he were back at the library, narrating a story for children, with rubbery facial expressions and broad gestures. "An avalanche of steel and glass came rushing down, sending out sparks as it slid along the mechanism that had held the cable. Then, when it was about halfway down toward us, the car went off balance and started tumbling. We had no idea where it would land. I took Juniper's hand and ran like the dickens until I heard the terrible crash. When we turned around to look, the steel behemoth had landed at the bottom of the mountain against a snowbank next to the station. Good thing that they'd recently plowed the snow and hadn't yet cleared it. It was softer than if you'd hit the stone wall of the station."

Juniper's eyes shone as if she were reliving the horror. "I was so frantic for the elf medics to get you out of there, but when they found you, you were unconscious. I worried—"

She burst into tears and in an instant Chip was at her side. "Don't cry, puddin' cup. April's going to be fine."

My gaze met Nick's. *Puddin' cup?* he silently mouthed.

I bit my lower lip.

"It's all over," Chip soothed. "The nightmare is over."

I closed my eyes and Nick cleared the room to allow me to rest. But sleep didn't come. For a while, it was just me staring up at those lights again. Trying to remember. Something had slipped my mind. I shut my eyes, willing myself to recall what it was . . .

I must have drifted off momentarily, because in the next moment I was startled out of sleep by a yowling shriek, a shout, and a crash. I bolted up to sitting, heart racing, a shout in my throat just as the bedroom door opened and Jingles, the castle steward, scurried in. He shut the door quickly and sank against it, gasping like a sprinter who'd just crossed the finish line.

An elfman—his elf mother had married a human—Jingles

was persnickety about his appearance. His black-and-white uniform was always neatly pressed, his booties polished to a high gloss, and his elf cap was worn straight. Tonight, though, his cap had slipped halfway down his forehead, showing how rattled he was. Yet a serving tray with a tea service for one remained expertly balanced on one arm.

"What happened?" I asked.

Still gulping in breaths, he said, "It's that horrid cat. He pounced on me! I had to fight him off with a spoon rest."

The cat was Lynxie, another pet of Lucia's. He was supposed to be a cross between a common cat and a lynx, but he'd grown up to be forty pounds of pure hellcat. He was allowed in parts of the house in hopes that he would rid the older wing of the occasional rat, but rodents seemed to terrify him. The only thing he was really good at was attacking us.

I sank back down. The fracas had caused a flashback to earlier tonight. I had to will my heart to stop racing. "I thought Lynxie had been relegated to the Old Keep."

"He keeps 'escaping.'" Jingles straightened and crossed the room with the tea things. "I think Lucia lets him in."

Lucia had a will of iron but was a complete pushover when it came to animals.

"I brought you some peppermint tea." He looked at me worriedly. "You look even more disturbed by Lynxie's attack than I am."

"The noise scared me. My half-asleep brain jumped to the conclusion that someone had come to finish me off."

While he poured, I propped pillows behind me so that I could sit up comfortably. He'd brought scones, too, I noted with anticipation.

He handed over a cup and saucer. "Finish you off? Do you think someone sabotaged the funicular on purpose?"

"I have no proof. Nick says they're looking into why the cable broke."

He sank into the visitor's chair. "Murder!"

"Attempted murder," I corrected. "And I only suspect."

"Suspect whom?" He reached absently for a scone. "Who would want to kill you, and in such a grisly, public way?"

"I'm not sure."

"Several people wanted to kill you last year, but they're gone now."

Amazing to think I went my entire life without anyone wanting me dead, and now in the space of a year I'd been the target of at least two murder attempts. Maybe three. "I don't *know* this was a murder attempt." It didn't hurt to remind myself—and now Jingles—of the real possibility that it had been an accident.

"You must have reason to suspect, though. Otherwise you wouldn't have been lying there wound up like a jack-in-the-box."

I wasn't sure if I should say anything more. But Jingles was my castle confidant. He would tell me if what I was thinking was crazy. "Does Tiny Sparkletoe strike you as the murdering kind?"

"The boot maker? The chair elf of the Christmastown Community Guild? Mr. Public Order?"

"You're right." I sipped my tea. "Stupid idea. I had a confrontation with him yesterday, so I just wondered . . ."

"Confrontation over what?"

I explained why I suspected Tiny of being behind the anti-Halloween campaign represented by the greenhouse break-in and the messages on the library's Elfbook page. Then I related Tiny's sharp words when I paid a visit to his shop. "I think he's Pumpkin Slayer."

Jingles ruminated over another scone. "Pumpkin slaying isn't person slaying."

"You're right." Why would Tiny have escalated so quickly? I drank some more tea to steady myself, but I couldn't shake

the feeling that I'd been targeted. When I returned the cup
to its saucer, the china rattled right along with my nerves. "It
was probably an accident."

Jingles frowned. "So why do you sound as jittery as
Waldo?"

I gasped. "Waldo!" *That's* what I'd been trying to remember.

His eyes narrowed sharply. "What about him?"

"I saw him right before the accident. At least, I think I
did. He was lurking outside the funicular station. When he
saw me, he turned quickly and hurried away in the opposite
direction."

"I always suspected that jitteriness of his signified a sneaky
nature!"

"This morning, he forgot to tell me about an appointment," I recalled.

He shot out of his chair. "This morning he told *me* that I'd
received a phone call summoning me to Kringle Lodge." The
Lodge, a Claus property at the top of Sugarplum Mountain,
was run by Nick's cousin Amory and his wife, Midge. It was
a half-hour ride away via snowmobile. "When I arrived, the
staff told me that no one had called here."

"I wonder what happened."

"Someone sent me on a snow goose chase, that's what."
Jingles yanked the bell bull.

Five minutes later, there was a faint knock at the door.
"Come in," I said.

When Waldo crossed the threshold and saw us both there
waiting for him, he looked as if he might come unglued.
Guilty, I thought. Of course, Waldo always looked anxious. It
didn't necessarily mean that he had attempted to murder me.
Why would he? I liked Waldo.

He cleared his throat. "It's good to see you looking so well
after your accident, ma'am."

"Thank you."

"Is there anything you, um, needed?" he asked, his gaze darting longingly back at the door.

Jingles swaggered toward him. As an elfman, he was slightly taller than Waldo, and now he used that extra height to his advantage. "Mrs. Claus has a few questions for you. And you'd better answer truthfully."

"Of course." Waldo's Adam's apple bobbed over his collar as he swallowed. "Ma'am?"

Though he'd named me as the one with the questions, Jingles began asking them with prosecutorial zeal. "Where were you earlier this evening around five o'clock?"

Waldo looked from me to Jingles and back again. "I—"

"Don't play innocent!" Jingles snapped. "You were seen lurking around the funicular station."

The elf's eyes bugged. "No! I wasn't anywhere near it."

"Then where were you?"

He swallowed. "I'd rather not say."

"Rather not, or can't?"

Waldo's face turned as crimson as a Christmas ball. "It's personal."

Jingles towered over him in full-on Perry Mason mode now. "Isn't it true that the real reason you don't want to give your whereabouts is because you're guilty, guilty, guilty?"

Waldo trembled. "I'm not! I have proof."

Jingles folded his arms again. "Let's have it, then. Where is this alibi?"

"In the kitchen," Waldo said.

"You were in the kitchen?" I asked, surprised. Why had I been so sure it was him?

"*I* wasn't in the kitchen. My, um, alibi, is in the kitchen. Cranberry, I mean. She works there. But when . . . I mean, at the time of the terrible accident, we were both in her— Cranberry's—room."

Jingles looked astounded. "You were having an assigna-
tion with Cranberry, a cook's helper, while Mrs. Claus was in
a horrible accident that nearly took her life?"

"There was no way for him to have known there was an
accident," I pointed out.

His mouth twisted. "I suppose not. *If* he's telling the
truth."

"If he's not telling the truth, all we have to do is ask Cranberry."

Waldo's head bobbed. "Yes, ask her. She'll verify everything I've said."

Jingles asked, "Will she tell us why you lied about a call
from the lodge this morning?"

"I didn't lie. There *was* a call."

"No one at the lodge remembered making one. To whom
did you speak?"

"I . . . I don't remember. A male voice, I think?"

Jingles lifted his arms and dropped them at his sides. "This
is pointless. If he's going to insist on lying—"

"I'm not," Waldo said, looking down at the rug. He produced a handkerchief from his tunic and mopped sweat from
his brow. "Must this story get out to the rest of the castle staff?
Cranberry wasn't exactly off work at that moment, officially.
She might get in trouble with Felice."

Felice, aka General Patton of the Pantry, was Castle Kringle's chef. I wouldn't want to be on her bad side, either.

"If she was trysting instead of working during her shift,
then she *should* be in trouble," Jingles said. "And so should
you, if you knew she was being derelict in her duties."

"I'm sorry." Waldo addressed the words to me.

I don't know why he thought he owed me an apology. If
anything, it was the other way around. I'd dragged him up
here for an interrogation based on a misperception. I'd been
so certain it was him, though.

"You don't have a twin, do you?" I asked.

"I'm an only child. It's just me and my grandmother." For a moment it looked as if he might weep. "Please don't tell my granny about this. I would die if I brought shame to her. I would do anything to protect her."

"All right," I said. "You've told us what we wanted to know. Thank you for being honest with us. I'm sorry to have troubled you."

Hope sparked in his big eyes. "Then I can keep my job?"

Jingles looked as if he would have gladly fired him on the spot. "If Mrs. Claus says you're free to go, you're free to go."

"Thank you, ma'am." Waldo bowed and scuttled away, fast, as if he expected me to change my mind. Perhaps he only wanted to escape Jingles's glare.

The moment the door closed, Jingles pivoted toward me, fists planted on hips. "That elf's hiding something."

"A love affair, evidently."

"We need to get Cranberry up here. I'll break her down."

I couldn't help laughing. "This isn't the Inquisition."

"Maybe it should be—if someone is trying to murder you."

"*If*," I said. "Apparently I was wrong about Waldo. He wouldn't have implicated his girlfriend and risked her losing her job, would he?"

Jingles's lips twisted. "I'm not sure."

"We should wait and see what a structural engineer has to say about that cable. Presumably they'll be able to tell if someone sabotaged it."

"Unless the engineer is in on the plot, too." Jingles's imagination was up and running.

"We shouldn't jump to any conclusions."

Sensing we were done, and probably also noting my growing fatigue, he began to gather the tea things. "All the same, I'm going to keep my eye on that elf."

In leaving the room, he passed Nick, who held the door for him.

"Jingles seems preoccupied," Nick said after he'd checked on me. "But you look better."

"I feel better."

"What were you talking about with your partner in crime?"

"Partner in crime *solving*."

I expected an argument of the don't-play-Sherlock variety. Instead, Nick sank onto the mattress next to me, his face thoughtful. "Did he have some information to give you?"

"We discussed Waldo. I thought I saw him earlier at the funicular station. He'd already been acting oddly all day. But it turns out I was wrong. Waldo told us that he was with a kitchen elf named Cranberry at the time of the accident."

"And did you talk to Cranberry?"

"No. I thought it better to give him the benefit of the doubt. Unless you found out for certain that the crash wasn't an accident."

Nick heaved a sigh, stood, and walked to the bell pull.

I sat up. "What are you doing?"

"I'm going to speak with Cranberry. An engineer examined the cable. He thinks it was cut deliberately."

Chapter 6

Cranberry was summoned to Nick's office, a spacious room on the castle's first floor boasting an executive-size desk, pull-down maps of various continents on the walls, a Christmas tree in one corner, as well as examples of possible toy favorites sent over from the workshop. Nick felt it was a more suitable place than our bedroom for questioning a castle employee. I had to agree.

Not wanting to miss anything, I hauled myself out of bed and went down to sit in on the interview. My head and bones ached, but my curiosity ached even more.

Jingles ushered Cranberry into the study and stood back, arms crossed, as if he intended to stay.

"Thank you, Jingles," Nick said. "That will be all."

The steward opened his mouth as if to argue, but one didn't argue with Santa in Castle Kringle—unless you were Santa's wife, of course.

I'd seen Cranberry many times, although our interactions had been limited. She was one of many cook's helpers, which, in a place the size of Castle Kringle, was a busy job. That she'd managed to sneak out for a tryst a few hours before dinnertime showed either considerable ingenuity or mad time-management skills.

Though dressed in a plain red chef's helper uniform with a white apron and hat, something in how she moved suggested Cranberry might be the siren of the kitchen elves. She glanced over at me, gave me a quick up-and-down, and seemed to sniff a little at my robe, a magnificent boiled-wool garment designed by Madame Neige. It wasn't as if I were sprawled in a chair in a tatty old housecoat.

Still, I sat up a little straighter in my corner chair.

It was my intention to let Nick to do most of the talking. He definitely looked more official in his Santa suit, minus the hat. His winter beard was already coming along nicely, too—not so scraggly as it had been over the summer. He said he liked to shave it off every spring and start a new one, like a reindeer starting a new set of antlers.

Her gaze softened when she looked at him, and she blinked several times. Before he could ask her a single question, she blurted out, "I'm sorry. I shouldn't have done it."

"Done what?" he asked.

"Invited Waldo to my room. That's what this is about, isn't it?" She sniffed and dabbed at her eye, as if wiping a tear with her apron. "It was only the once, I swear."

"What time was this?" I asked.

She sucked in a ragged breath and directed her reply to Nick. "J-just fifteen minutes or so. Around five o'clock."

Waldo didn't own a sleigh, traditional or motorized. He couldn't have been both at the bottom of the mountain at the funicular station and with Cranberry in her room around five o'clock. No one could have reached the castle that quickly even by sleigh bus or thumbing a ride on someone's snowmobile.

As Nick and I made silent calculations, Cranberry tensed. "Am I going to lose my job?"

"Of course not," Nick said.

"I didn't mess up anything," she insisted. "I'd peeled all the parsnips and rutabagas, like Felice ordered me to."

"Well, then," Nick said. "There's nothing more to say. We just needed to know where Waldo was."

"Why?" She inclined her head. "What's he supposed to have done?"

"It doesn't matter," Nick said. "As long as he was with you."

She crooked a hand on her hip. "Then I can go?"

"Of course. I'm sorry to have had to ask questions concerning your personal business," Nick said, as if he'd put her through a terrible ordeal. "I didn't mean to make you feel threatened. We just needed to double-check something."

Her eyes narrowed. "And you won't tell Felice, or Jingles?"

"No." He looked over at me, as if expecting me to agree to the impossible.

"Jingles already knows what Waldo told us," I said.

"But he'll have to keep it under his cap," Nick assured her.

"Right." She obviously had a more realistic take on the castle grapevine than Nick did. She chewed her lip. "So . . . I'd better get back, then. We're still finishing cleaning from dinner."

"Thank you, Cranberry," Nick said.

When she was gone, I leaned back. "Not sure how much of that I believed."

He looked shocked. "Didn't you see her? She was upset."

My dear husband. How could he have arrived at the ripe old age of thirty-eight with so little cynicism? "It could have been an act."

"If it weren't the truth, why would she have confirmed Waldo's story? You saw her—she was fearful she'd lose her job."

"She certainly seemed more worried about her job than about Waldo."

Nick tilted back in his chair, frowning. "Would that be unusual?"

"Depends on how much she likes Waldo." From what I'd witnessed, the answer to that was *not much*. The two seemed a mismatch all around. But then why had she vouched for him?

Maybe Nick was right and she was simply telling the truth.

"If it wasn't Waldo, that leaves us with no suspects," he said.

I scooted forward in my chair. "Actually, it leaves us with one suspect." I filled him in on my suspicions about Tiny Sparkletoe, telling him about my recent visit to the Bootery, followed by the trip to the constabulary. "Crinkles didn't take my suspicions about Tiny seriously," I said. "All I got out of my visit there was a bunch of raffle tickets."

Nick groaned. "Not you, too."

Oh, no. "How many did you buy?"

"Ten."

I tilted my head. "Which wallpaper did you like—hens or wreaths?"

"Hens."

"Me, too."

He frowned. "Odd that they didn't mention that you'd been at the constabulary or anything about Tiny."

"He probably wanted to steer clear of the subject of me so that you wouldn't wonder if I'd already bought tickets. Honestly, Nick, those two lawmen worry more about the wallpaper in the jail than they do about crimes committed."

"They'll be investigating this funicular crash now that we have proof it wasn't an accident."

I tried but failed to hold back sarcasm. "I'm sure the culprit is quivering in fear at the thought."

Nick laughed. "Anyway, let them take care of the inves-

tigating from here on out." His smile melted away. "If someone's already tried to kill you once . . ."

At his unspoken meaning, fear knotted in my gut. For
some reason, I'd been so focused on what had happened earlier tonight that I hadn't considered what could happen in
the future. If the sabotage of the funicular wasn't a random
act, and if the mastermind behind the crash was targeting me
specifically, they surely knew by now that this attempt on
my life had failed. What if they had something else up their
sleeve?

It's hard to get a good night's sleep when your unconscious brain keeps reminding you that someone's out there
watching for the next chance to kill you. My nightmares did
make getting out of bed the next morning more appealing,
however. I was awake and showered before Jingles came in,
not just with coffee, but with a large box from the Order of
Elven Seamstresses.

"The dress," he announced, placing it on the bed. "I don't
suppose you'll need it now."

"Oh, yes, I will."

Nick and I were determined that no change should en-
sue from the accident last night, which we were still calling
an accident even among the family. Gossip spread quickly,
and we didn't want to alert the population at large that the
cable had been cut. For one thing, we didn't want the culprit to know that we'd twigged to the fact that the funicular
had been sabotaged. The night before, Nick had paid another
visit to Constable Crinkles to tell him about the engineer's
findings and direct him to have a word with Tiny Sparkletoe concerning his whereabouts at the time of the accident.
Hopefully Crinkles would catch him off guard and wring the
truth out of him.

"You can't go cut ribbons now," Jingles insisted. "You almost died last night!"

As if cutting ribbons required Herculean strength. "I'm fine now. In fact, think I'll go down to breakfast." I was eager to test exactly how spry I was feeling . . . and to hear what the rest of the family was saying about what had happened yesterday.

Everyone was gathered in the breakfast room except Nick and Tiffany, the early birds. Nick was in his office, I knew, and Tiffany always liked to be the one to open her tearoom.

Nick's nephew, Christopher, greeted me with excitement. "You look pretty good for someone who rolled down a mountain."

"Only halfway down," I said modestly as I sidestepped Quasar on my way to the sideboard covered in silver chafing dishes and bowls of fruit. Quasar was having a bowl of what looked like raw cereals and lichen, the reindeer breakfast of champions.

At twelve, Christopher was in that last stage of boyhood— chipmunk cheeks and a body just one growing spell away from adolescence. He still had a child's relentless inquisitiveness, too. "Was it scary?" he asked.

Lucia shot him a sharp look. "What do you think?"

From the head of the table, Pamela said, "Are you sure you should be up and about so soon, April?"

"I feel fine." I loaded scrambled eggs and French toast onto my plate.

"What was the crash like?" Christopher asked. "I bet it was like plunging through space."

I fought a brief but terrifying flashback as I took my place at the table and snapped open a napkin. "It was a plunge, all right."

"Like when Neldor drops the little elves he steals," he

continued, all enthusiasm. "They free-fall through the air until—*splat!*—they hit the ice."

"There's no need to be gruesome, Christopher," Pamela said.

He shrugged. "It's what Neldor does."

"That's fiction." Lucia's voice took on an edge. "It's not good fiction, either. That story's highly prejudicial against reindeer. There's never been a case of a reindeer with weird antlers harming an elf child," she lectured. "And yet that's all kids are talking about now—dressing up as Neldor."

"I'd rather be a snow monster," Christopher said. "That's what I'm going to be for Halloween."

I shook my head. "I just remember kids dressing up as witches, ghosts, and Ninja Turtles."

"What's a Ninja Turtle?" Christopher frowned. "It sounds dumb."

"No dumber than Neldor," Lucia said.

Pamela smiled in memory. "When I was a girl, I always liked to be something pleasant, like a princess or a fairy."

Christopher scowled. "I thought the point of Halloween is to be scary."

"The point is to have fun," I said. "Spooky fun."

"Fairies aren't spooky," he insisted. "Princesses, either."

"That's only because you don't know your North Pole history," Lucia said. "If you did, you'd know about Crazy Princess Lucasta, the hunchback. She ordered an entire elf village to be covered over in ice bricks because one of its elves laughed at her."

Christopher frowned. "Did the elf ever apologize?"

"He couldn't," Lucia said. "He suffocated along with the entire village."

"Harsh," he said.

I slanted a dubious look at Lucia. "How does someone

cover an entire town in ice bricks without the elves inside escaping?"

Lucia shrugged. "Maybe she did it while they were all asleep."

"She was either a lightning fast ice-brick layer, or those were the most hapless elves ever."

"Okay, maybe it didn't happen *exactly* like it's been passed down to us," Lucia admitted. "The point is, a scary princess makes a lot more sense than a scary reindeer. People are better equipped to be villains than animals."

Given my recent experience, I couldn't argue with that.

When breakfast was over, I returned to my room and got myself ready for the day. After fixing myself up and putting on the dress and cape, I felt like a new person. Only a few aches and pains reminded me of yesterday's misadventure. I'd been very, very lucky.

I went down to Nick's office, where he was waiting in his best Santa suit. I hadn't expected him to be formally dressed, too, but it was nice that the orphans would be getting the full Santa effect. It's hard to explain how impressive it is to see the genuine Santa in full Santa regalia. *Santa* and *sex appeal* weren't words I associated together before my marriage, but Nick took my breath away. If my mother-in-law hadn't been standing there next to him, I might have pulled him down onto the musk-ox-hair rug.

The Santa-suit lust worried me a little, to be honest. Maybe the North Pole was getting to me. Could eggnog cravings be far behind?

"You look fantastic," he said. The glint in his eye told me the musk-ox-rug scenario had crossed his mind, too.

"So do you," I said.

Pamela beamed. "Doesn't he? Born to don the suit," she said, choking up a little.

The truth was that Nick was wearing the suit only because his beloved older brother had died, and Christopher was too young to step into his inherited role. Nick was the Santa regent, and coping the best he could. But the role was definitely growing on him.

"Are you sure you want to go?" he asked me. "Everyone would understand if you weren't able to make it."

"No, I'm going."

Whoever had tried to kill me would see that I was not an easy person to get rid of.

Chapter 7

The new Santaland Home for Orphaned Elves was located in a former park on the north side of Christmastown. Gray stone walls rose from a looping drive up a short hill. Small evergreens, seedlings started from the trees of the Christmas tree forest, pushed up through the snow on either side of the drive. Someday this would be a spectacular boulevard, but even now, driving up with Nick in Santa's ceremonial sleigh, I was struck by the stark beauty of the building and its prospect.

The residents of the orphanage had just recently been relocated from their old home in Tinkertown, the neighboring town where most of the worker elves lived. The abandoned building was going to be used as transitional housing for young craftsmen training at Santa's workshop. Today the orphans were all dressed in their best tunics and stockings, their booties polished to a high gloss. Groups of them sang in corridors as the town dignitaries were escorted through the new facilities by Miss Gladgoose, the head of the orphans' home. She had a helmet of dyed black hair and wore round wire-rim glasses that kept slipping down her nose. I couldn't help wondering if Chip, Juniper's boyfriend, had made those specs. I was ready to add slapdash lens crafting to his other faults.

In the dormitories, the classrooms, the activity halls, and the dining room, there was always an elf or two on display. *Props*, I couldn't help thinking as I looked at the orphanage's resident nurse taking the blood pressure of an older elf child. Who knows how long they'd been sitting there waiting to perform this pantomime.

At first I didn't recognize the elf on the business end of the blood-pressure cuff. He looked so different than he did the last time I'd seen him. The black tunic and jeans tucked into booties had been exchanged for the orphanage uniform of red and green.

"Quince," I said.

"Hey there, Mrs. Claus," he said casually, saluting me with his free hand.

Miss Gladgoose looked surprised, then appalled. "You know this orphan?"

"We met"—I bit off my words before I let slip to the tour crowd that the model elf patient before them had been in jail yesterday—"recently."

Our tour guide's already thin lips pursed to the point of disappearing completely. "Quince is one of our most senior orphans. Soon he'll be out in the world on his own. Another Santaland Home for Orphaned Elves success story."

Quince barely held back a smirk. Even I wondered if Miss Gladgoose had laid it on too thick, but my fellow VIPs all nodded approvingly.

Part of the older orphans' day, we'd learned, was spent in one of the mini-workshop rooms, which gave them a taste of the various Santaland trades and prepared them for making their own way when their time at the home came to an end.

"Where will you be going to work?" Nick asked Quince.

He shrugged. "Dunno yet."

Miss Gladgoose cleared her throat. "We're trying to se-cure a place for Quince at the Wrapping Works."

The lack of enthusiasm on Quince's face told me exactly how he felt about his future life in wrapping.

"Well!" Miss Gladgoose said. "Moving right along—"

"I'd like to find something to do that would allow me to be with Pocket," Quince interrupted.

Nick was all ears. "Who's Pocket?"

"Pocket's my best friend, but while I'm here, he has to sleep outside."

"Because he's a snowman," Miss Gladgoose reminded him with a scowl.

"I don't see what's wrong about that. Pocket and I would like to do something outdoors. And adventurous."

Miss Gladgoose tsked. "Santa and Mrs. Claus didn't come here to engage in your pointless speculation and daydreams."

Nick smiled. "Pointless speculation is one of April's favorite pastimes."

I could see the kid's dilemma. Snowmen were all around Santaland; once created, they could live a long time in our climate. But they definitely couldn't stay indoors. I tried to think of elves I knew who did outdoor work. Maybe I could find a position for Quince, although I didn't want to get his hopes up. . . .

"We should finish our tour," Miss Gladgoose said. "We have a schedule, you know."

"Good," Quince muttered. "My arm's sore."

"Continuing on," Miss Gladgoose trilled over his lament, hustling our group down the hallway.

Halfway down the corridor we reached a nursery school room of younger, rambunctious elves wearing costumes that had been made for them by older orphans in their sewing class.

"They were so excited when they heard you were coming, Mrs. Claus—they know you're responsible for bringing Halloween to Santaland."

I was uncomfortable taking credit for a holiday that had been around for centuries, at least where I came from, but before I could protest, we were rushed by twenty tiny snow monsters, demented reindeer, something that looked like an eagle, a polar bear, and a ghost.

I turned to Miss Gladgoose and said in a low voice, "If I'd known they were going to be in costume, I would've brought candy to give them."

"No sense in that," she said brusquely. "They'll all be having refreshments after the speeches. Cake and eggnog for everyone."

At the mention of treats, the room erupted in shrieks. Nick dived into the melee and ho-ho-ho'ed good-naturedly for them, and asked more questions about their costumes. He seemed to be enjoying himself.

When we all left the warmth of the building to look at the outdoor amenities before heading to the area set up for the dedication ceremony, a snowman stood sentry close by, facing the orphanage. I knew at once this was Pocket. He was diminutive for a snowman. Instead of the three-blob kind that most snowmen were, he had just a head stacked on a fat base—which made sense, since he'd been made by an eight-year-old. He wore a hodgepodge of clothes. His hat was a battered brown herringbone wool cap, his eyes were coal, and his scarf was an obviously handmade black-and-red striped one that was far too long and so was wound around his neck several times, almost as if it were choking him. His stick arms were stubby and short, but he had the friendliest smile I'd ever seen on a snowman.

Breaking away from the Gladgoose herd, I went over and introduced myself.

"Quince mentioned you to me. It's a pleasure to meet you."

"The pleasure's all mine," the snowman said. "Gosh, what

an honor. And Santa, too," he added as Nick came up behind me. Apparently the whole tour was trailing after me.

"Pleased to make your acquaintance," Nick said.

Quince appeared, slipping in next to his frozen friend. "I was just telling Mrs. Claus we don't want to go to the Wrapping Works."

Miss Gladgoose's demeanor had chilled right along with the temperature outside. "We're not here to discuss your future employment, Quince. We're only here to look at the pond and the sleigh slide."

For recreation, orphans had something called a wavy pond, which was a sort of skate park, only done in ice. Tiffany was there with several young elves. A few daredevils showed off their skating prowess, flying across the course and performing maneuvers that made my stomach flip to watch. On the flat part of the ice, Tiffany oversaw a demonstration of spins and figures. There's nothing cuter than a group of elves barely out of toddlerhood on ice skates.

Beyond the pond was a sledding slide—a super-slide coated in ice that the elf orphans could sled down. It looked incredibly fun, and for a moment I regretted being in my nice togs.

After the ice skating show had received its applause, I pointed to the slide. "Is anyone going to demonstrate that?"

"Not today." Miss Gladgoose glanced at her watch. "The speeches should begin soon . . ."

"Looks like Mrs. Claus would like to try it," a familiar voice called out.

Tiny Sparkletoe pushed to the front of the crowd. He must have been a late arrival. I hadn't noticed him among the VIPs on the indoor tour—and he was hard to miss. He was dressed in a velvet and wool tunic with crimson breeches and forest-green stockings. His boots, of course, were elaborate creations made from the richest leather dyed red, gold buckles in the silhouette of a Christmas tree, and squared-off toes that curled inward multiple times. Sparkletoe originals, no doubt, and they were impressive. They looked like something that might be on display at the Museum of Modern Art.

His smile put me on edge. "Or would climbing something the ladder up to the slide be too traumatic after your recent ordeal?"

I glanced to my side to get Nick's reaction, only to discover he'd gone over to talk to the kiddies at the skate pond.

"I guess we should just be thankful that you were able to make it today," Tiny said, the corners of his mouth turning down in faux concern.

Maybe he hadn't expected to see me at all because he thought I'd be dead from the funicular accident. I lifted my head. "I'm perfectly fine, as you can see." Not for anything would I let myself appear weakened.

"Probably too nervous to want to try sledding anytime soon, though." He grinned. "That's a big drop."

Yes, it was. I swallowed. "If Miss Gladgoose says it's not on the program . . ."

"Well, to be honest, it hasn't been tried and tested yet," the lady said.

"Yes, it has," Quince said. "A bunch of us snuck out and sledded on it this morning before all the people got here. It's fun!"

Miss Gladgoose's expression turned stormy. "Who did this? I want names."

Great. This VIP tour was going to end up getting a lot of orphans in trouble.

Too late, Quince realized his error. "I just thought that if Mrs. Claus wanted to try it . . ."

"Ladies do not shoot down slides," Miss Gladgoose said.

"Actually, this one does." I smiled at her. "Show me the way, Quince."

Miss Gladgoose's jaw dropped, but she said nothing as I turned and marched toward the intimidating staircase that led to the platform at the top of the slide. Maybe making a spectacle of myself would make her forget the orphans' misdemeanor and get them off the hook. And I would prove to Tiny that his attempt on my life had not intimidated me.

It was a good thing boots were de rigueur in Santaland. If I'd been at home, I would have been wearing slinky pumps with my outfit, and I never would have made it up the long, twisting metal staircase that led to the top of the slide. Even in dress boots, the climb was difficult. The staircase seemed to go on forever. A handrail had been installed with elves in mind—child elves, at that. The higher I climbed, the queasier I felt. And it wasn't just the memory of Tiny taunting me that made me feel that way. I hadn't noticed the wind before, but now it pierced right through me, making my teeth chatter. I held the cape around me with one hand while with the other leaned onto the railing for dear life. But not so far that I would topple off.

If it hadn't been for the pressure of Quince behind me, I might have turned back. I couldn't forget Tiny's smile as he challenged me to go up on this thing. What if he'd done that because he knew there was something wrong with the slide? Could he have sabotaged this contraption the way I suspected he had the funicular?

"You say you were on this just this morning?" I asked Quince.

"Yeah."

"And it was okay?"

"Sure. It's fun."

Fun, he says.

I finally wobbled onto the platform at the top of the slide and looked down. A wave of dizziness hit me. Dizziness and cold, stark fear. This was lunacy. What was I thinking? Yesterday I'd fallen down a mountain, and now I was going to purposefully hurl myself down a slide?

A steep, icy slide.

"Don't look directly down," Quince said.

He was a mind reader. I lifted my gaze to look out on the snowy lawn by the orphan home. The faces in the crowd tilted up at me. More people and elves had gathered for the ceremony than the group who'd taken Miss Gladgoose's tour. I looked for Nick, but instead my gaze alit on Tiny, grinning.

Was he smiling because he knew I was terrified or because I'd fallen into a trap he'd set for me?

"I guess I can't back out now," I muttered. I just had to trust that Tiny was playing mind games, not truly trying to kill me this time.

Sleds were lined up like balls in the feeder at a bowling alley. Quince guided me over, set one at the top of the slide, and helped me onto it. "Just kneel and lean back," he said. "You'll have a blast."

I did as directed, although I was skeptical about the blast part. *Here goes nothing.* He gave me a quick push, tipping me from horizontal to what felt like a sheer vertical drop-off, and down I plunged. A scream stuck in my throat. My stomach hadn't flipped so much since I'd ridden in a flying sleigh the year before. But I felt the same rush and excitement. I finally let out a long shriek. The world was a blur around me. This was pure sensation—air rushing, my flapping cape. The ground was careening toward me as if I were in free fall, but instead of feeling terror, I was exhilarated. I caught sight of Miss Gladgoose below, her arms akimbo. I let out another whoop.

Too soon, the curve of the slide flattened and my sled projectile slowed as I reached the end. Nick was there to hand me up. Good thing, too. I might have forgotten yesterday, but my muscles hadn't. I was as stiff as an old lady as he pulled me to standing.

"That was fantastic!" I cried. "Do you want to try?"

He looked at me as if I were a madwoman. "Maybe some other time."

"We must be getting back," Miss Gladgoose said, unable to hide her irritation at the way I'd gone off-piste. Maybe it *had* been juvenile, but her tone made me want to do it all over again. "The other guests are waiting. If you'll just come this way . . ."

"Just a moment," Nick said. He nodded up where Quince was halfway through with his sled ride down. When he arrived at the bottom, Miss Gladgoose shot the orphan a look that probably made Quince wish he were back in the cozy Christmastown jail cell.

We all proceeded to the front of the orphanage for the official ceremony. Pamela and Tiffany were standing together; Pamela smiled her tightest Queen Mother smile as I walked over. I didn't have to guess what she thought of my slide stunt. Other Claus relatives were mixed in among the upper-crust elves of Christmastown, including stout Cousin Amory, taking the morning off from his job at the Candy Cane Factory, standing next to his wife, Midge, who always reminded me of a pouter pigeon. I smiled at them all as I headed to the front row with Nick.

Tiny Sparkletoe had also claimed a place up front next to Mayor Firlog and his wife—right where Nick and I were directed to stand.

Tiny grinned when our eyes met. "Have fun?"

"As a matter of fact, I did."

The mayor took a step toward me. "We heard all about your accident. So terrible! And now the city's going to have to find the funds to fix the funicular. Where's that going to come from?"

The budget was always uppermost in Mayor Firlog's mind. When he looked at the new orphanage, you could almost see the dollar signs spinning in his eyeballs.

"Time to cut the ribbon," Nick said before the gathering could devolve into a discussion of revenue.

But first, Miss Gladgoose made a speech full of gratitude and reminders of how necessary the new home had been. After that, Mayor Firlog had "a few remarks," which went on and on . . . and on. Everyone who'd ever donated anything was thanked. My cape was warm, but standing still for so long in the cold made me feel as if my blood were congealing. By the time the mayor wrapped up his speech, I was surprised my frigid fingers could still manipulate the giant pair of scissors Miss Gladgoose had handed me to cut the ribbon.

Luckily, the refreshments were served inside the orphan home's main hall. The only orphans present were a few who were serving eggnog and tea or handing around trays of finger food and cookies. I looked around for Quince, but he was gone. The orphans were having their party elsewhere.

For a few minutes my concentration was so focused on thawing out that I forgot that I was standing in the same room as my nemesis. I had to give Tiny credit, he had nerve to spare, and gall. He found me as I was holding my teacup with both hands, hoping the heat from it would get my blood circulating again.

"I suppose I have you to thank for the visit I received from Constable Crinkles early this morning." His whiskers twitched in irritation. "He came to my workplace to interrogate me. Me! The head of the Christmastown Community Guild."

"To ask you about . . . ?"

"You know very well what," he said. "Your accident."

"What did you tell him?"

"That I was in the Bootery all day yesterday. Louie was there, too, and confirmed it for the constable."

"Well, I guess that's all there was to it, then." I couldn't help feeling disappointed. Not that I wanted to persecute Tiny, but someone messed with that cable, and Tiny already had a bone to pick with me. I hated to think there was another elf in Christmastown who wanted me dead . . . but if Louie could back him up on his alibi, there had to be someone else.

Nothing like an unseen enemy to unsettle your nerves.

"That wasn't all," Tiny continued, carrying on with his grievances. "He wanted to know the names of all my clients who wear a size four and a quarter."

Mayor Firlog flinched. "*I* wear a size four and a quarter."

"It's the most common size in Santaland," Tiny said. "Louie and I will be going through our records forever trying to draw up that list. And then those clients will be pestered with questions, too."

"Again?" the mayor asked. "The constable's already been to my house once."

"Why?" I asked.

Tiny explained, "Because I told the constable that at the end of the day, when the funicular accident took place, I was talking with a client. Who just so happened to be Mrs. Firlog, who was trying on the boots she's wearing now. But would he take my word for it? No! Thanks to you, every law-abiding elf is under a cloud of suspicion. The constable went to the mayor's wife and asked her if she really was at the Bootery when I said she was."

Behind him, someone turned. It was Mrs. Firlog, round and doughy. Her yellow hair was piled high atop her head, the bun at the crest of the pile set off with its own tiny tiara. "He actually interrogated us!" she said, trembling in remembered offense. "We've never had the constable in the house before."

"He was only asking you to corroborate what Tiny told him," I explained.

"As if I were a criminal!" the boot maker yelled. "I had nothing to do with that cable being cut."

His incensed voice pierced through the chatter around us. A hush fell and everyone turned toward us.

I could hardly believe Tiny had blurted that out. *Gotcha,* I thought.

"The cable was *cut?*" Firlog asked.

"And how would you know that, Tiny?" I asked.

His lips turned up in a tight smile. "The constable told me."

I groaned inwardly. I guess Crinkles hadn't understood that the information about the cable was supposed to be kept on the q.t. for as long as possible. Now that all the movers and shakers of Christmastown had heard the news, it would spread like a river overspilling a dam.

Firlog scratched his chin. "Maybe that'll relieve the city of liability."

"The liability should all be on April Claus here." Tiny grew even more voluble. "Constable Crinkles insinuated that someone was trying to kill her. Again. That's why the cable was cut—but *I* didn't do it. No one can prove I did!"

"Of course it wasn't you," Mrs. Firlog said soothingly. "Why would you kill anyone? You're chairman of the Christmastown Community Guild."

That declaration was met by nods all around. Big Guild presence in that room.

"There are better ways the constable could be spending his time than questioning me," Tiny said. "Why not talk to the three other witnesses? There must be other suspects they could dig up."

Who? If the attack was targeted at me, what enemies had

I made over the past year? Even my acquaintance with Tiny had been mostly cordial until recently.

"Didn't I warn that Halloween would bring mayhem to this town?" He posed the question to the group in general, and the crowd was with him.

"It's certainly creating havoc," one well-dressed matron said. "An elf in a snow monster suit scared my reindeer team yesterday. They nearly crashed into Gert's pretzel cart."

"There!" Tiny said, vindicated. "You see?"

The mayor's wife leapt in to agree with him. "When we're encouraging people to run around town in disguise, is it any surprise that they'd go a step further and start doing something criminal like sabotaging our transportation?"

A hubbub about the cost of fixing the funicular grew until I worried we were going to have an impromptu, contentious council meeting right there. But just then a latecomer elf swaggered into our midst. Walnut Lovejoy, rising entrepreneur of Christmastown and Tiny's rival in the shoe trade, was dressed in green velvet with red-and-purple stockings in a diamond pattern. The outfit's extravagance topped Tiny's, something that didn't escape Tiny's notice.

"Well, well." Walnut's smile showed blinding white teeth. He was a handsome elf, with a head of wavy brown hair that he'd blow-dried and sprayed into a pompadour worthy of *Saturday Night Fever*–era John Travolta. To show it off, he went around bare-headed, which was unelfin of him. "I hear you enjoyed my slide, Mrs. Claus."

"*Your* slide?" I asked.

He shrugged modestly. "Of course it belongs to the orphanage now, but I paid for it."

"And will brag about it until you're blue in the face, evidently," Tiny sneered.

It did seem bad form to toot one's horn so loudly at a charity event, but then again, the whole togged-up crowd was here because they were donors to the cause. Still, Walnut Lovejoy, only recently wealthy and a relative newcomer to social functions like this one, came across as an outsider.

"It was a fun slide," I said, trying to nip an argument between the two men in the bud. "So nice of you to donate it to the orphans."

"Unlike some, I don't balk when it comes to spending on those less fortunate than myself." He stared pointedly at Tiny.

Tiny bristled. They were like two velvet-clad roosters squaring off. "Was that crack about me?"

Walnut laughed. "Funny you should assume it was. Maybe if you think of yourself as a cheapskate, you might be one."

"I'm not a cheapskate, I'm just prudent."

"Stingy," Walnuts translated.

Tiny went as red as a new Santa suit. "I certainly don't go wasting my money opening businesses I know nothing about."

"Nonsense," Walnut said. "Bootie World is even more profitable than Walnut's Sleigh Wash."

Tiny scowled. "You know nothing about quality."

"I sell booties every elf can afford."

"That's lucky, because if elves buy your cheap product, they'll have to buy new booties every six months."

"Keep telling yourself that, Tiny. Next year I'm going to be launching our custom line." Walnut grinned. "*If* I can find the right elf boot maker for the job, and I think I can."

Did he intend to seduce Louie away from Tiny? If Tiny's apoplectic expression was any hint, the answer was yes. "You upstart!"

Walnut laughed. "That's right—you don't like rivals, do you?"

"I play to win," Tiny said.

"And even when you win, you don't know what to do with the prize. You're a small, miserable elf, Tiny Sparkletoe."

"I'm a pillar of this community, which is something you'll never be. I'm also Pixie Sparkletoe's husband. You'll never be that, either."

"No?" Walnut asked, looking amused. "Anything can happen, you know."

"Is that a threat?"

Walnut laughed. "Just a statement of fact, Tiny. Just a statement of fact."

The escalating hostility between the two had drawn a crowd. If a fistfight had broken out between the two bootie sellers, I wouldn't have been surprised. But in the next moment Miss Gladgoose marshaled in a large group of orphans to sing "Winter Wonderland" for the guests. I tried to catch Nick's eye, wondering if he'd heard the exchange. But he was busy being a jolly, attentive Santa and was focused on the orphan singers.

What had Tiny meant about Walnut never being Pixie's husband? What an odd thing to say. I looked around to see if Walnut and Tiny were still fuming at each other, but Walnut had disappeared. And Tiny was back to glaring at me.

Chapter 8

For the next two days, the world seemed relatively quiet. Halloween approached, and everyone focused on the fun. The band had another rehearsal for the festival program. More window displays appeared, households stocked up on candy treats, and sewing machines whirred overtime to transform little children into snow monsters, Neldors, and even, occasionally, traditional witches and ghosts.

Madame Neige sent a package to me with my own Halloween outfit, which I tried on and then tucked away with giddy impatience. Even if we were just going to Midge's Halloween party at Kringle Lodge, I was looking forward to it. Halloween was the rare time when I longed to be twelve years old again. Old enough to dress up and run around trick-or-treating with friends, still young enough to stuff myself with candy and not care.

A text came in from my friend Claire in Cloudberry Bay. It was her first response since I'd sent her Damaris Sproat's editorial in the *Cloudberry Bay Weekly Chronicle*. If I hadn't been so preoccupied with my troubles here, I would have worried she was ghosting me.

Claire's text message was: **Are you okay? I'm worried about you.**

I frowned at the screen and then typed, **I'm fine. Just a small accident.**

I hit SEND before I realized that there was no way Claire in Oregon could have heard about a funicular accident in Santaland. She didn't even know Santaland existed outside of department store displays and Christmas cartoon specials. I hadn't been up-front with her about who Nick was or where he was from.

Her response was immediate. **OMG! Accident? Are you sure?**

Me: It's fine, honestly.

Claire: Are you SURE it was an accident?

Actually, no, I wasn't sure. But I couldn't exactly explain to Claire now that there might be a malevolent shoemaker elf who wanted to kill me.

Claire: You need to be careful. Especially around Nick.

Me: ???

Claire: Was he with you during the accident?

Me: No, he was at work.

Claire: And you aren't suspicious?

Me: LOL. No. Do you think I married a psycho?

Psycho Santa, qu'est-ce que c'est, my brain riffed.

The three dots indicating Claire was typing pulsed for several minutes. Maybe she had a customer at her shop. Finally a little burp alerted me that a new message bubble had popped up.

Claire: I don't want to alarm you, but I think you should keep an eye on Nick. Maybe it's not my business, but while I was dusting around the Coast Inn, I found a few things that seemed . . . weird. One was a list. It was tucked inside a book I'd seen Nick reading that was left on a bedside table. The list had "Naughty" and "Nice" written at the top. And it included actual

**names (both sexes!) written under both categories!
I'm pretty sure it was Nick's handwriting.**

Uh-oh. I tried to think how to respond. Before I could
decide whether to lie or merely evade, another bubble from
Claire appeared.

I also found some sketches of Santa suits. Like, several. I think your husband might have some issues.

The honest thing to do would be to put her mind at ease
and let her know that Nick wasn't a creep with a Santa Claus
fetish but that he was, in fact, Santa Claus. It would have been
such a relief to type those words. But over the summer, I
never gathered the nerve to confess Nick's identity to Claire.
It wasn't an easy subject to bring into a conversation. *"By the
way, I live at the North Pole now!"* or *"Guess what? I sleep with
Santa!"* seemed too ridiculous.

Claire was a levelheaded businesswoman. Her business
was selling ice cream, yes, but she didn't suffer fools. If I'd
taken her aside over the summer and announced that I'd married Santa Claus, she'd have thought I was insane. So I'd told
her Nick ran the family business up north, which wasn't exactly a lie. When Claire had tried to do an end run around me
and questioned Nick directly for more details, he'd followed
my lead and responded with bland generalities or changed the
subject.

Now this was the result. She believed I'd married a lunatic.

What is friendship without honesty? My feelings would
have been hurt if I'd found out Claire had hidden a huge part
of her life from me. Yet here I was, concealing the identity of
the man I'd married. Concealing my own identity. Lying to
my friend.

And I still didn't know how to introduce the subject. Especially via text.

**Me: I'm sure there's a reasonable explanation.
Claire: ???**

Me: I'll talk to Nick.
Claire: I'm here if you need me.
Another wave of guilt hit me. She was offering support, and I was tap-dancing around the truth. I didn't know what else to say, so I did what I hated to do. I emojied my way out of the conversation, sending her a smiley face.

It was always Claire's and my contention that emojis were the new "I should let you go" passive-aggressive sign-off. Yet here we were.

I didn't have time to brood about it too much. The reindeer were having a cross-country sled pull and Lucia was refereeing one of the heats. In a moment of weakness, I'd agreed to go along and watch. It wasn't that I didn't enjoy reindeer races, but in Santaland they were endless. Half the young reindeer in the country took part in a series of tournaments throughout the year, the outcome of which would determine the team that pulled Nick's sleigh on Christmas Eve. Obviously, that was an important job, but . . .

All. Year. Long.

It was bound to be cold standing in a snow-covered field watching reindeer run around, and, wouldn't you know, it had started snowing heavily during the night. I put on my warmest clothes, boots, and parka and brought an extra blanket for the ride over in Lucia's sleigh. I also suggested we stop off at We Three Beans on the way. A hot beverage seemed essential.

She grumbled about worrying we'd miss the warm-ups, but in Christmastown she parked the sleigh outside the coffeehouse and told Quasar we'd be right back. "You want anything?" she asked him.

He stood thinking, his red nose fizzling to black as he tried to make up his mind. "A w-warm milk?"

In the past two days, We Three Beans had undergone a transformation. Neldor cardboard cutouts were propped in several places, and spiderwebs draped across the ceiling. Plastic spiders dotted the fake webs and pumpkin lights were strung across the counter where customers placed their orders. Over the speakers, Christmas music had been set aside for "The Monster Mash." It was only a little after nine in the morning, but it seemed like every elf in the place was singing along, and some were even dancing in a kind of jerky fashion, with raised arms that seemed a pretty poor imitation of Frankenstein. Lucia set me straight on that.

She was watching them, too, and shaking her head. "Never thought I'd see elves treating snow monsters as a laughing matter."

I'd never seen a snow monster, so I hadn't recognized the imitation.

At the counter, Trumpet greeted me with a big grin and gestured around his establishment with pride. "What do you think?"

"Very Halloweeny," I said approvingly. I put in my order for a non-eggnog latte. Lucia ordered a warm eggnog for herself and a warm plain milk for Quasar.

She couldn't stop scowling at the Neldor cutouts. "No reindeer ever looked like that."

Trumpet and I exchanged looks. Before he said anything that could set Lucia off on a reindeer advocacy tirade, I asked him, "Where'd you find the lights?"

"Ordered them off Elf-bay. The *Spooktacular Hits* CD, too. Winkie's Chocolate Shop down the street went all out with the decorations last week and siphoned off some of my business. I had to get the stuff delivered ASAP from Santaland Parcel Express."

After we got our drinks, Lucia and I headed back outside. I was surprised to nearly run into Quince. I introduced him to Lucia, who was polite but clearly impatient to get going.

"What are you doing here?" I asked.

He lifted a jar full of coins. "Pocket and I are fundraising to start an Old Snowmen's Shelter."

"A snowman shelter?" Lucia frowned. "We've never had one of those before."

"I know, but last year . . ."

He didn't have to finish. Last year one of the oldest snowmen in Christmastown had been melted to death. After that tragedy, the snowmen had been skittish around people for a while. I could see why they might want a little more protection.

I dug some change out of my purse and put them through the slot. A pointed look from me spurred Lucia to do the same. "This is turning out to be a more expensive morning than I was expecting," she grumbled.

"Thank you!" Quince turned excitedly to Pocket. "We just made more than we did from an hour standing in front of the library."

"There was such a to-do there," Pocket said. "Constable Crinkles donated, though."

"Only after we bought a raffle ticket from him," Quince said.

For heaven's sake. The constable's shaking down everyone for that raffle was getting out of hand. "What was Crinkles doing at the library? Just selling tickets?"

"Someone broke in overnight and tore up the decorations the library had put up," Quince said. "The ones the children had made."

"The pumpkins?" I asked.

He nodded.

Pumpkin Slayer! It had to be. After the funicular, I'd almost forgotten about him.

I turned to Lucia. "I need to talk to Juniper, and the constable, too, if he's still there."

"He probably won't be," Quince warned. "Pocket and I left there a while ago. It took time to get here."

Snowmen move slowly.

"I can't take time out to go to the library," Lucia said. "I'm late as it is."

"I'm sorry. I'll have to catch a reindeer race another time." There were only hundreds of them.

She shook her head at my screwed-up priorities. But Lucia's best friend was a reindeer. Mine was a librarian.

"Thanks for letting me know," I told Quince. "Good luck with your fundraising."

I hurried to the library.

Crinkles was already gone by the time I arrived, but I could see for myself that the walls had been stripped of construction-paper pumpkins. What was left were children's drawings of various monsters—snow monsters and Neldors, but also some ghosts and three Frankensteins. I felt slightly misty-eyed to see the latter. *My influence.*

Other than the missing pumpkin drawings, the library seemed to be having a normal morning. There was a story hour going on in the children's area. Chip was reading a story about snow monsters. Toddler elves, eyes round with fright, were cringing at all the scary parts.

Lucia would be glad to know *some* residents of Christmastown still had a healthy fear of snow monsters.

I found Juniper in the back stacks, in the process of shelving a cartful of books. "Who broke in?" I asked. "How much damage was done?"

"It was just the decorations, although whoever it was broke the lock on the back door. I had to call Christmastown Hardware to get it fixed. I'm glad it wasn't worse. They didn't touch any of the books."

"Have you checked Elfbook?"

"Someone left a message. 'Stop the madness' was all it said. But it wasn't from the Pumpkin Slayer account."

Hm. Who else would have sent it? "Did Crinkles see it?"

"I showed it to him, but he didn't seem to have any idea who it could be."

Even though I'd given him the name of the likeliest suspect days ago?

I remembered Tiny's sputtering protestations at the orphan home opening. *I didn't do it. No one can prove I did.* The words struck me as odd now. Would an innocent person have phrased his denial like that? Something else Tiny had said bothered me, too. I frowned.

"What is it?" Juniper asked.

"Did Crinkles ask you about the funicular accident?"

"Sort of."

Leave it to Constable Crinkles to "sort of" conduct an investigation. "Did he ask who you saw by the funicular station?"

Her expression turned confused. "I didn't see anybody. Aside from you and Chip, of course."

She and Chip had been immersed in conversation when I'd spotted Waldo, or thought I had. I was the only one who suspected there had been three witnesses to my accident in the funicular.

Yet at the orphanage Tiny had said, *Why not talk to the three other witnesses?*

Tiny swore he'd been in his shop, fitting Mrs. Firlog with a new pair of booties. How could he have known that in addition to me there'd been three others at the scene?

I needed to talk to Crinkles. But I worried about Juniper. She seemed too lackadaisical about this break-in. "You need to be careful," I said.

"Because of Pumpkin Slayer? He seems fixated on doing harm to gourds, not elves."

I lowered my voice. "Pumpkin Slayer might be the same person or elf who sabotaged the funicular."

That got her attention. "*Sabotaged* it?"

I told her about the cable. She had to be the last elf in Christmastown to find that out.

"Holy doodle!" she exclaimed. "That's attempted murder."

"That's why I'm worried. Be careful."

"I'm well protected." She nodded to where Chip was marching around, arms raised as if his hands were claws. He was making a vicious snow monster face, and the children were shrieking in delighted terror. Then he took up his book and started reading to them again.

He did have a flair for drama.

"My protector," she said. "He's always around when I need him. Even sometimes—"

She bit her lip.

I watched her face sharply. Had she been about to say that he sometimes was around when she didn't want him to be? Not that I blamed her for being exasperated. Chip was half elf, half barnacle.

"It's odd that he's taken to forgoing his own work to show up at yours all the time," I observed.

In an instant, the mixed emotion that had shown on her face disappeared. "His business has never been better, according to him. He just squeezes all his clients into a shorter space of time. It's more efficient, he says. And it gives him more time to be with me."

Whether she wanted him to be with her or not.

My expression must have been as readable as a billboard. "You were just telling me to be careful," she pointed out, "and now you seem to disapprove that Chip likes to watch over me."

There was watching over, and there was sticking like glue . . .

"I've never had anyone enjoy my company so much that

he wants to be with me all the time," she said, a little defensively.

"I'm happy for you." I forced myself to add, "And it's a good thing Chip's around—especially now, with all these incidents happening."

The pumpkins, the funicular, the break-in . . .

Could they all have been done by the joker on Elfbook? One of the attacks was so much more vicious than the others. I couldn't square attempted murder with the childish shredding of construction-paper pumpkins or even with the wanton destruction of actual pumpkins.

I left Juniper in the stacks and hurried across town to the constabulary.

Crinkles smiled when he saw me. "You're just in time to sample Ollie's latest. Ginger plum pull-apart bread."

Annoyance with his lack of law-enforcement focus lasted only until the aroma from the kitchen reached me. "Wow, that smells fabulous."

He beckoned me in. Ollie, oven-mitted up to his elbows, presented me with a piece of perfectly sweet, buttery bread. Before I knew what was happening, I'd bought another fistful of raffle tickets.

"Juniper told me about the break-in," I said, after the transaction was completed and I was wiping sugar off my fingers.

Crinkles rocked back on his heels. "Not too much damage there. Just the door and a few little decorations. Might've been kids."

"It's Tiny," I said.

"Now, I spoke to Tiny and he was none too happy to see me, I can assure you. Was he, Ollie?"

"Said we were wasting our time before we even told him what we were there to ask him."

If that wasn't a giveaway in itself. "He inadvertently said

something that added to my suspicions." I explained about
Tiny mentioning the three witnesses. "Did you talk to him
about how many people were at the funicular stop before the
crash?"

Crinkles scrunched his face in thought. "Not that I recall.
But he might've heard it from someone else."

"From whom? The only ones there were Juniper, Chip
Pepperbough, and me."

"Maybe he was counting you as a witness. Or maybe Chip
or Juniper mentioned the other person. Once one person
knows, it takes no time at all for it to snowball into common
knowledge in this town."

"But Juniper didn't see Waldo. Neither did Chip, as far
as I know. And I certainly didn't say anything to him. Tiny
could only have known if the other person told him—or if he
was there himself."

"We know he wasn't there," Crinkles said. "He was helping the mayor's wife try on shoes when the crash happened."

"He could have cut the cable before that, though."

The constable's eyes went wide. "Are you insinuating that
Tiny would have done something that diabolical just to cause
random chaos? What if the funicular had been full when the
accident had happened?"

"Yes," I said. "What if."

Ollie's jaw dropped. "Tiny Sparkletoe—terrorist!"

A tremor went through Crinkles, as if the very idea shook
the foundations of all he believed in. "That can't be! Tiny's
the chairman of the Christmastown Community Guild. A
model citizen. He reports more by-law violators than anyone
in this town."

"He's bought more raffle tickets than anybody, too," Ollie
said.

I couldn't help rolling my eyes. "Well, he *must* be innocent, then."

"I just don't see Tiny doing something like that," Crinkles said. "Bad enough when you thought he was Pumpkin Slayer."

"I still believe he is. He hates Halloween and told everyone there would be chaos—and he's been creating it. If he isn't the culprit, he certainly knows more than he's letting on. Otherwise there was no way he could have known how many people were at the funicular stop before the crash. I think you should speak to him."

Crinkles's chin sank into the ones below it. "But I already did."

"Again."

"Tiny won't like that."

"Is Tiny the law in Christmastown or are you?"

"I am," he admitted unhappily. "He yells, though. It's so unpleasant."

"I'll go with you. That way all his yelling will be focused on me."

It was an offer Crinkles couldn't refuse.

We rode across town on snowmobiles, Crinkles on one, me sitting behind Ollie on his. Light snow continued to fall. All the new Halloween decorations were getting dappled with white, creating a Halloween–Winter Wonderland mash-up.

When we arrived, Sparkletoe's Bootery had no customers. It also had no Tiny.

From his workbench, Louie looked up at us, his eyes wide. It wasn't every day that the constable, his deputy, and Mrs. Claus marched into his store at once. We obviously weren't there for booties. "Has something happened?" he asked.

"Just wanted to have a chat with Tiny," Crinkles said.

"He didn't come in this morning. I haven't seen him since yesterday evening when we closed."

Relief spread across Crinkles's face. "Oh, too bad. Just tell him—"

"Is it normal for him not to come in until almost noon?" I wasn't about to walk out without getting more information.

"Well . . . it's not unheard of," Louie allowed. "Sometimes he has to go meet with suppliers, but I don't think that's where he is this morning. He would have mentioned that to me. And I don't think he's sick. He would have called, in that case."

"You haven't heard from him at all?" Crinkles asked.

"Not a word."

The constable pressed his lips together. "Hmph."

"Do you know if Tiny was in the shop the whole day, the day of the funicular accident?" I asked Louie.

He frowned. "Gosh, I couldn't say. You should know that—I spent part of the afternoon in rehearsal with the band, like you."

"That's right." With Louie gone from the Bootery, there was no way to know Tiny's movements the day of the funicular accident. Unless we could trace every customer who'd come in that day and have them verify that Tiny was there.

"He did tell me to draw up this list," Louie said, handing over a scroll. "It's all our customers with size four and a quarter."

Crinkles took the list and I stood over his shoulder, skimming the names. There were hundreds, as Tiny had predicted.

"Half the elves in Santaland are on here." Crinkles scowled. "*I'm* on here."

"It's a common size."

"Well, never mind this now." Crinkles rolled up the paper. "We'll go check on Tiny at his cottage. Maybe he is sick and just forgot to call."

Louie's wide eyes blinked. "That wouldn't be like Tiny at all. He's never forgotten to call before."

"First time for everything," Crinkles said.

We set out on the snowmobiles for Tiny's cottage. You'd

expect one of the community's most successful businessmen to live in Christmastown proper, but apparently Tiny insisted on staying in the old Sparkletoe cabin that had been passed down to him from his parents.

"What about Bella?" I had to yell in Ollie's ear to be heard above the roaring engine of the snowmobile. "Why didn't Tiny's sister get the cabin?"

"Probably because she didn't want it," Ollie said. "The place is . . . well, I won't say a dump, but it's pretty rustic."

A thundering sound grew louder and all at once Crinkles and Ollie stopped the snowmobiles. We all cocked our heads, and then panicked when we realized what we were hearing. This country snow path must have been designated part of the route for the reindeer races. The two elves fired up their engines again and got us out of the way moments before a herd of young reindeer dragging weighted sleds charged through. They were followed by Lucia and Quasar bouncing along on her sleigh. Lucia held a bullhorn in one hand and the reins in the other.

She didn't see me—she practically flew by. I'd have to tell her I got to witness a reindeer race, after all.

"Does Tiny's wife like living so far out?" I asked Ollie when we were underway again.

"I doubt she complains. Pixie was a trapper's daughter, and they weren't too well off. Tiny probably seemed like a big step up. Even so, she still cleans for people."

I frowned. "Tiny's wife cleans houses?"

"Oh, sure. She does work for a lot of elves all over. I think that's how she met Tiny. Cleaned the cottage for him after his mom died."

I bit my lip. I did plenty of housework at the Coast Inn, and even enjoyed chores like that sometimes. At the same time, it was hard to imagine Tiny Sparkletoe, who strutted around town almost as if he were the mayor, and who was so vain about his appearance, sending his wife out to clean bathrooms. Maybe she didn't want to give up working . . .

"Do she and Tiny have any children?" I asked.

"No, not yet."

I'd never seen Pixie, so I didn't know much about her. That was odd, too, now that I considered it. Tiny was a fixture in Christmastown, yet I'd been there a year and had never crossed paths with Mrs. Sparkletoe. She hadn't been at the orphanage ceremony. Tiny attended the event alone. Maybe I was about to meet her this morning. The interchange I'd heard between Tiny and Walnut at the orphanage made me curious to know what she was like.

The reindeer hooves had created ruts in the snow, which made for a bumpy ride the rest of the way out to the Sparkletoe cottage.

Rustic exactly described the place. The logs that had been used were massive and gleamed dully like wax from at least a century of standing up to the elements at the North Pole. We walked up to the door, cut in the shape of an oval.

Crinkles rapped on the thick wood. We waited, me hunched slightly because of the stoop's low overhang. I leaned toward a window and peered in.

"No lights on inside," I said. "None that I can see, at least."

The constable frowned. I would have expected him to use my observation as a pretext for leaving as soon as possible. He clearly still dreaded this encounter with Tiny. But a few worried wrinkles appeared on his forehead below the bill of his constable's hat.

"I could have sworn I glimpsed his bright blue snowmobile around back," he muttered. "I'm going to have a look around."

Ollie and I followed him.

Sure enough, there was a snowmobile parked under what

looked like the snowmobile equivalent of a carport. Crinkles circled it as if it might tell him something, then he knocked on the back door.

"Walk around, Ollie. See if you notice anything."

While Crinkles waited again for his knock to be answered, I went to another window and peeked into a small but tidy kitchen. A knotted wood table with only two chairs stood in the middle of it. The cottage wasn't big enough to have a dining room. It appeared Tiny and Pixie weren't big entertainers.

A strangled cry came from behind us. "Unc!"

Crinkles and I turned. The cottage stood on a small rise that was almost a plateau—the backyard stretched for about an acre, and then the ground dipped. Ollie was standing at the top of that dip, looking down in horror. Crinkles and I exchanged an anxious glance and then rushed to join him.

At first it was hard for me to believe what I was seeing. Several yards down from where we were standing, a smear of color showed through the snow—an elf form. I knew who it was from the colors—a bright purple tunic with yellow and red embroidery, with a matching hat. His stockings were purple and his dyed red leather booties had chunky heels and a square, elaborately curled toe. Tiny had been wearing them at the orphanage.

The oddest aspect of what I was seeing, though, was the way his body lay. He was planted facedown in the snow—not as if snow had fallen around him, but as if he had been pressed down into it. And all around his body, the snow had been depressed, in a peculiar shape. It was much larger than Tiny—a long oval, except wider at one end, and that end had three triangular formations, like toes.

I squinted, confused by what I was seeing. "It almost looks like a footprint."

Only then did I notice that my two companions had gone white with shock.

"It *is* a footprint," Ollie said. "The footprint of an abominable."

I sucked in a breath. After a year in the North Pole I was still ignorant about a lot of things, but that word, *abominable*, was enough to strike fear in me. "You mean . . ." It seemed so improbable, so foreign to my experience, that I couldn't make myself form the words.

Crinkles took off his cap and rubbed his coat sleeve across his brow. "Tiny got squished by a snow monster."

Chapter 9

Come to Tiny Sparkletoe's cottage ASAP, I texted Nick. **Tiny is dead. Possible snow monster attack.**

"Now, we shouldn't jump to conclusions," Constable Crinkles said for about the hundredth time. Nevertheless, he bobbed on his heels and anxiously scanned the area as if expecting the snow monster to leap out at us at any moment.

"What other conclusion could you come to when Tiny's found smooshed in the middle of a giant footprint?" Ollie asked, quivering in panic.

I'd never seen a snow monster in the flesh, but I'd heard stories of past depredations the snow monsters had committed. The creatures lived in the Farthest Frozen Reaches, mostly in the crags and valleys around Mount Myrrh. Occasionally, though, one or several would breach our forest border, crush an elf cottage or two, or even come right into towns and flatten beloved landmarks. A plaque in front of the community center marked the site where once had stood a magnificent building of ice called the Christmastown Ice Palace. A snow monster had made short work of the structure after the accidental—according to the elves—shooting of one of his relatives. Now the elves' inclination was to send out a hunting party at the mere whisper of a snow monster near Santaland.

And here was proof that one had come here and killed a prominent citizen. The monster whose foot had crushed Tiny must have been colossal, bigger than any animal I'd ever seen.

I looked across the rest of the yard. Several inches of snow had fallen, and last night had been windy. Small indentations in the snow indicated a faint trail where Tiny's booties had sunk into the snow during his run from his house to the place where he'd met his demise. The footprints lay next to a long path that had also been covered in snow—a walkway, I guessed. It was strange that Tiny, in fleeing, hadn't run on the pathway.

But I was even more curious about where the snow monster had come from.

"Doesn't it seem odd that there's just one snow monster print visible?" I asked.

"One's enough if you're the elf getting stepped on," Ollie said.

"But shouldn't there be other prints around?" The surrounding snow revealed no other large prints. "They can't fly, can they?"

I tossed out the question as a joke, but Ollie cringed and glanced skyward as if some kind of diabolical snow monster hovercraft might appear.

"Flying snow monsters!" He shuddered in horror. "That's all we need."

Crinkles shook his head, chins jiggling. "Marshmallows! Snow monsters can't fly."

"So how did the monster get to this spot, crush Tiny, and get away without leaving any traces?" I asked.

"If this happened last night," Crinkles said, "the blowing snow probably covered the tracks. Look at the drifts." Small banks of snow rippled across the expanse beyond Tiny's yard.

My gaze couldn't help darting toward Tiny's prone figure.

"The wind blew away traces of all the prints—except that one?"

"The monster probably mashed his foot down extra hard just there," the constable said.

Poor Tiny was in the bull's-eye of that footprint. "It couldn't have been accidental, I suppose."

"Monsters never kill by accident," Crinkles said. "They're demons, no matter what crazy people who live in the Farthest Frozen Reaches will tell you."

Along with the snow monsters, there were a few people, elves, and other beings who lived in the Farthest Frozen Reaches. A penal colony had been set up there, as well as a few scattered settlements. Jake Frost, a detective I'd met last year, made his home out there.

Bells sounded in the distance, and Doc Honeytree's sleigh came into view, followed by Nick's.

"Good," Crinkles said. "I'd like to get Tiny out of here before Pixie comes back from wherever she is. A wife shouldn't have to see this."

It was kind of him to be concerned for the widow's feelings, but I would think he'd want to talk to her. "Has anyone broken the news to her yet?"

Crinkles shook his head. "I don't know where she's cleaning today."

"Would you like me to make some calls? She should be told what's happened to her husband."

"I guess it wouldn't hurt to try."

I got out my phone and put out feelers among my acquaintances in Christmastown.

It was Juniper who came through. "I'll send her a text," she said.

"Wait. You have Pixie Sparkletoe's number?"

"Unless she's changed it. She used to clean at the library.

She stopped about a year ago, not long after she married. What would you like me to say to her?"

"Why don't you send her number to me? I'll pass it on to Crinkles."

"Oh." Juniper's voice changed when I mentioned the constable. "Is this something serious?"

I cast another glance down at Tiny. "I'm afraid so, but I can't say more right now." I didn't want the news to spread before Pixie could be notified.

She texted me the number and I ricocheted it to Crinkles by the time Nick and the doctor arrived, a feat that impressed the constable. "You're a fast worker!"

"It pays to know librarians," I said.

As Nick and the doctor walked up, Doc Honeytree raised his bushy brows at me. "You're looking better, Mrs. Claus."

"I feel fine today."

"Good." He sighed. "I guess I'd better take a look at our unfortunate victim."

I gestured down the hill, where Tiny lay undisturbed except for having been checked by Crinkles to identify him and verify that he was dead.

"You won't need your stethoscope," Crinkles said. "He's frozen as solid as Peppermint Pond in January."

The doctor half walked, half slid down the hill behind the constable and his deputy. I tugged on Nick's sleeve before he could follow them. "Doesn't that footprint look strange to you?"

He shook his head, not in contradiction but in awe. "It came from a big snow monster. The biggest I've seen."

"It's the only print around."

His expression changed to a frown, the lines of which deepened as he looked back at me. "Let Doc and the constable do their work before you jump in. We have to tread carefully here."

The words seemed ill chosen, given the manner of Tiny's death, but I could tell Nick was anxious. "This is all unfortunate. If anything can stir up a panic in Santaland, it's a snow monster sighting. At the very least, it'll trigger a hunt for the rogue monster."

Knowing what he was thinking of, I reached for his hand and squeezed it. His older brother had died during a snow monster hunt just the year before.

When we joined the others, Doc was kneeling by the body. "Evidence of blunt trauma on the back of the head," he said.

"Was that the cause of death?" I had no idea how death occurred when one was stepped on. It wasn't anything I'd ever had to think about. There had never been a *CSI: Santaland* to familiarize me with the forensics of snow monster attacks.

"Might've been," Doc replied. "When I examine him further I expect to see lots of evidence of bruising all over, if he was crushed by a foot. I only hope the force of the blow killed him quickly and he didn't suffocate while facedown in the snow."

"Why would he have been hit on the back of the head?" I asked. "Do snow monsters carry weapons?"

"Clubs and sticks," Crinkles said.

Doc Honeytree scratched his chin. "That could have done it."

I couldn't imagine the terror Tiny must have felt to be chased from his house by a club-wielding snow monster. "Why didn't he just stay inside?" I wondered aloud.

"Staying inside is no guarantee of safety," Crinkles said. "Snow monsters have been known to flatten cottages, and by the looks of things, this one was big enough that he could have done that."

I still would have felt safer cowering indoors than making

a run for it out in the open. "He could have at least made a run for his snowmobile." The vehicle was parked right by the house. "Do you think he was already outside and was caught unawares?"

They all stared at me as though I'd taken leave of my senses.

"What?" I asked.

"A snow monster wouldn't be able to creep up on someone unawares," Nick explained. "They lumber, and their noses make a snuffling sound. Most of all, they grumble."

My eyes narrowed. "Grumble?"

"They sure do," Ollie said. "My uncle was hunting once and got trapped in a snow monster cave and said the thing never stopped talking to itself, even in its sleep. He had a heckuva time figuring out whether it was awake or not so's he could sneak past it."

"How does a monster ever manage to catch anything?" I asked.

"They aren't the best hunters, that's for sure," Ollie said.

Crinkles put his hands on his waist. "That's why they end up eating so many walruses. They're the one thing too slow and stupid to get out of the way of a snow monster."

Poor walruses. They got no respect.

The doctor stood. "I'll take a closer look at Tiny back at my office, but I think it's pretty safe to say, given the circumstances, that it was death by snow monster foot."

"This'll hit Christmastown hard," Crinkles said as the doctor and Ollie lifted Tiny's frozen body, aided by Nick. I tried not to watch. I hadn't liked Tiny much. I even suspected he'd sabotaged the funicular and tried to kill me. But getting stepped on seemed a particularly ignominious end for anyone.

I followed the procession back up toward the sleighs. "How long has he been dead?" I asked Doc.

"It's hard to say. He's frozen pretty solid, so it's been at least since early this morning. Maybe even last night."

Wouldn't his wife have noticed him missing?

As the thought crossed my mind, Lucia's distinctive sleigh appeared in the distance, pulled by four reindeer thundering in our direction. The sleigh wasn't moving quickly enough for the female elf sitting in the passenger seat next to where Quasar's head hung between Lucia and her. The thin slip of an elf hopped out even before Lucia's reindeer team had stopped. She raced up to where the others were loading Tiny onto the doctor's sleigh.

"Tiny!" She fell to her knees in the snow.

I'd never seen Pixie Sparkletoe before, but this wasn't what I'd expected. Wearing a puffy blue coat, plain booties, and a navy-blue hat, she seemed as different from the dandy-ish Tiny as she could be. Yet she was pretty, I could see that now. She had a wispy, delicate beauty, with big blue eyes.

Nick broke apart from the others and pulled her back up to her feet. I saw him whispering comforting words to her, but she wasn't having it. She broke away.

"What happened?" she asked through sobs.

"We think he got . . . stepped on," Crinkles said. "Snow monster attack."

Her eyes widened in horror, and a mittened hand covered her mouth.

"When did you last see Tiny?" Nick asked.

"Last night! I went to stay with my sister. I had to clean the Firlog place this morning, and they like me to start early, so I sometimes stay with Rosemary so I don't have to drive as far in the morning. Tiny was fine last night. Complaining about Halloween, of course. But that's how he's been for weeks." She stared up at me through teary yet curious eyes.

"This is my wife," Nick said.

"I'm so sorry about Tiny," I said.

"Mrs. Claus." Her gaze narrowed. "Tiny didn't think much of you."

I shifted awkwardly. "I know we had our differences—"

"When did you get here?" she interrupted. "And what were you doing here?"

There was a crackle in the air when what she was implying sank in. My cheeks heated. She thought *I'd* killed her husband? Did I look like someone with the power to summon snow monsters to do my bidding?

"Say, now!" Crinkles quivered uncomfortably. "Mrs. Claus was with me for a good part of the morning. And before that . . ." He shook his head. "Well, I don't know where she was before that, come to think of it. But I doubt she was stepping on your husband."

"Of course she wasn't," Lucia said. "I drove April into town myself this morning. And I assume Nick can vouch for where she was last night, so you can nip that crazy idea in the bud."

Fresh tears flowed down her face and she fell against Nick's red coat. "I'm sorry! I don't know what I'm saying! I just can't believe he's gone. Why would Tiny chase after a snow monster?"

"Sounds more like the monster chased him," Lucia said. "Where'd it happen?"

We all went back over to survey the scene of Tiny's last moments. Pixie, still attached to Nick, shook uncontrollably. "How awful! I want the monster who did this killed!"

"You can bet he will be," Crinkles said. "This is an outrage. We haven't had an attack this brazen in decades."

Lucia's face tensed as she surveyed the scene. "I was at the Reindeer Games this morning. No reindeer mentioned a snow monster in the area, did they, Quasar?"

Quasar had been hanging back. He looked a little queasy

at the idea of such a horrible death, and his nose was flashing red uncontrollably, like an emergency vehicle. "N-no."

"Reindeer can scent snow monsters a long way off," Lucia said. "They're usually the ones who send out a warning."

Crinkles shook his head. "They didn't this time."

Nick's expression was solemn. "We should probably wait until the doctor finishes his report before letting others know what's happened."

"Others?" Crinkles asked.

"The townspeople," Nick specified.

"Shouldn't they be warned?" I asked. "After all, if there's a snow monster wandering around stomping on elves . . ."

"The monster seems to have left the area. Lucia's right— the reindeer would have smelled danger if he'd stuck around."

Crinkles sighed. "How long will an autopsy take, Doc?"

"Not more than a day."

"I want justice," Pixie insisted. "Soon. Tiny deserves that."

Nick patted her comfortingly. "He'll get it. I promise you."

How could he promise that? We had one footprint, no snow monster, and Laurel and Hardy on the case. The odds were not in justice's favor.

"Make sure word of this doesn't get out yet," Nick said. "We don't want mass hysteria."

Ollie's eyes bugged. "You mean . . . tell no one?"

Nick nodded.

The deputy's Adam's apple bobbed as he gulped. "We might have a problem."

Chapter 10

On the drive home, Nick and I didn't speak for a while. What we'd just seen deserved a respectful silence to absorb. The end of a life under any circumstances is the passing of a whole history; under mysterious circumstances, the tragedy is compounded by uncertainty. And in this case, a sense of danger.

Crinkles had offered Pixie a ride back to her sister's house. They were probably having an even more somber ride. I felt sorry for her, even if her first instinct had been to wonder if I'd been involved in her husband's death. Tiny must have been vocal in his opinions about me.

The dimming afternoon light shone pink against the white landscape. As we trundled along the icy path, I burrowed in a fleece-lined blanket and sifted through what I'd seen at the Sparkletoe cottage. Finally, I said, "What if we have it backward? What if Tiny was investigating the print in the snow *before* he died?"

Nick's expression didn't change. "Then there's still a snow monster on the prowl in Santaland. And a murderer besides."

Not a comforting thought. "To be honest, I imagined that a snow monster attack would cause more damage. That it would be, you know, bloodier."

"Tiny's dead. That was all the damage required."

I'd probably seen too many horror movies. That's where most of my experience of violent death came from. But things like *Blood Freak* and *Theater of Blood* weren't made with forensic accuracy in mind.

"I suppose they'll be putting together a hunt for the snow monster." The thought filled me with dread. Elves and men against snow monsters. I didn't like the odds. And Nick would feel compelled to lead the hunt.

"I think we should wait," he said.

His declaration eased my alarm somewhat, although I wondered if Santalanders would agree with him. "If there's a murderous creature on the loose . . ."

"I'm not convinced there is. From what I've heard of past snow monster incursions, they create havoc and make their presence known. The way Tiny died . . ."

"It was a precision kill."

He looked at me in surprise.

I'd probably seen too many spy movies, too.

"I'm hoping Doc finds that whatever was used to club Tiny wasn't made of wood," he said. "Snow monsters don't use metal tools, as a rule."

"So you'd rather believe another elf murdered Tiny?" I asked. "Or a human?"

"This isn't about my preferences. If there had been other snow monster sightings, I'd be more worried. But from the moment you texted, this felt all wrong to me. Lucia's telling us that the reindeer herds hadn't reported anything confirmed that what we saw might not be the whole story."

A current thrummed through my blood. Thoroughbreds hearing the starting gun couldn't be any more energized than I was by the words *might not be the whole story.* I was cursed with the irrepressible curiosity to know the rest of the story.

Nick, noticing me sitting forward, looked worried. And resigned. "Wait until we hear from Doc Honeytree before you jump to any conclusions."

"Of course." I only wished I could go camp out in Doc's waiting room and be the first to receive his verdict. "Who could have wanted Tiny dead?"

Nick hitched his throat. "When I said we need to wait, I meant that we need to keep an open mind. Maybe it *was* a snow monster. I just hope we can find out quickly, before too much damage is done."

"What kind of damage?"

"Folks can get a little irrational when it comes to snow monsters. There haven't been any attacks in generations, but even rumors can set off a panic."

"Lucky thing you asked Crinkles to keep the attack on the q.t., then."

"I'm a little worried about that text Ollie sent."

I shrugged. "It was just one text."

We chatted for the rest of the way into town, until we came to a dead stop at a bottleneck on Festival Boulevard. Christmastown isn't known for its traffic jams, so this seemed . . . odd. The air was thick with exhaust from idling snowmobiles and foggy puffs from the impatient snuffling of reindeer. Meanwhile, the sidewalks teemed with elves and people dragging wagons and carts to and from nearby Sparkletoe Lane. Those who lived above shops had shuttered their windows. Those who lacked shutters were hammering pieces of wood over them.

Tempers were short. While we were stalled, I watched two elves collide on the sidewalk, which sent two sacks of groceries spilling to the sidewalk. The elves started yelling at each other and then engaged in a tug-of-war over a bunch of beets.

At that moment, Nick's cousin Amory tried to cross in front of us in his sleigh, causing our opposing reindeer teams to start bickering over right of way.

"What's going on?" I called out to Amory.

"As if you didn't know," he said. "There's a snow monster on the loose!"

Dread settled over Nick's countenance.

"Thanks for the warning, Cousin." Amory's tone was sharp with sarcasm. "You could have at least given your own family a heads-up about the danger."

"We don't know that there was a snow monster attack," Nick said.

Amory sputtered incredulously. "I saw the picture with my own eyes. That was a snow monster print, no doubt about it. It's a good thing I got down here double-quick before Sparkletoe's Mercantile ran out of lumber." He nodded toward the back of his sleigh. "I'm going to board up all the windows at Kringle Lodge. Loaded up on ammunition, too. There's going to be a big meeting tonight at the Community Center. We've already sent for Boots Bayleaf to lead the expedition."

"We should wait to hear from Doc Honeytree first," Nick said.

"Wait for what? Tiny was stomped to death, wasn't he? Let that go unavenged, and pretty soon we'll all be squashed like bugs."

A sharp sound like a bicycle horn hooted impatiently at Amory, who was still stopped crosswise in the street. He twisted toward the sleigh behind him, annoyed. "Hold your reindeer, bub! Can't you see I'm talking to Santa Claus?"

The elf behind him was unimpressed. "Can't you see you're blocking traffic?"

"Just wait until you hear from me, Amory," Nick called

out when his cousin reluctantly gave in and began to drive away.

"It's too late for waiting. You'd better be at the Community Center tonight."

I understood now why Nick had hoped it wasn't a snow monster that had attacked Tiny.

After Amory was gone, an elf darted in front of our sleigh, carrying as much lumber as his sled dogs could pull. A bazooka still in its packaging lay on the driver's seat beside him.

A line of elves snaked around the corner from Hollywell's Christmastown Cornucopia, the largest grocery. An Armageddon mentality had taken hold of everyone.

More horns blared and frustrated reindeer teams hurled trash talk at one another. Just as it looked as if we might get moving again, a group of elves carrying a chopped-down tree crossed in front of us.

"What are you doing?" Nick called out.

"Building a bonfire pile in Mistletoe Park," one elf replied.

"Piles are going up all over town," said another. "Snow monsters are afraid of fire!"

Nick shook his head. "This is madness."

Maybe it was, but the madness started to claw at me. Could all these people and elves be wrong? That footprint *had* been colossal. What if a monster really was on the rampage? My heartbeat raced as I imagined being crushed by a big furry foot.

Our reindeer were finally able to get away from the main boulevard. Nick steered us through back streets to reach the main road up the mountain.

My hands gripped the edge of the bench seat. "Wait. Shouldn't we be getting supplies before it's too late?" I asked. "I could text Jingles and ask him to take stock—"

Nick put a hand on my arm before I could pull out my

phone. "The castle is well provisioned. Think about it. If the snow monster killed Tiny overnight, where is it now? Why hasn't anyone seen it? Why didn't it come into Christmastown when it could have taken us all unawares?"

My lips twisted as his questions sank in. I'd begun to panic like Cousin Amory. Like everyone.

"The hysteria could be the aim, couldn't it?" I asked.

"Might be," Nick said.

I thought about that. "But if there's a snow monster out there doing this on purpose just to create a panic, he would have to be cunning. I understood that snow monsters are more slow-witted."

"There's still a lot we don't know about them," Nick said. "They usually try to keep to themselves, and they definitely prefer the wilds of the Farthest Frozen Reaches to Santaland."

"Maybe there's an enemy of Tiny's out there who has a snow monster acquaintance who was willing to help him pull off this sick killing."

"Not many elves have snow monster friends or even acquaintances, and even if they did, what would be the point?"

"Look how hysterical everyone is. Nobody cares about looking any further into the murder than that footprint. The whole town's in an uproar from just a single text sent from Ollie's phone. What would dissuade them now from believing Tiny was killed by a snow monster?"

Nick's expression became grimmer, then he gave his head a shake. "I don't want to speculate yet. Tiny's death might not be a snow monster's doing. But it might have been."

We continued home. Even after a year as Mrs. Claus, I still found Castle Kringle an impressive sight. Perched three quarters of the way up Sugarplum Mountain, its gray stone edifice had darkened over the years so that it created a stark contrast to the snowy white world around it, especially the tower of the Old Keep that rose above the "newer" wings of the castle, which were merely hundreds of years old. The grounds were dotted with impressive ice sculptures and Christmas trees that remained decorated all year round. At the castle's back was Calling Bird Cliff, a place where the mountain fell in a steep drop into the snowy valley below. From various vantage points at the front of the castle, though, you could see down the mountain into Christmastown, and beyond the Christmas Tree Forest past the jagged peak of Mount Myrrh and into the icy wilderness of the Farthest Frozen Reaches.

Out where the monsters lived.

There was nothing terrifying about Castle Kringle and its lighted, manicured grounds, though. It was home to me now. "Feels like we're returning to a little sanity," I said.

"And peace," Nick agreed.

In the next instant, Salty's work sleigh careened across the road, barely avoiding a collision with our reindeer team.

"Watch it, short stuff!" our lead reindeer shouted. He was from the Comet herd; they had a reputation for being hot-heads.

"Sorry, Santa," Salty called out.

I peered behind Salty's wagon. He was hauling a contraption I'd never seen before. "What's that?" I asked.

"I'm setting up a catapult to guard my greenhouses with," the elf called after us. "No snow monster's going to stomp what's left of my pumpkins!"

That evening, the Christmastown Community Center was surrounded by sleighs, sled dog teams, and snowmobiles. Cross-country skis and snowshoes leaned against the wall near the building's entrance. Everyone was at the meeting.

Nick was still in a grumbly mood after seeing that one of the bonfire piles had been lit.

"Will it scare away the snow monsters?" I asked him.

"Who knows? But at this rate half the Christmas Tree Forest will be chopped down for kindling."

The Community Center's auditorium, so often the site of concerts, pageants, and plays, was pandemonium. Elves and people crowded wall to wall, and they all had something to say. Finally a voice I recognized rose above the cacophony. A craggy old elf named Boots Bayleaf stood on a chair to get attention. For the occasion, he'd dressed in his best winter camouflage tunic, plus a white cap.

"The only thing an abominable understands is force," Boots declared. "We have to retaliate, and most of all we have to strike while the iron is hot. If we wait, the snow monsters will likely forget what we're mad about. They'll convince themselves that *we're* the aggressors."

I hadn't noticed Nick leaving my side, but now I saw him striding toward the front of the room, and up the steps toward the stage. Boots had a booming voice and was able to speak without amplification, but Nick went right to the microphone that had been set up and pulled it off its stand. A shriek of feedback silenced the room before he started to speak.

"There's no reason to send out a militia group yet," Nick said. "And we certainly shouldn't raze our forest to build bonfires and risk burning our cities down. We still aren't sure this was a snow monster attack."

Several people jeered. "What else could it be?"

"We saw the picture!"

"It was a footprint, plain as day."

Nick raised his hands to appeal for calm. "I've asked Doc Honeytree to examine Tiny and establish a cause of death."

This was met with skepticism. Elves and people around me muttered about a cover-up.

"Until we know more, we need to stay calm," Nick continued. "Go home and lock your doors, by all means. Be vigilant, but don't panic. Even if Tiny was killed by a snow monster, this has the looks of an isolated incident."

"Isolated or not," Boots said, "it doesn't rightly matter. Dead is dead."

"Vengeance for Tiny!" someone yelled, and several others took up the cry.

"Remember the Ice Palace!"

Nick looked despairing, and my heart plummeted. This was starting to seem like a mob. A mob comprised mostly of diminutive beings in pointy hats and curly-toed boots, it was true. But without the happy facade, even a vigilante posse of angry elves could be terrifying.

A side door banged open, and Doc Honeytree appeared. He stumped up the stairs to the stage and grabbed the microphone out of Nick's hands.

"I've looked at Tiny carefully. While he did suffer significant bruising and a bone fracture as a result of being stepped on, it wasn't the crushing that killed him. It was a blow to the head."

"Who hit him?" someone called out.

"Someone or something with a heavy chunk of metal."

Not wood, then. I seized on this clue, remembering what Nick had said about snow monsters mostly using wood clubs and sticks in attacks.

"A snow monster could wield a hefty chunk of metal," Amory called out.

"He could, but this was a piece of metal like a thin pipe. If that snow monster's foot was indicative of his overall size, the monster would have had a difficult time holding a little iron rod like that. They aren't dexterous creatures, and their hand-eye coordination is poor."

Boots's whole face, including his handlebar moustache,

drooped at the logic of the doctor's words. "But you can't prove definitely that it *wasn't* a monster," he said.

"No, I can't," the doctor allowed.

Nick took the microphone back. "No one else saw the monster, but from the size of the print, it would have been huge. A true abominable."

The words created another stir. Abominables were the largest of the snow monsters, and the fiercest. They were also usually the ones sent to attack elf and human settlements.

"Please," Nick implored the crowd, "let's hear what Constable Crinkles has to say."

I hadn't even realized that Crinkles was in the hall. He tottered up the stairs onto the stage, looking uncomfortable. "If what Doc says is true, we'll be doing more investigating. And you can bet we'll find the culprit. Until we do, you should . . ." He frowned in thought. "Well, um, just do what you normally do. Do your work, and . . ." An idea occurred to him. "And keep preparing for Halloween. It's going to be a great evening for the town—and for the constabulary. Ollie's there in the back, and if anybody wants to buy a raffle ticket, he's got a whole roll on him."

No one seemed appeased by his speech, but the collective call for patience by the constable, the doctor, and Nick persuaded everyone that raising a monster hunt would be premature. Instead, the crowd selected several elves and people to form an anti–snow monster vigilance committee to draw up and implement a preparedness plan. Nick was chosen to lead the effort—as if he didn't have enough on his plate with Christmas two months away.

Nevertheless, from the look on his face, I could tell that Nick felt as relieved as I did that the worst of the panic seemed to have passed.

"Thank goodness Nick was able to defuse the situation," I

told Lucia, who'd been standing in the back, next to Quasar, throughout the meeting.

"He did a good job," she agreed. "There's just one possible hitch."

I glanced over at Quasar. Neither of us understood what she was driving at.

"What if it actually was an incredibly dexterous snow monster that killed Tiny?" she asked. "In that case, we're up against an abominable with the agility of a ninja. Good luck with that."

Chapter 11

Snuffling reached my groggy ears first, followed by a raspy muttering. "Why sleeping? Always sleeping."

To forget, my half-awake brain wanted to reply. I already had recurring nightmares of last December and, more recently, funiculars. Yesterday's scene of Tiny face-planted in the middle of that snow monster footprint was a new addition to my nightmare loop.

What had Ollie told me about snow monsters? They snuffled and muttered.

"Sleeping . . . ," the guttural voice hissed.

My eyelids fluttered just as something hairy landed on my arm outside the coverlet. I rocketed fully awake and sat up, a shout in my throat. Then, seeing what had woken me, I collapsed back against my pillows, trying to steady my breath.

A snow monster hovered over me, but it was the size of a twelve-year-old boy. Christopher laughed delightedly. "You should have seen your face!"

His face had chalk all over it. The rest of him was white fur. He even had claws.

I groaned. "You're a demon."

"Nope, a snow monster." He parked his hairy carcass

down on the edge of the bed. "You like it? I made it myself last night."

Whatever he'd used for his pelt looked like shaggy, man-made pile like you'd see on old shag rugs. "The 1970s called. They want their rumpus room carpet back."

"It's not carpet. I found this in the doll cellar." The doll cellar in the basement of Castle Kringle was a repository of outmoded dolls and stuffed toys. "There was a big plush polar bear down there, so I unstuffed it and cut out the face."

I could see it now. The head was ragged—the execution lacked expertise there—but the plastic claws had been realistic enough to scare the stuffing out of me. "That's not a half-bad job," I said. "You might have a future with the Order of Elven Seamstresses."

"I'm not an elf," he said. "Besides, I'm going to be Santa Claus."

"You won't live to be Santa Claus if you go around terrifying people in their sleep like that. How did you ever get past Jingles?"

He swung his furry feet as if he were sitting on the edge of a fishing dock. "I told him that I thought I'd seen someone creeping around the shed where he keeps his snowmobile."

Jingles's snowmobile was his pride and joy. He wouldn't take a threat to it lightly—even a false threat.

"Kid, I think your days are numbered."

The light sound of Jingles's tap at the door gave me a chance to see if I was correct. "Come in," I said.

The steward sailed into the room, coffee tray steady in front of him, taking no notice of the snow monster sitting next to me. He set the tray down and then straightened, keeping his eyes trained on me. "There seems to be a mangy creature on your bed, madam," he observed with over-the-top formality. "Would you like me to remove it?"

"No, thank you, Jingles."

"I should warn you. It fibs."

"It also apologizes." In case he missed his cue, I bumped Christopher on the arm. "Doesn't it?"

"I'm sorry, Jingles," he said. "I just wanted to scare April with my snow monster costume. What do you think of it?" He hopped off the bed and vogued in his ersatz fur suit.

A trace of a smile appeared on Jingles's lips. "You're a fright, I'll grant you that. But you've got the face all wrong. You'll have to do something about the mouth."

"I don't have the teeth right," Christopher agreed. "They need to be spaced apart, and pointy."

That didn't seem insurmountable. "You've got a whole week to get it right."

"If Christmastown lasts another week," Christopher said excitedly. "Now that real snow monsters might be on the loose . . ." He fidgeted as I took a sip of coffee. "Did you see what happened to Tiny when he got squished?"

Jingles intervened. "You've been ghoulish enough for one morning. It's not fair to interrogate someone before they've had their coffee."

He escorted my nephew from the room. The moment Christopher's footsteps had receded, Jingles ducked back into the room. "What *did* you see?" he asked.

I laughed. "Hypocrite."

"The downstairs elves are saying ridiculous things."

"Like what?"

"That Tiny was trying to use the snow monsters to scare everyone from celebrating Halloween, and it backfired when the snow monster turned on him instead."

"Ridiculous." Even Tiny didn't hate Halloween *that* much. Did he? "How did that rumor get started?"

Jingles fluttered his hands. "You know how rumors are. Of course, some are saying there might not be a Halloween celebration at all now."

I tapped my fingers against my mug. Rumors often had a germ of truth to them, and I didn't like the sound of canceling Halloween. So many had put serious effort into the plans. "I think I'll go into town today."

"You'd better hurry if you're going to catch a ride from either Lucia or Tiffany."

I gulped down the rest of my coffee and climbed out of the massive four-poster.

"You have that investigator's glint in your eye," Jingles said. "Do you know something everyone else doesn't?"

I belted my robe. "This doesn't have anything to do with Tiny. I just want to see if I can salvage Halloween."

I might have asked myself if the holiday was worth salvaging. I'd always loved Halloween, but maybe, all things considered, it wasn't a good fit with Christmastown. Judging from Christopher and the elf children I'd seen at the orphanage, though, they were looking forward to the fun. Canceling Halloween would be a big letdown to them. Also, part of me just didn't like the idea of letting Tiny win—even posthumously.

I hitched a ride with Tiffany. My goal was to speak to some of the merchants in town, but halfway down the mountain I remembered I was sitting right next to one. "Are you planning on scaling back your Halloween decorations or plans?" I asked Tiffany.

She sent me an are-you-kidding-me side glance. "Christopher would never forgive me if I removed even one pumpkin."

"You aren't nervous about Christopher trick-or-treating?"

"Why should I be? He'll be with a bunch of kids from Kringle Heights. It's hardly a hotbed of danger up here."

Her nonchalance was remarkable. After her husband's death on Mount Myrrh, Tiffany was the Boeing Chinook of helicopter parents, but she'd eased back on that this year and busied herself more with her own projects. I worried that talk of the snow monster would set her back.

"What happened to Tiny doesn't make you nervous?"

"What does that have to do with Halloween?"

I repeated the gossip Jingles had told me.

Her lips twisted. "I don't like to speak ill of the dead, but some of the talk I've heard about Tiny hasn't been the most complimentary."

Toward me, he'd been officious, querulous, and down-right aggressive at times. But I didn't realize others had had difficulties with him, as well. "What have they said?"

"Nothing specific. I've heard grumbles. Seems Tiny threw his weight around a lot."

Now I was curious to discover who might have had a motive to kill Tiny.

It felt awkward approaching merchants just to squeeze gossip out of them, but I shouldn't have worried. Everyone in town knew I had been at Tiny's cottage yesterday when the gruesome discovery was made, and they were as eager to wring details out of me as I was to question them.

Toggle Hollywell—Tog—the owner of the Christmas-town Cornucopia, pulled me inside his office when he saw me speaking to one of the cashiers. The usual questions about the footprint, its size, and its freshness followed. Then he asked me something puzzling.

"You're sure it was Tiny?"

The query confused me. "Who died, you mean? Yes, of course."

"You saw his face?"

No, I saw his footwear. "I didn't see his face, but Constable Crinkles did, and so did Doc Honeytree."

"That's all right, then." He caught me regarding him

curiously and said, "I mean, I'd hate to think a mistake had been made. That it was someone else out there lying in the snow for all those hours."

"Who else could it have been?"

Tog lifted his shoulders and gestured as if to say, *Just a crazy notion I had.* "You're right. Such a tragedy, isn't it?"

It was the opening I'd been waiting for. "I worried Tiny's death would cancel everyone's Halloween plans, but I notice the Cornucopia still has pumpkins, and Neldor drawings in your windows."

"Of course. This holiday has been a boon for us. Everybody's baking and making candy. I've sold some of Salty's pumpkins, too." His lips turned down and he stood, as did I. He clearly wanted to get back to work. "We erased the snow monster drawings on the plate glass, though. Out of respect."

After I left the Cornucopia I strolled down the boulevard to Dash's Candy and Nut Shoppe, where I was greeted with the usual good cheer. I was a regular. "We got a fresh order of pecans in," Dash told me, grabbing a scoop and a bag, ready for my order. "Tippi just whipped up a batch of chocolate-pecan fudge, too."

Tippi's fudge was a weakness of mine. Some preferred the fudge at Winkie's Chocolate Shop, but I was a Dash's fan all the way. I asked for a half pound of candied pecans, too. It was all in the name of fact finding, after all.

I wasn't the only one after information, though.

Scooping up pecans, Dash said, "I heard you were at Tiny's cottage last night—that you found him in that footprint."

"Deputy Ollie found him, actually, but I was there, yes."

"So you saw him." He slapped the bag of nuts onto the scale. "Tiny, I mean."

How odd. Because of the conversation I'd just had with Tog, I specified, "I didn't see his face, but Constable Crinkles and Doc Honeytree made a positive ID. You were at the meeting."

"Oh, sure, but you know how rumors are around here."

"Is there a rumor that someone other than Tiny died?" I asked.

"It's obviously untrue." He smiled. "How much fudge you want?"

"Several pounds," I answered honestly. "But I'd better just take a few squares."

He obliged by slicing off a good chunk. He weighed it, slipped it in a bag, and pushed my purchases across the counter. "I'll put them on your tab. Got your Frequent Fudger card on you?"

I reached for my wallet, dug out my card, and handed it over to be punched. Yes, I was a Frequent Fudger.

"Are you planning anything for Halloween?" I asked.

Tippi laughed. "Come over and see." She pointed me to a counter filled with Halloween treats—chocolate Neldors and snow monsters, and fudge squares individually wrapped in orange foil. "We're doing big business this week."

They didn't seem inclined to pull their candy snow monsters, either. Maybe eating the enemy was fine.

Gert's Pretzel Stand was my next stop. I didn't expect information from Gert, I was just thirsty and Gert had hot cider. She gave me a cup and I handed her a square of fudge.

"This from Dash's?"

"Of course."

She nibbled at it happily. "So much better than Winkie's."

I nodded as I sipped my cider. "Is someone besides Tiny missing from Christmastown?" I asked.

Gert's face screwed up. "Not that I know of. Why?"

"Everyone keeps asking me if I know for sure that the body we found was Tiny's. Almost as if they were afraid it was someone else."

She snorted. "I think you've grasped the narwhal by the horn."

"Who else could it have been?"

"Doesn't matter. So long as it was Tiny, that's all anyone cares about."

Call me thick, but up to that moment I hadn't understood what was going on. People weren't asking me about the victim's identification because they were afraid someone else had died. They were nervous that Tiny might still be alive.

"I know Tiny could be annoying," I said, "but what did he do to all these elves who want to make sure he's dead?"

"I can't speak for everyone. But did you ever wonder why an elf who ran a successful business didn't mind that his wife was cleaning other elves' houses?"

"There's nothing wrong with being a cleaning lady."

"Nope," Gert agreed. "Not a thing in the world. Only you didn't see him escorting Pixie to fancy dos, did you? You never saw *her* swanning around Christmastown in expensive duds."

"I never saw her around Christmastown at all. I only met her yesterday, after she found out her husband was dead."

"There you go." Gert crossed her arms as if an obvious point had been made.

If so, it had whizzed right over my head. "You mean the whole town resented Tiny because of the way he treated his wife?"

"You could say that." Her lips twisted into an enigmatic smile, as if to indicate that one could also say something else. "More cider?"

"No, but thanks. It was delicious."

"Thanks for the fudge."

As I walked away from the pretzel stand, I mulled over what everyone had told me. There was something about Tiny that I wasn't grasping. Gert had implied that everyone's attitude about him had something to do with Pixie. I needed to talk to Tiny's widow again. . . .

I stopped short. I'd told Nick that I'd let Crinkles pursue this investigation, and I fully intended to. I'd already poked around more pointedly than I'd intended to, but wasn't it natural for me to be curious? I'd thought Tiny tried to kill me. It would do my peace of mind a world of good to find out whether he'd been the real threat . . . or the threatened.

I walked another half block and stopped at the corner while a large delivery sleigh driven by musk oxen passed through the intersection. *I'm Mrs. Claus. Perfectly natural that I'd pay a bereavement call on the widow of one of Christmastown's most prominent citizens. . . .*

I'd need to find out where her sister lived, though.

"Hi, Mrs. Claus!" Salty called out to me from the driver's seat of his sleigh wagon loaded up with pumpkins. He'd drawn to a stop nearby, waiting for the same sleigh to pass.

"Taking those to the Cornucopia?" I asked.

"I've already been there. I'm selling door-to-door now. I was getting calls all morning for them, so I decided just to bring a wagonload into town."

"The Halloween spirit is alive and well," I said, gratified.

"More like the need to burn things is," he said. "Santa convinced everyone not to light bonfires, but people will still feel safer to have something burning in front of their house. So now everyone's stoked to put a jack-o'-lantern or two or three on their porch."

"A little jack-o'-lantern would scare away an abominable snow monster?" I asked.

"Doubt it, but ours is not to question why. Ours is just to make the pumpkin patch pay for itself."

If Salty was delivering door-to-door . . . "Maybe you could help me. I'm trying to find someone."

"Who?"

"The sister of Pixie Sparkletoe. Rosemary Something."

"Oh, heck—I know where she lives. She's married to a fellow who works out at Santa's Workshop. They have a place in Tinkertown."

"Right." Tinkertown was beyond walking distance.

Salty sensed my dilemma and smiled. "Pumpkins should sell like elfcakes out there. I can take you."

Chapter 12

The large Christmas enterprises that dominated Tinker-town—the Candy Cane Factory, the Wrapping Works, and the many warehouses that comprised Santa's Workshop—were all surrounded by elf homes, forming distinct neighborhoods. Around the Wrapping Works, bungalows were spaced close together, set back far enough from the street to allow for an evergreen in the front, most of which remained strung with lights all year long.

As we approached the neighborhood around the old Santa's Workshop, however, the houses started to appear older, and on some streets the front doors of the adjoined buildings were flush against the sidewalk. Salty pulled up in front of one of these. The house, like the ones flanking it, was three stories high and narrow, with one first-floor bay window.

"This is where Pixie's sister lives?" I asked, perched on the seat next to him, a tinned fruitcake in my lap. Fruitcakes were an all-year-round dessert here, and Salty had assured me it would be an appropriate gift to take to a bereaved family. Luckily Tiffany had had a spare, Castle Kringle–made cake in her tea shop when we'd stopped by Tea-piphany on the way over.

Salty nodded, but the guardedness in his expression made me wary. "You've never met Rosemary, have you?"

"No, I haven't."

"She's something." The way he said the words, it didn't sound like he meant something good. "When should I pick you up?"

I cast a nervous glance at the Doveball residence. "I'll need about a half hour."

Salty was already driving away before I reached the door. As I knocked, I heard high-pitched screams coming from inside the house. The door jerked open and a dark-haired elf with a blunt-cut bob, brown eyes, and round cheeks peered out at me impatiently. A couple of children were shrieking in play somewhere behind her. "What do you want?" Before I could answer, she saw Salty's wagon disappearing down the street. "*Hey!*" she yelled after him. He didn't stop. "Was that Salty selling pumpkins? We could use one of those."

"He'll be back," I said. "He gave me a ride here."

Her beetly gaze looked me up and down, then rested on my face, unimpressed. "And who are you?"

I shifted self-consciously. This wasn't a question I received too often. Most Santalanders knew the Clauses like Brits know their House of Windsor. "I'm Mrs. Claus."

"Oh, yeah?" She grunted. "I'm the Tooth Fairy."

I looked down at myself. I wasn't wearing my best outfit, but I looked respectable enough in a forest-green coat lined with white wool. Of course the snow boots I had on weren't the most elegant. . . .

I tried again. "My name is April Claus. I was at the scene of the . . . where they found Tiny yesterday. I came to pay my condolences to your sister."

As the truth in my words sank in, her eyes widened. "Right, sorry. Well, I *am* the Tooth Fairy around here, come to think of it." A brassy laugh gusted out of her. "Name's Rosemary. Come in if you want to see Pixie, but try not to upset her. It took me half the night to get her to calm down. The second night in a row I barely got a wink. Night before that I was just dropping off when some idiot's snowmobile backfired on the street. Then it woke me again. Folks have no consideration. But I guess I'm just naturally sensitive to sound."

I nodded in sympathy as she stepped aside to let me in. Before I'd taken two steps into the house, though, I had to hop back to avoid two young elves racing through the entryway—the source of the shrieks. The one doing the chasing had some kind of stick tied to his head, crossed with a large wooden spatula. The boy being pursued screamed in terror.

Rosemary yelled, "Boys, don't run in the house! And *no shouting!*"

The one with the spatula on his head skidded to a stop in his striped socks. "I'm not a boy, I'm Neldor the Evil!"

"You're going to be Joey the Sent to His Room till Doomsday if you don't pipe down and if that spatula doesn't find its way back to the kitchen by the time I start dinner."

The kids complied, at least until they were out of sight. Then the shrieking started back up again.

Rosemary rolled her eyes. "They swore they were too broken up about their Uncle Tiny to go to school today. I should've known that was a load of reindeer flop." She poked her hand in the direction of the house's parlor. "Pixie's in there. Don't worry about the boys bothering you. They're not allowed in the parlor until they're thirty-six."

The room was obviously the showplace of the house. A fire was going in the hearth, beneath a mantel festooned with figurines, framed pictures of elf ancestors, and an evergreen swag that I assumed was plastic, since the room didn't have the smell of evergreen at all. The parlor was crammed with furniture and bric-a-brac, and a round, barely worn carpet dominated the center.

Pixie languished on the sofa, a crocheted afghan over her small frame.

"Pix, you've got a visitor," Rosemary said. "Mrs. Claus, if you can believe it."

"Call me April," I said.

"I guess you'll want refreshments," Rosemary said, without real enthusiasm.

"That's not necessary," I said. "I brought this for you, though."

I presented the fruitcake tin to Rosemary. It was decorated in a beautiful red-and-gold wreath design around the drawing of a waving Santa that was the Claus logo.

"Thanks." Taking it, Rosemary went over to a table loaded with similar tins and stacked mine on the top of the pile. There had obviously been a lot of fruitcake condoling going on.

Over on the davenport, Pixie pushed herself up to sitting. "It's nice of you to take the time to come here, especially after the things I said yesterday. I hope you'll forgive me. I was in such shock."

"Naturally." I felt awkward towering over her, so I perched uninvited on the other side of the couch. I was a little too large for the furniture, but I was accustomed now to that bull-in-the-china-shop feel of visiting elf houses. "What happened to your husband would have been a shock to anyone."

I heard a grunt behind us. Rosemary had settled on a stiff-looking embroidered chair.

"Oh, Rosemary," Pixie said with a sigh, as if they were in the middle of a conversation they'd had a million times.

"There's no reason to try to put him on a pedestal now, Pix." Rosemary slanted a knowing glance at me. "Tiny was no saint."

"He was just busy," Pixie told me. "He had a lot of irons in the fire."

Rosemary crossed her arms. "Maybe all those irons were what made him think he was better than everybody else."

"I *told* you," Pixie said, "he didn't grow up in Tinker-town. He just wasn't comfortable here."

Rosemary was having none of her sister's rationalizations. "You don't have to defend him anymore. He's dead. I get it—two years ago you thought he was the handsome prince and let him sweep you off your feet, but it's way past time to admit that your prince was a pill who was happy to let you keep on doing your Cinderella act as long as you were bringing in money." She shook her head at me. "I don't suppose you ever had much to do with Tiny."

"We did speak on a few occasions," I said.

Her brows raised. "What did you think of him?"

My instinct not to speak ill of the dead warred with my burning desire to keep Rosemary talking freely. "We crossed swords once or twice, mostly over Halloween."

She blew out a breath. "Halloween! Now *that's* the one topic where Tiny and I saw eye to eye."

Oops.

"If you had two boys running around talking about Nel-dor and snow monsters twenty-four/seven, you'd agree with me," she said.

Pixie whimpered and raised a handkerchief to her face. No wonder. I wouldn't want to hear about snow monsters if I were her, either.

"I'm so sorry," I said. "I didn't come here to upset you."

"Pix has always been that way," Rosemary said dismis-sively. "Sensitive. That's why I never understood her staying with Tiny. He never appreciated her. Just look at her." She gestured at her sister nestled delicately on the couch. It's ri-diculous to describe someone as *elfin* when she actually was an elf, but Pixie did have that particular quality. Yet I'd seen that delicate facade break out in real anger.

Perhaps it was unfair to judge how someone reacted when she was in the first shock of grief. The first time we'd met was a stark contrast to now, though. Now she seemed adrift on that sofa, or just numb. Or . . . distracted.

"Our Pix could've married anybody," Rosemary continued. "Walnut Lovejoy was mad to marry her at one point. But *noooo*, he wasn't good enough for her. It was Tiny or nothing for Pix. But look at Walnut now. He'll own half of Christmastown soon, and Tiny . . ." Her lips blew out a flaccid half-raspberry.

"Oh, Rosemary, stop it," Pixie said. "I didn't love Walnut."

"I can't believe you ever loved that puffed-up shoemaker, either. You should be glad some snow monster came and put you out of your misery. Let's just hope it doesn't come back and smoosh the rest of us."

"You're awful," Pixie said.

"I'm only saying what you'll be admitting yourself is true in a few weeks. You're better off without him. Everybody will be, from what I've heard."

"What have you heard?" I asked.

"Rosemary, please, that's all been just gossip." Pixie looked at me sharply. "My Tinkertown relatives never liked Tiny because he was proud and wore fine clothes and was so wrapped up in the community of Christmastown. They thought he was too big for his booties, but he was just a proud man."

"An s-n-o-b," Rosemary said, and then she lowered her voice and said to me as if Pixie couldn't hear, "And if you left out the *n*, that would work, too."

Pixie tensed. "You should be ashamed of yourself! I would never speak that way about Alv."

"Of course not, because there was never a more honest or true elf than Alvin Doveball, and everyone knows it." Somewhere in the house, crying began. Rosemary reddened. "Those darned kids. They've woken the baby." She got up, hurried to the door, and bellowed. "If you kids don't pipe down, you'll *wish* Neldor had dropped you in the Farthest Frozen Reaches!" A hush fell, which just made her tilt her head suspiciously. "Excuse me." She stomped out of the room.

"You shouldn't pay Rosemary any mind," Pixie said. "She's a little gruff, but it's just her way."

"She's protective of you, isn't she?"

"She always has been, ever since I was little. She never liked Tiny—never thought he was good enough for me. That's how Rosemary is. No one would be good enough for the people she loves. She'd do anything for her family."

Would she do murder? I could imagine Rosemary having the power to summon snow monsters. Well, at least the lung power.

"She said she stayed up with you half the night last night," I said.

Pixie nodded. "I was pretty upset."

"Even though she was tired from the night before. She mentioned she hadn't slept well." The very night Tiny was killed . . .

"Rosemary's always tired," Pixie said with a dismissive shrug. "Three kids. And Alv is always around nights, which takes her attention."

"He never works nights or goes out to the tavern?"

"Alv?" Pixie laughed. "Oh, no. He's a family man."

"I thought maybe he'd clear out to give you two some quality sister time." And time for Rosemary to sneak out in the night and kill Tiny.

From her puzzled frown, I guessed the concept of quality time with Rosemary bemused her. "No."

"Do you think you'll be staying here with your sister for a while?"

She plucked listlessly at the tassel on a throw pillow. "I don't know. Rosemary already has her hands full with the children. I offered to help some, but she's the type that likes to do things herself. Then she gets cranky because she's doing everything."

"I'm sure she just wants you to take it easy. You've had a terrible shock."

She nodded. "I'm not going back to work anytime soon, that's for sure."

I assumed that meant Tiny had left her well fixed. That was a mercy. "Then Sparkletoe's Bootery will stay open?"

She blinked as if surprised the question would be asked. "Of course. Louie will keep it going."

"Perhaps he'll be in a position to buy you out."

She didn't respond.

The silence stretched. I'd never been so relieved to hear a knock at the door. Rosemary bustled to answer it, a bundled baby on her hip. "There you are," she greeted Salty. "I called out to you earlier and you didn't stop."

He took off his cap as he stepped inside. "Sorry, Rosemary. I must not have heard you."

"I need to buy a pumpkin. Maybe two."

"I thought you didn't like Halloween," I said.

"It's not for Halloween," she said, as if explaining something to a dim-witted pupil, "it's to keep the snow monsters away. Whether a lighted pumpkin can actually scare one away is anybody's guess, but better safe than sorry." She lowered her voice. "Especially if there's one stomping around with a grudge against the Sparkletoe-Doveball clan."

I said good-bye to Pixie, who had already sunk back down on the sofa. When I went to the wagon, Salty was unloading two of his biggest pumpkins. He wouldn't take money for them.

"Consider them a gift for Pixie," he said when Rosemary protested.

As Salty and I drove back, he seemed more satisfied with this trip to Tinkertown than I was. I'd learned that Pixie's sister didn't like her choice of husband. But most in-laws had friction at some point, didn't they? They rarely murdered each other.

"Only ten pumpkins left," Salty mused. "Maybe I could sell those to Bella Sparkletoe for her store. She's got a big display, I noticed."

"Sure, let's go."

While I was there, I could talk to Bella about her brother's death. Not that I was investigating.

Not officially, at least.

Bella bought all the pumpkins, but she didn't have much to say about Tiny. There was black bunting across the front of Sparketoe's Mercantile in memory of her late brother, but she was bustling about the store as if it were just another day. Strangely, the black bunting seemed to complement the graveyard tableau window display.

"I suppose the Christmastown Community Guild will have to choose a new leader," I said. "Maybe you'll be stepping into that role?"

She shook her head. "That's a time suck. Tiny didn't mind doing it, but then Tiny liked to be up in everybody's business."

"I did hear Tiny had some contentious business relations . . ."

"That's an understatement." She laughed. "You wouldn't think the bootie biz could be so rife with drama, but when Walnut's Bootie World opened, it was like a declaration of war."

Sounded to me like the war had started before that. "Did you know that Walnut had been in love with Pixie?"

"Half of Santaland has fallen for those big blue eyes of hers at some point. Tiny just happened to be the idiot who had the bankroll she was looking for."

"You think Pixie's a gold digger? She cleans houses for a living."

"Right, because she misjudged Tiny. He was always resentful of other people having things—even his own family! When our parents left me this store, the way he took it, you'd have thought they'd done it just as an insult to him."

"Well, he was their son."

"A son who'd never shown any interest in the mercantile. Instead, he'd forced my parents to buy out the old boot maker so Tiny could anoint himself the Christmastown bootie king. And when the old boot maker died, he found Louie to take his place."

"So Tiny couldn't make boots?"

"He did a fine job, but he was never the artisan he wanted everyone to believe. And he never made as much money as he tried to project, either."

Hearing that his own sister didn't like Tiny any more than his sister-in-law almost made me feel sorry for the guy.

Her brow wrinkled. "Tiny also owned some property in town. That probably caused more disputes than booties did."

"Rental property?" I asked.

"I think so. He was never interested in talking business with me. He always considered my success just a bit of unearned luck."

"I just visited Pixie at her sister's in Tinkertown," I said. "She mentioned holding on to the Bootery, but not any rental property." When Bella didn't respond, I continued, "I might have someone who'd be interested in it. Do you know which building it is?"

"I couldn't give you details, and I'm not sure Pixie could, either. She's a good sort but not the brightest light on the string. Louie might be able to tell you more about it. He's been slaving away for Tiny forever, so he probably overheard a lot of business talk over the years."

Of course I stopped by the Bootery. Even today of all days, Louie was at his workbench, hovered over a pair of high-heeled booties. "Another pair for Mayor Firlog's wife," he explained. "She was always Tiny's best customer. He'd want us to keep on providing excellent footwear service for Christmastown."

There was something sad yet noble about his keep-calm-and-cobble-on attitude.

"I saw Pixie this morning," I said.

He stopped what he was doing. "How is she?"

"About how you'd expect."

"Of course." He looked back down at his work. "I guess it'll be a while before she'll want to come here and decide what to do with this place."

"Have you considered buying her out?"

"I wouldn't presume . . ."

No, it wasn't in Louie to presume. He was too modest for his own good.

"Pixie—Mrs. Sparkletoe—and I don't talk much," he said.

"I heard something about Tiny having a rental property, and some conflict about that."

He squinted in concentration. "Oh, sure, I remember. Someone wanted to buy it, but Tiny wouldn't sell. I think he had dreams of expanding this place. Especially after Walnut horned in on his territory."

"So it's the building next door that he owns?"

"Yeah, the optician wanted to buy it. One day he and Tiny were yelling so loudly at each other, it felt as if both buildings might come down. Mr. Pepperbough sounded as though he was ready to kill him."

The name jolted me. Of course I knew that Chip's busi-

ness was right next door and that he was the only optician in
town. But it wasn't until the name Pepperbough came out of
Louie's mouth that I put it all together.

"Chip Pepperbough threatened Tiny?"

Louie's face fell. "Oh, now, I didn't mean to say he was
threatening him. They were just angry, like people get when
they've got a business conflict. You know how Tiny could be.
He wasn't the relenting type."

"So things got heated between them . . ." I'd never heard
Chip so much as raise his voice, except when he was reading
to children at the library. Sure, his niceness had always seemed
suspicious to me. But would he have killed someone over a
property dispute?

Then again, why not? Property disputes had been leading to murder probably for as long as there had been private
property.

"Gosh, don't go spreading around that I think Mr. Pepperbough did anything wrong. I'm sure he didn't." Louie
gulped. "I mean, it was a snow monster that killed Tiny."

I stared at him.

"Wasn't it?" he asked.

"It was a monster of some kind," I said.

Chapter 13

Hearing Louie name Chip as the elf who'd fought with Tiny over property already had me reeling. Then, as I left the Bootery, I walked right into him.

"Whoa," he said, grabbing my elbows to steady me. "Are you all right, April?"

"I'm fine," I lied. Seeing him so soon after I'd talked to Louie about him flustered me.

Chip darted a glance around me, then met my gaze in mock inquiry. "Buying some booties?"

"No, I was just checking . . ." I didn't want to tell him what I'd just heard. Not outright. "I paid a condolence call on Pixie Sparkletoe this morning, and I sensed that she was a little concerned about the shop . . ."

Chip held up his gloved hands. "Say no more. Just Lady Bountiful, checking up on things." The backhanded barb was delivered with an ingratiating smile. "Well, whatever brought you to Sparkletoe Lane, I'm glad it's given me the chance to run into you. Literally!" He chuckled. "Seriously, though, I've wanted a chance to speak to you. On our own, I mean."

I didn't like the sound of this. "Without Juniper?"

"I've always sensed that you . . . well, I won't presume to say you don't like me, because why should you? Right now you just know me as Chip Pepperbough, Juniper's boyfriend. Or maybe as Chip Pepperbough, optician. I'd like you to get to know me as Chip Pepperbough, elf and friend in his own right."

Oh, brother. "That would be fine, but I was just heading back to the castle—"

"Wonderful! I'm going to the library. We can walk together a little ways."

He gestured for me to accompany him down the sidewalk. What could I do? I didn't relish his company. All that eagerness to be liked made me ill at ease . . . especially after I'd just heard about his screaming fight with Tiny Sparkletoe. On the other hand, this was an opportunity to verify what Louie had just told me.

We covered half a block in strained silence.

"Juniper said you met through the band," was his conversation opener.

"That's right."

"I have to confess, I'm a little jealous of that band," he said. "It eats up a lot of her time."

It takes time she could be spending with me, I translated. As if spending half his afternoons at the library weren't enough togetherness during her day.

"I'm always curious about what she's up to," he said. "I guess that shows how in love with her I am."

"Maybe you should take up an instrument."

"I wish I were musical. Unfortunately, I'm tone deaf and don't even have a good sense of rhythm."

"Excuses, excuses," I joked.

He laughed. "That's right—you're rhythm challenged, too."

My smile disappeared. "What?"

"That's what I heard, anyway."

"From Juniper?"

"Oh, no," he said quickly. "I must have heard it from . . . well, I can't remember now. Okay, maybe it *was* Juniper, but"—he smiled—"on the whole she has nothing but glowing things to say about you."

On the whole.

Rhythm challenged.

It's not that a lot of my ego was wrapped up in my dubious percussion skills, but they had improved. Or I thought they had.

I was lost in thought until Chip said, "I think it's marvelous that you condescend to be such a good friends with Juniper. Really admirable."

The words surprised me so much I nearly tripped off the sidewalk. He caught my elbow and I shrugged it off. *Condescend?* Were we in Jane Austen territory now? "There's no condescension involved. Juniper and I just hit it off."

"Of course. But she also knows that you live in the castle, while she . . ."

My face reddened. Was this how Juniper saw our friendship—as if I were some kind of Lady Bountiful coming down from Kringle Heights to grace her life with my presence? A wave of queasiness hit me. Was that why she spoke well of me *on the whole*? My mind sifted through our recent encounters. Had I ever been dismissive, condescending?

I caught a sidewise glimpse of Chip's slight smile. He was planting these ideas in my head, and I doubted it was by accident.

"Juniper and I enjoy hanging out," I insisted.

"Of course you do. Why not? I know there are no two ladies whose company I enjoy more. Though you'll understand if I have a slight preference for one of you over the other."

I didn't even bother to respond to that dumb remark.

Don't let him get to you. It was time to take charge of the conversation. "Did you ask Tiny Sparkletoe to sell you a piece of property?"

The disappearance of his oily smile let me know I'd hit a nerve. "Who told you that? The widow?"

"I heard it through the grapevine."

He continued several steps before responding. "For once, the grapevine is correct. I did want to buy the building my business is in, which I've been renting from Tiny for years. I thought we could come to an agreement, but he was a stubborn elf and wouldn't budge on price. I think he expected me to keep offering more, but I'm not crazy. There are other buildings in Christmastown. At some point one of them will come up for sale and I'll be ready to pounce."

"Did you tell him you were going to leave as soon as something good came along?"

"Oh, yes. He thought I was bluffing."

"But you weren't."

"I try to be up front in my dealings whenever possible. Guile has never been one of *my* qualities."

His tone implied that Tiny was the wily one. Or was that gibe directed at me? Maybe he suspected my motive for asking these questions about Tiny.

I took a deep breath. If Chip was a suspect in Tiny's murder, I needed to tread carefully. "Sorry to sound so nosy."

"Juniper said you have a probing curiosity, but I never thought you'd be poking around in my business." A half-hearted laugh barely concealed his annoyance.

It would be very un-Chiplike for him to be openly hostile, but after what Louie had told me, Chip's affable exterior struck me as more artificial than ever. It seemed unwise to risk letting it slip that I suspected him in what had happened to Tiny.

"I should be heading back to the castle now." Although

the funicular was no longer operating, a sleigh bus went up and down the mountain every hour.

He appeared equally eager to be shed of me. "It's been fun to talk a little with you," he lied. "I've always gotten the sense that you didn't like me as well as I liked you—but I hope that will change."

I tried to keep my smile from slipping. "I'm sure we'll have a lot more opportunities to talk." *Unfortunately.*

As I hurried away from him, I worried about Juniper. Chip's resenting the time she spent in the band was a bad sign. And his manner with me was so passive-aggressive and repellent. Almost as if he wanted April to have fewer friends.

Fewer friends. If I had died in that funicular accident, Juniper would have had one less friend.

I gave myself a mental shake. *This is paranoia talking.* Chip had been there during the funicular accident, standing right in the path of the runaway car. He'd saved Juniper's life.

But what if acting the part of heroic rescuer had been his grand scheme?

My footsteps slowed as my mind replayed the afternoon of the accident. After rehearsal, Chip had shown up unexpectedly, and then insisted on walking me to the funicular stop. True, my taking the funicular hadn't been at his suggestion, but Juniper could have told him that I regularly rode it home after rehearsal. He might have sawed the cable before arriving at the band hall . . . and then nonchalantly escorted me to my would-be doom. And positioned himself to be Juniper's savior-hero.

Could Chip be that cold-blooded?

A mother came toward me with two young elves in tow. One was dressed as a snow monster, the other had the inevitable shovel horn on his head.

The kids were singing "The Monster Mash," and walking in the awkward flat-footed way that I'd seen Chip doing at the library when he was narrating the story of the snow monster. The little elves could barely sing for laughing at their own antics.

Their mother noticed me looking at the children, then rounded on them sternly. "Stop that," she admonished. "Today isn't the day to make fun of monsters . . . mashing people."

Let them have their fun, I wanted to tell her. Wasn't this why every culture told spooky and scary stories, be they about witches, snow monsters, or vampires? Fictional horror was a release valve for our fears.

I'd almost reached the place to catch the sleigh that would take me up the mountain, but I remained frozen in my tracks across the street. *Stories.* The first story Chip had read at the library was the story of Neldor. And what had Christopher said of the funicular accident? That my plunge down the mountain was *like Neldor*. Then, yesterday, Chip had been reading a story about the snow monster the same day Tiny, the elf who'd refused to sell him the property he wanted so much, had been discovered smashed to death by a snow monster foot.

Coincidence?

Jangling bells brought me out of my trance. The sleigh bus was arriving, and I had to run across the street to catch it. Once the passengers were all seated, the elves started to do what elves normally did on sleighs, or whenever they were together and feeling convivial: they started singing. Not a Halloween song. They broke into "The Twelve Days of Christmas," which I'd come to think of as the Santaland equivalent of "99 Bottles of Beer on the Wall." A good-for-all-occasions time killer.

Not to have sung along would have seemed as strange to elves as singing a Christmas song in October did to me, so I joined in. It was good to turn off my brain for a while. Maybe by the time I reached Castle Kringle, my suspicions about

Chip would seem as crazy as I wanted them to be. I didn't like Chip, but I didn't want to believe Juniper had hooked up with a killer. Aside from being dangerous, something like that would be a serious blow to her self-esteem. She'd had enough bad boyfriends in her life already.

Waldo was in the castle's foyer as I came through the door. "Oh! Mrs. Claus!" He hopped back as if surprised to see me walk into my own home.

"Hello, Waldo." I wondered briefly if there was Xanax for elves.

"Has there been any news about Tiny Sparkletoe?" he asked.

I assumed he wanted to know the same thing the elves in Christmastown had wanted to find out. "He's really dead."

"And they know for sure it's a snow monster that did it?"

My gaze narrowed on him. "Why? Do you have any other ideas?"

"No!" he said quickly. "No, I've just been worried. Snow monsters have always made me nervous."

Everything made Waldo nervous. Including, evidently, me. Having exhausted his conversation, he pushed the hulking door behind me closed and scurried away.

There was still time before dinner to wash up and change, so I headed up to my room. I showered, changed clothes, then sat at my dressing table, lost in thought. If Chip had attempted to kill both Tiny and me, he'd had a busy week. With mixed results. *A hit and a miss.* There was also the question of method: death by funicular crash was quite a bit different than death by snow monster foot. How would one arrange to have a snow monster step on an elf?

I was still pondering that last question when someone knocked. At my "come in," Jingles entered. "Good, you're here," he said. "Mrs. Claus—the dowager Mrs. Claus—wasn't sure you would make it back in time for dinner. Santa won't be dining with the family. He's gone out to the first meeting of the Anti–Snow Monster Vigilance Committee."

That was disappointing. I'd wanted to talk to Nick about what I'd learned today. But maybe Jingles could help. "Are there such things as assassin snow monsters a person could hire?" I asked.

His brows rose. "Who's made you angry?"

"*I* don't want to assassinate anyone. I was wondering if someone could have arranged for a monster to step on Tiny. Would a snow monster do something like that for . . ." Snow monsters probably didn't use money, but there had to be something they valued. "Maybe a walrus carcass or two?"

"That would be an unusual modus operandi."

Yes. "So odd no one else might think of it as murder. Just like a funicular crash."

He caught my gist. "Are you thinking that whoever tried to kill you also killed Tiny?"

"Let's just say it's a possibility."

"But why? You and Tiny . . . well, there's not much linking the two of you."

"Not unless one person wanted to be rid of both of us for his own particular reasons."

Jingles gasped. "You know who it is."

"I only have a suspicion."

"Who did it?" he asked eagerly.

"You mean whom do I suspect?"

He let out a long-suffering sigh. "All right, Prudence. Whom do you suspect?"

"Chip Pepperbough."

He gaped at me. "The optician? Why would he want to kill you?"

"Because he's the most clingy boyfriend I've ever seen,

and from what I gathered talking to him this afternoon, he doesn't want Juniper having outside interests or friends."

Jingles didn't look convinced. "And Tiny? Why would Chip Pepperbough kill him?"

I told him about the real estate argument Louie had overheard. "When you think about it, two entirely unrelated murders with such vastly different motives and methods is almost ingenious. Who would ever link them?"

"Especially to the town's affable optician," Jingles agreed.

"Outwardly affable."

"Since he missed you the first time, he might make another attempt."

"That's a comforting thought."

"Shouldn't you tell the constable about this?" Jingles asked.

"What would that get me? Frustration and more raffle tickets."

"But if Pepperbough's as diabolical as you say, you might not be the only one in danger. If *you* pieced this together, someone closer to him might be able to connect the dots, too."

Juniper? "He wouldn't hurt Juniper. I've never seen a guy so crazy for someone as he is about her."

"Obsessive about her, you mean. And how do relationships like that usually end?"

He was right. If I truly thought Chip was a murderer, that wasn't information I could withhold from my best friend. "I have to tell Juniper."

"Send her an anonymous note."

I drew back. "Why would I do that?"

"Because if you tell her in person, you'll have one less friend. No one wants to hear that her boyfriend is a calculating killer."

"*Might be* a calculating killer." I could see his point, but . . .
"An anonymous note seems so cowardly. Besides, she might
just dismiss it as being from a kook or the work of the Pumpkin Slayer. What if something happens—what if Chip were to
attack *her*? I wouldn't be able to forgive myself if I didn't warn
her myself. He's already murdered one elf."

"You *suspect* he has," Jingles reminded me.

Now who was playing Prudence?

Maybe the smartest thing to do would be to tell my suspicions to a responsible, sharp law enforcement officer. But
that was something in short supply at the Christmastown constabulary. No telling how Crinkles would handle this. I doubt
it would be with finesse.

I made up my mind. "I'm going to warn Juniper—in
person—before talking to Crinkles." I looked at Jingles to
gauge his level of doubt about this plan. On a scale of one to
ten, he was at thirty-two. "I could use some help, though," I
added.

His expression brightened.

Chapter 14

I wasted no time calling Juniper to ask if she could meet for coffee. "Not tonight," she said. "Chip is making a cassoulet. You know—romantic dinner for two. It's our seven-and-a-half-week anniversary."

Seven and a half weeks? What constituted a half week in terms of milestone counting? Three days? Four?

"What about an early lunch tomorrow?" I pressed. "Could you get away?"

"I think so. I have something I want to talk to you about anyway."

"What is it?" Maybe *she* wanted to talk about Chip, too.

"It's not a big deal—library business."

We made plans to meet the next morning at Tiffany's place at eleven.

After I hung up, I began to worry about the delay. Had I been a wimp not to come out and voice my suspicions? If Chip was a maniacal killer, he would have over twelve hours to do his worst while Juniper was still blissfully unaware of his true nature. That seven-and-a-half-week-anniversary dinner was rife with the potential for evil. Just the fact that he was cooking made me nervous.

It wasn't Juniper he wanted to do away with, though. It was me.

Maybe.

When Nick got home from the meeting, I went down to his office to pick his brain. As I walked in, he was staring distractedly at a map of Santaland. He was also wearing a new, odd outfit—a Santa suit made from winter camouflage material of gray and beige blotches on a white background. It looked like Santa wear designed by Jackson Pollock.

"What happened?" I asked.

"We need to come up with a snow monster warning system," he said. "I'm trying to figure out where we could place cameras at the border."

"Studying maps requires camouflage?" I also noted a crossbow leaning against the office wall.

He glanced down at himself. "Boots decided we needed uniforms. He had this made up for me." And that's about all the interest he could muster in sartorial choices. He gazed back at the map. "It's incredible that no system was put in place before now. We've been remiss."

"I thought you were skeptical that this was a snow monster attack."

"My doubt about Tiny's death doesn't mean that a warning system wouldn't be a good idea." He squinted. "The question is how closely spaced do the cameras need to be for this to be effective?"

"Did any other ideas come out of the meeting?"

He laughed. "Well, someone suggested putting up an electric fence that would zap any monster that tried to cross it."

"I can just imagine Lucia's reaction the first time a reindeer gets zapped."

He nodded. "Cameras were all that we could agree on today. But they'll take time to order and install."

When it came to snow monsters and guarding against

them, I was out of my depth. Besides, another worry preoccupied me.

"Are there any North Pole stories that involve deadly cassoulets?" I asked.

Nick looked at me with dread in his brown eyes. "Do I even want to know what prompted that question?"

"It's not as strange as it sounds. Until a few days ago I was ignorant of stories about shovel-horned reindeer . . . and I'd never had personal experience with snow monsters. I was just wondering if there was some story about an elf who poisons his true love. Possibly with a cassoulet."

To Nick's credit, he gave the question serious thought before answering. "If there is, I've never heard it."

"Good." I stood and went over to hug him. "You've put my mind at ease."

"You don't think someone's trying to poison you, do you?"

"Not at all," I assured him. "Something Juniper mentioned got me thinking about it."

"How's Juniper?"

"Fine, I think. I'm going to see her tomorrow morning." Assuming she survived Chip's romantic dinner for two.

"Good—she always cheers you up."

I wasn't sure that would be the case after I informed her that she might be romantically involved with an evil elf.

I arrived at Tea-piphany a little early the next morning, so I was already seated in the window when I saw Juniper coming down the sidewalk. The sight of her alone made me breathe a sigh of relief. I'd taken steps to ensure this would be a Chipless lunch, but Chip had confounded my best-laid plans before.

She was in a buoyant mood, especially when she saw the tower of food I'd ordered, with all her favorite sweets and sandwiches. Soon Tiffany deposited a pot of tea in front of us, and we were set.

"Isn't this nice?" Juniper said. "We haven't had a lunch like this since . . ."

"Since I got back from Oregon." I added, "And you were going out with Chip."

She shook her head, still smiling. "I suppose I haven't had as much time for things like this as I did before. But I've never felt so much a part of a couple before. You're probably used to it, but all this togetherness is new to me. It's . . . a lot."

I leaned forward. "You're happy, aren't you?"

"Golly doodle, yes," she said quickly. "How could I not be? Chip is so . . . so attentive." She poured tea. "All the time."

The hint of exasperation I detected offered me an opening. "I need to talk to you about something."

Her face brightened. "I had something that I want to talk to you about, too, remember? Chip thought of it, actually. He thinks the library should have a costume contest. We've put up a few signs encouraging patrons to dress as their favorite fictional character for the Halloween carnival, and yesterday Chip suggested that we make it into a contest. Don't you think it's a good idea?"

"Yes," I admitted.

"Guess who we want to judge the costumes."

"Nick?"

"Close—you!" She beamed at me. "Please say yes. When I said we'd need a judge, Chip mentioned your name right away. You know how much he likes you. He said you two had a great chat yesterday."

"Mm."

"I guess I should have felt my ears burning. Did he say anything about me?"

I coughed uncomfortably as I swallowed a bite of scone.

"Are you okay?" she asked.

I took a sip of hot tea. "Scones are a little drier than usual."

"They look delish," she said, slathering clotted cream on one. Her eyes brightened. "I'm sorry. You wanted to talk about something else. What was it?"

"It's a . . . sensitive subject."

"Oh, a problem." She put her knife down and gave me her full attention. "Dr. Juniper is in. What's going on with you?"

"It's not about me. It's about you."

The slightest hint of a frown lined her brow.

"I'm worried about you," I said.

An anxious laugh sputtered out of her. "Why?"

"Well, to be honest, it's because of Chip." Was there a delicate way to put this? I couldn't think of one in that moment, so, fool that I was, I plunged ahead. "I have reason to believe—or to suspect—that Chip has been involved in the two incidents this week."

"Incidents?" Her gaze went glassy with confusion.

I nodded. "The funicular accident."

"But that's impossible."

"Think about it. Do you trust Chip?"

"Of course!" Confusion filled her face, then she leaned forward. "Wait. Is this a joke?"

"I think he should be considered a suspect," I said.

"Last I heard, you thought Tiny was behind the funicular accident. Or that elf who works in the castle—what's his name?"

"Waldo," I said. "That was what I thought in the beginning."

"But you *know* Chip couldn't have been involved." Her voice grew more forceful. "We were there with you. We walked you to the funicular station."

"Just hear me out. I realize—"

"You think Chip tried to *murder* you? And what was the other incident you're talking about?"

"Tiny."

Her jaw dropped. "You think he tried to kill Tiny, too? You think Chip Pepperbough, my Chip, is a serial killer?"

A couple at a nearby table glanced our way.

I lowered my voice. "Technically, a serial killer has to have three victims before being so designated."

A sarcastic laugh escaped her. "Chip better get busy, then."

"Please believe me, Juniper, it's not easy for me to say this to you. I have good reasons for believing what I'm telling you."

"Oh, I know your reasons. You don't like Chip. You never have."

"That's—" The lie caught in my throat. "I want to protect you."

As calmly and quickly as I could, I told her what I'd heard from Louie about Chip's grievance with Tiny. Then I explained how I'd stitched together the similarities between the stories Chip had chosen to read at the library and the crimes that had followed. And, reluctantly, I added that although he proclaimed to have nothing but Juniper's best interests at heart, yesterday Chip had spoken to me in a way that actually made me suspect that he wanted to separate her from activities and friends.

She heard me out, but by the time I finished, her face was fiery red. "I know Chip has his faults, but how anyone could think he would actually be a cold-blooded killer is beyond me. And your proof? He read a few children's stories. And because of an offhand comment of Christopher's—who's twelve—you suddenly imagine that a falling funicular has something to do with Neldor, and that the town optician somehow has the ability to convince snow monsters to assassinate his enemies. It's ludicrous!"

I could feel my own face reddening. "It was when Louie

told me about Chip's fight with Tiny that I started to put these things together."

"Because Chip wanted to buy the building he's been renting? I agree that it's unlike Chip to yell at someone, but have you forgotten how irritating Tiny could be? I'm sure plenty of elves and people yelled at Tiny over the years."

As she spoke, any certainty I'd felt girding my suspicion of Chip melted away, leaving me on ever-thinning ice.

I couldn't tell if her face looked more hurt or angry. "I thought you were my friend," she said.

"I am. That's why I'm telling you all this. If Nick were a murderer—or even if you thought he was—I'd want to know."

"So this is you being a good friend?"

"Well . . . yes."

"I've found someone who wants to be with me all the time and shower me with affection, and instead of being happy for me, you're trying to sabotage my relationship."

The accusation stung. "Don't you think there's something strange about someone who wants to be with you *all the time*?"

"No," she retorted. "I think it's wonderful. And you know why? Because I can appreciate how rare it is. I've been alone most of my life, April. Unlike you, I haven't been married twice. I've never been married at all. Or even in a long-term relationship. I've lived thirty-five years with the creeping suspicion that I might be one of those elves who just never finds her soul mate. But now I have, and, yes, he's a little overattentive sometimes. Yes, it's unusual that he likes to hang around my workplace. But those things are unusual in good ways, aren't they? I was alone for years, except for the time I went out with jerks. And Chip had a horrible experience, too—he was engaged to someone who cheated on him twice, with two different elves! So, yes—we're both happy to have found someone who cherishes every day, week, and even every half week we're together."

By the end of her speech I'd sunk so low in my chair, we probably appeared around the same height. "I was honestly worried."

"You don't respect me enough to give me a little credit for not falling for a psychopath."

It wouldn't be the first time.

I didn't say the words, but they must have shown in my face, because she looked as upset as if I'd called her a psycho sponge. I needed to learn to guard my expressions better.

"You've been a false friend," she said.

"False would be saying nothing when I'm worried for you." Judging by her glare, she didn't agree. "Okay, maybe I've jumped to the wrong conclusion—"

"Maybe?" Her voice looped up so that the whole room swiveled toward us. "After all I've said, that's all you're willing to concede?"

"I'm your friend and I'm worried," I said. "But fine. Maybe I should just keep my mouth shut."

She tossed her napkin onto the table. "No, you should show a little tact and not act like a lunatic, voicing every crazy idea that pops into your head."

I'll admit, I don't like being called a lunatic. That's probably what caused me to blurt out, "That's rich, coming from you."

"What do you mean?"

"How much tact did you display when you told Chip I was rhythm challenged?"

A flash in her eyes revealed her surprise that Chip had let that slip. But it was gone in an instant. "You are, April. And, unlike Chip's being a murderer, your poor percussion skills are easy to prove. All anyone has to do is come to one of our concerts."

Or they could have just watched the jerky way my foot was bouncing under the table. I couldn't believe we were arguing this way. We'd never argued at all. But now I was so mad myself that I didn't feel able to offer a conciliatory word.

Juniper stood. "I don't think we should be socializing if you can't respect my choices." Hitching her purse over her shoulder, she said, "Chip warned me that a friendship with a Claus from the castle was bound to end unhappily someday. I guess he was right about that, too."

So Chip had been talking against me? I wanted to point out that those were not the words of someone who liked me—as Chip had claimed to. But one more criticism of Chip might have pushed her over the edge into never-ever-speaking-to-you-again territory.

Although, to be honest, there was a good chance she'd reached that point already.

She slapped several bills on the table. "This will cover my lunch."

"Juniper . . ."

She lifted a hand, palm out, to stop me. "And don't bother yourself about judging the library contest. We'll find someone else. I don't think you're a good judge of anything—even costumes."

And with that, my best friend in all of Santaland turned on her heel and walked out. The bell over the door jangled with a cheer completely incongruous with my sinking mood. I felt sick. I'd made a huge mess of everything.

And the terrible thing was, I still wasn't ready to exonerate Chip. I sipped my tea and seethed with a growing resentment that bordered on the illogical. As if Chip himself were responsible for my ham-fisted attempt to warn Juniper that he was a murderer.

Except, if he *was* a murderer, then he actually was responsible.

The bell above the door tinkled again and I looked up, hoping Juniper had returned to say she forgave me and maybe even thanked me for worrying about her welfare. Instead, Jingles appeared, sporting a pair of spectacles. In order to ensure that Juniper and I would have lunch to ourselves, I'd sent him to Chip's office for an eye exam.

He spotted me right away and hurried over, plopping himself down in the chair Juniper had just vacated. "Chip Pepperbough is a miracle worker!"

"You've got to be kidding."

"He gave me an eye exam and fixed me up with a pair of glasses to wear until the new frames I special-ordered arrive." He turned his head one way, then the other, modeling his eyeglasses. "What do you think?"

"Mm." I took a swig of tea. I just couldn't bring myself to compliment Chip's professional handiwork at the moment.

"Wait until you see the ones I ordered," he continued. "They're more square, with tortoiseshell accents. I'd picked out a rounder pair, but Chip said I had a face that cried out for the executive look in frames. Did you know Chip has all his frames made in a special workshop?"

"You're on a first-name basis with him now?"

"It's what he asked me to call him. I hadn't even realized my eyesight had deteriorated to the point that I needed glasses, but Chip caught it right away." He drew his glasses down the bridge of his nose and then pushed them back up again and peered around the shop. "Now I can see things with perfect clarity."

I was beginning to see perfectly, too. I saw that I'd screwed up the best friendship I'd made since moving here, all because, as Juniper had said, I lacked tact. And hard evidence.

"Did you find out anything?" I asked. "Apart from Chip Pepperbough's professional genius?"

"Well . . ." Jingles chewed a scone and considered. "He's worried about you, I know that."

Aha. "He thinks I'm on to him?"

"No, he thinks someone from the castle sabotaged the funicular. He told me we should be extremely careful."

"Big of him," I said.

Oblivious to my sarcasm, Jingles munched on an egg salad sandwich. "I thought so."

Seeing how completely Chip had won over Jingles's allegiance, I had the unhappy feeling I was all alone in my suspicions of him now. My moping was cut short, however, when what looked like a monster appeared in the street just outside the tearoom.

Chapter 15

Customers leapt to their feet and hurried to the window. It wasn't a snow monster trundling up the street but a mammoth wood-and-iron contraption resembling a giant grasshopper. It creaked across the snow-packed cobblestones, driven by a team of eight musk oxen. Several elves in camouflage and hardhats marched alongside it, urging on the animals. They obviously belonged to the Vigilance Committee, but I had no idea what the contraption was.

"Is that some kind of construction vehicle?" It looked medieval.

"A trebuchet," Jingles said. "For defense."

"Defense against what, a Viking invasion?"

"Snow monsters. That long arm will act like a snowball catapult."

Tiffany appeared next to me, fists planted on her hips. "They can't park that monstrosity in front of my shop."

Evidently they could. When we went outside, a stocky female elf in a hard hat showed us a permit signed by Mayor Firlog authorizing the placement of defensive equipment. Tiny's death had triggered a state of emergency.

"Believe me, ma'am," the elf told Tiffany, "you'd much

rather have this here than have a snow monster squish your place of business."

"If Tiny Sparkletoe were alive," Tiffany said, "he'd be all over this. Look at that wheel—it's on the sidewalk. That's bound to be in violation of city laws."

The irony was that Tiny's death had brought about the necessity of ordinance-defying trebuchets being rolled into town.

I left Tiffany vowing to take her complaint to the town council and returned home. Overnight, Christmastown had become a study in odd contrasts. People were clearly wary— loud noises were spooking elves and reindeer these days—but the supposedly protective jack-o'-lanterns on display were cheery and bright. Meanwhile, children too impatient to wait for Halloween dressed up in their costumes and played on the sidewalks. I had to smile at little snow monsters hurling snowballs at each other.

Back at Castle Kringle, Pamela heard my footsteps in the foyer and came out almost at a run. Seeing me, her expectant expression sagged in disappointment. "Oh, I thought you would be the delivery man from the Cornucopia. The kitchen is dangerously low on the icing sugar I'll need to make my spice cookies for the Ladies' Guild Halloween bake sale."

"I thought the Ladies' Guild was against Halloween."

She slanted an impatient glance at me over her bifocals. "If you attended more meetings, you'd know we decided it was too good an opportunity for a fundraiser to miss out. We'll be selling baked goods outside the Christmastown Community Center all day on Halloween."

"Why do I get the feeling that 'we' includes me?" I said warily.

"Of course it includes you. You're Mrs. Claus." She reconsidered. "*One* of the Mrs. Clauses, at any rate. I signed you up for two shifts and some cookies. Surely that's not too much to ask?"

She was right. Between the funicular accident and all my poking into Tiny's death, I hadn't been attending much to official Claus business. And where had that gotten me? I was down one friend, and no closer to knowing what had happened to Tiny.

"Cookies sound easy enough," I agreed.

She gave me an approving pat on the arm. "That's the spirit."

"How many should I make?"

"I signed you up for fifteen dozen reindeer cookies."

I froze. Had I heard correctly?

Fifteen *dozen?* "That's"—I was so appalled I resorted to doing math in my head—"a hundred and eighty cookies? Isn't that a lot?"

"We want to make a lot of money, don't we?" She smiled. "I'm sure you can handle it. You're always talking about how you baked things for guests at that hotel of yours."

The Coast Inn had ten rooms. I'd never baked more than two dozen anything.

"Oh, and your shift is from eleven to one." She raised a hand before I could object. "I checked the festival schedule, and you should have plenty of time after your shift to get to the band shell for the Santaland Concert Band performance. So it's all settled."

She turned and marched away, her sensible heels tapping purposefully on the marble floors.

Fifteen dozen cookies. Reindeer cookies, which meant there would be elaborate decorating involved. I'd have to look online for ideas and scrounge up a cookie cutter in the appropriate shape . . .

As I trudged distractedly up the staircase to my room,

Lucia blocked my path. "I have a bone to pick with you," she announced.

"Can't it wait? I'm a little tired." After the morning I'd had, I wasn't up for a harangue from my sister-in-law.

"Why should *you* be tired? I've been up since before dawn, officiated at two reindeer races, and this after I was up half the night with Lynxie."

"What was the matter with him?" I asked.

"He threw up a hairball the size of a chinchilla."

Delightful. I preferred being griped at to hearing about hairballs. "What's the bone you have to pick with me?"

"Halloween," she said. "I don't mean to sound like the ghost of Tiny Sparkletoe, but someone really needs to put a stop to this holiday. It's gotten out of hand."

"How?"

"Have you seen all kids running around in snow monster costumes?" she asked.

"Sure, they're cute."

She let out a strangled sound of disgust. "You certainly aren't putting yourself in a reindeer's hooves and trying to see it from their perspective."

I remembered Jingles saying that Chip thought someone in the castle was trying to kill me. Could he have meant Lucia? She was on the verge of annoying me to death.

"Imagine being a reindeer and seeing snow monsters every time you turned around," she said. "You know what snow monsters consider tasty snacks?"

"Twizzlers?"

"Reindeer," she said. "Can't you perceive how terrifying that would make coming across a snow monster in the street?"

I tilted my head. "Reindeer can't distinguish between a real snow monster and a kid in a costume?"

"Of course they can tell the difference, under the right circumstances. But just picture yourself trotting down the road and out pops a scary fur ball, even a tiny one. Quasar nearly fell out of the sleigh today, he was so spooked. He started running and didn't stop till he was all the way back here. Now he's exhausted, poor thing."

Though Quasar lived in the castle, not everyone relished having a large gassy ruminant wandering around the place. If she'd had sole control of the castle, Pamela would have banned him and Lynxie both. I was in rare agreement with her about Lynxie, but I liked Quasar and even considered him a friend. Yet the fact that he'd run back to the castle from town didn't exactly pluck at my heartstrings. "I'm sorry he was startled, but isn't running sort of what reindeer do?"

Lucia leveled a withering gaze on me. "I can't believe you could be so callous."

"I wasn't trying to be dismissive or flippant. But I'm sorry, we can't tell kids not to dress up as snow monsters now."

"Why not?"

"Because costumes have been made, and the kids are excited about dressing up."

Her lips curled down. "The whole town is snow monster crazy now. They're either terrified one is coming or they're dressing up like them. Does that make sense to you?"

My head began to ache. Actually, it had started aching when I learned I was on the hook for fifteen dozen cookies. "I need to lie down."

"Oh, sure," Lucia said testily, "just go ahead and let the reindeer bear the brunt of this holiday that was all your idea."

All my idea. What had I done? Just a tiny suggestion last year—a nostalgia for a holiday I thought of as harmless fun. And look at the result: vandalism, threats, terrified reindeer . . .

I continued upstairs and attempted to shut my brain down

with a nap. Instead, I stared at the ceiling, returning to the mystery of Tiny's death. If it wasn't a snow monster attack, and if Chip hadn't killed him, then who? Bella and Tiny didn't get along, but what would she have gained by his death? She already had the store. Pixie might have been a disappointed Cinderella figure, but even so, she'd been staying with her sister the night Tiny was killed. Rosemary clearly disliked Tiny, but Rosemary had an alibi . . . unless she'd sneaked out of her house in the middle of the night, run out to Tiny's family cottage, murdered him in a way that made it look like a snow monster had stepped on him, and returned home without anyone noticing. And of course there was always Walnut, the rival bootie seller. But he seemed the type who would want to kill Tiny in a duel—something public. Not arrange a death by snow monster.

That snow monster footprint kept tripping me up.

When napping proved elusive, I took a shower, dressed for dinner, and went downstairs an hour early. I wasn't usually a big drinker, but this day called for a stiff belt of something.

In the large evening sitting room, I scanned the contents of the liquor cabinet. It was heavy on fussy spirits like liqueurs and spiced rum, but I did spot a bottle of gin in the back. I rang the bell.

A minute later, Waldo came in. "Oh!" he said when he saw me kneeling by the liquor cabinet, digging out the gin.

"I need a lemon," I said. "Do you think they'd have one in the kitchen?"

Citrus was a valuable commodity at the North Pole, but tonight I felt like pulling out all the stops.

His expression turned anxious. "I can ask. Would a lime do?"

"Yes. Thank you, Waldo."

"I—" Whatever he was going to say died on his lips. He turned and scurried out of the room. I got to work, pulling an ice cube tray from the little cabinet refrigerator there. Someone came back while I was wrestling chunks out of it and into my glass.

"That was fast," I said, assuming it was Waldo.

A shadow was cast over me—a shadow too big to be an elf's. I couldn't help remembering Juniper's warning relayed from Chip, about someone in the castle wanting to kill me. My heart roared into overdrive, and I pivoted, ready to clock whoever it was with the ice cube tray.

Nick jumped back, arms raised in surrender. "Watch it," he said, "you almost cubed me."

I lowered my arm and sank against the bar in relief. "Sorry. Rough day."

He leaned forward and kissed my forehead gingerly, then nodded at the bottle of gin. "I sensed that. I think I might have something to make you feel better." He looked back toward the door. "He's just outside making a phone call."

He? "Who?"

The door pushed open and a person I knew sloped into the room. I use the term *person* loosely. I hadn't seen Jake Frost, the detective from the Farthest Frozen Reaches, in nearly a year, but he hadn't changed a bit. He wore a black suit, and his face, with an ever-present stubble across his jaw, had a pallor that stood in stark contrast with his dark hair.

Nick was right. Jake's melanin-deprived features buoyed my spirits, although his wasn't a face I would've called friendly. It was as if Robert Mitchum had been released after having been locked in a cellar for a few months.

The slimmest of smiles touched his lips. "You're looking well."

"What brings you to Christmastown, Jake?"

"A case." He glanced at Nick. "And there's another matter that your husband and I were just discussing."

Nick stepped away from me. "Unfortunately, I can't stay longer to talk more. I need to go into Christmastown. One of the Vigilance Committee members says Boots has gotten hold of several flamethrowers online. I need to nip this in the bud."

After Nick had left, I asked, "Did Crinkles send for you?"

The constable sometimes called on Jake Frost if a case grew so contentious that an outsider's perspective seemed necessary.

He shook his head. "I've got a new client in town, which has nothing to do with Crinkles. But I'm also on a mission from my side of the border. That's why I needed to talk to Nick. He got me up to speed on everything that's been happening around here."

"Who from the Farthest Frozen Reaches would have sent you here?"

"Ermlau the Abominable."

I frowned. "A snow monster?"

"An important one. He's a member of the Council of Snow Monsters."

"Snow monsters have a government?" This was a new one on me.

"Well, it's not the best-organized governing body in the world."

A mysterious, unknown world lay beyond the Christmas Tree Forest, and my ignorance was almost as vast as the territory itself. "What do the snow monsters have to say about Tiny Sparkletoe's death?"

"They'd never heard of him until word of what happened filtered to the Reaches. They claim they know nothing about how he died."

"I saw the footprint myself. It was massive."

"Yeah, I went over to the crime scene and saw what little there was to see. I have questions."

"So did I," I said eagerly. "We only found the one print."

He nodded. "And then there was the layout. . . . I heard Tiny was found facedown, with his head pointed *away* from the house."

I saw what he meant. "Whatever was chasing him was coming from the house."

"But the snow monster, if he'd come down from the north, would have chased him in the opposite direction."

"Did you notice that Tiny didn't run on the walkway from the house? The footsteps were beside it."

He shook his head. "That wasn't a walkway. Someone shoveled a path and then the snow covered it. I thought it looked like a walkway, too, but there was just hard ground there, same as everywhere else."

"The killer cleared his tracks. They must have known the snowfall would make it look as if Tiny had cleared the pathway himself."

"Well . . . maybe he did. We don't know what Tiny was doing outside before he died."

"There was no snow shovel on the ground. And if Tiny had been shoveling something, wouldn't he have used it to fight off the monster?" I asked.

For some reason, Jake chuckled. "Not sure how much good that would have done him."

"It doesn't matter, because there wasn't any tool found near him." I drummed my fingers. "No, I think you're right. This was a human or elf crime, not a snow monster."

He scratched his stubbly chin. "I'm not saying that snow monsters are immune to lying, but guile isn't their strong suit. Even taking into account the normal amount of confusion when it comes to interspecies communication and interpreters, I'm inclined to believe Ermlau. The snow monsters had heard rumors about the measures Santaland is taking, and now they're stirred up. They're worried Santaland is gearing up to start hunting them in retaliation."

"*They're* worried! Everyone around here is panicked that we're all going to be squished like Tiny. But now it seems we've been looking across the border for a monster when we should be focused on someone among ourselves."

"Your husband was telling me that there have been other incidents in town, including an attempt on your life."

I gave him a quick review of recent events in Christmastown—from the greenhouse incident to Pumpkin Slayer at the library, the funicular accident, culminating in the death of Tiny. "The reason his death shocked me most was that I was so sure of his being behind all the mayhem. Now . . ."

The swinging door from the kitchen opened. It was Waldo, back with a sliced lemon on a silver salver. When he saw Jake standing with me, his eyes bulged and his arms began to quiver so that the lemon threatened to slide off the tray.

"I f-found one," he said.

"Wonderful," I said. "Bring it here before it drops."

He hurried over and I took the lemon. The salver slipped through Waldo's fingers and went clanging across the floor. Jake scooped it up and handed it to him.

For a moment Waldo looked as if he might faint. When he took the tray, his gaze didn't meet either Jake's or mine. "Will that be all, ma'am?"

"Yes, thank you, Waldo."

He left as fast as an elf could move without running. It was almost a relief when the door swung shut behind him. All that nervous energy made me nervous, too.

I mixed my drink and also prepared one for Jake.

"Waldo . . ." He frowned. "That was the elf you saw by the funicular stop?"

"He's always a little shaky."

"Strange that an elf so jittery would be a footman."

"His grandmother worked in the castle for years. Waldo's a bit of a butterfingers, but he's always been reliable . . ."

One of Jake's brows arched in an inverted V. "Until recently?"

I didn't want to cast more suspicion on Waldo. He had an alibi. And my instincts were obviously not infallible. "He has been acting more oddly than usual, but I'd be a mess, too, if my employer accused me of attempting to kill her."

"Good point."

"Besides," I added, "he has an alibi for the evening of the accident."

"A reliable one?"

I thought about Cranberry. "The servant who vouched for being with him at the time risked her job by sticking up for him."

I handed him a glass. He drank, thought for a moment, and began going over the Christmastown crime wave again. "So what we have here is a Halloween hater—"

"Pumpkin Slayer," I said.

"Who might have escalated his crimes from vandalism and threats to murder."

"Or Pumpkin Slayer might have had nothing to do with what happened to Tiny."

His face didn't betray an opinion. Which made me suspect he disagreed.

"You think that's wrong?" I asked.

"Too early to say."

I'd forgotten how maddeningly noncommittal Jake could be. My biggest worry was that I wouldn't be privy to what he was doing. I needed to find some pretext for why he should have me along on his investigation. Otherwise I'd be spending the next days wondering what he was up to and wanting to tag after him like a bothersome kid sister. I was drumming my fingers against my cool glass, wondering how to finesse myself into his investigation when he spoke again.

"I have a favor to ask you."

My tapping stopped. "Ask away."

"Your husband suggested, and I agree, that it would help me to have you along on my interviews about Tiny's death."

The unexpected request startled me into momentary silence. *Nick* had suggested this? I almost suspected there were hidden cameras recording my reaction—that in a moment Jake would burst into a completely uncharacteristic laugh and tell me that he was just kidding.

Instead, those smoky gray eyes of his continued to stare at me evenly. Expectantly, even.

"I thought you were a lone-wolf detective," I said.

He swirled the ice cubes in his glass. "A second pair of ears and eyes never hurts."

"When shall we start?" I hadn't felt this upbeat in weeks. "Tonight?"

"I'm working tonight." The other client—that would be another mystery for me to solve. "First thing tomorrow, though. Snow monsters aren't the most patient creatures."

I froze. "Do you mean that if the Santalanders continue to blame the snow monsters for Tiny's death, they'll launch an attack on us?"

"I wouldn't rule it out. Hearing about bonfire piles and vigilante committees has them antsy."

"It's a vigilance committee, not vigilante."

"Try conveying that distinction to a twenty-foot primate with a Neanderthal brain."

Antsy snow monsters. I'd been worried that if we didn't find Tiny's killer, he might strike again. Now it seemed that a lot more was at stake in this investigation. Like the safety of the whole country.

No pressure, then.

Chapter 16

"You'll see what I mean as soon as anyone starts talking," I told Jake when we met up outside the Christmastown Cornucopia the next morning. "There's a palpable animosity toward Tiny."

"If too many elves disliked him, it could be hard to find out who killed him out of all the pool of suspects."

That was true. "How much of a time crunch are we under? The snow monsters aren't going to march on Christmastown today, are they?"

"They won't invade as a group. They'll send their biggest abominable."

That seemed like invasion enough to me.

Inside the Cornucopia, I escorted Jake straight back to Tog Hollywell's office.

"Well, well, Mrs. Claus." Tog smiled, flicking a curious glance at Jake. "What brings you back so soon?"

"Just came in to visit, actually. All right if we talk here?"

"Sure," he said. "Take a seat, both of you."

"Do you know Jake Frost?" I asked.

"Can't say I've had the pleasure, although of course I've heard of you," the elf said, jovially shaking Jake's hand. "Say, are you any relation to Jack Frost?"

Jake shrugged. "Distant cousin."

We all sat down. "I hope there's been nothing wrong with the deliveries we've sent to the castle," Tog said from his side of the desk.

"Not at all," I replied. "I actually came by to ask you more about Tiny. The day before yesterday, you seemed to want to make sure that it really was Tiny who'd died."

He clasped his hands together and leaned on his elbows. "I guess I was still in shock. It was so hard to believe he was gone. It still is. Tiny was a force of nature around here. Christmastown won't be the same without him."

I shot Jake a glance as if to say, *Just wait till I really get him talking.* "Tiny was probably a pain in the neck at times, too."

The grocer's eyes widened. "Tiny? Gosh no."

"It's not pleasant to speak ill of the dead, I know. But—just between us, mind you—there were bound to be times when Tiny's officiousness stuck in your craw."

His mouth twisted one way, then another. "No . . ."

Was he kidding? "Oh, come on. Everybody knows Tiny was a pain in the butt."

The elf's eyes widened. "Who's saying things like that? I hope it never gets around to Pixie." He continued in the overly sincere tones of an undertaker. "The poor widow has enough to grieve her without anyone slandering her recently departed husband."

Oh, brother. Our conversation sputtered along a few minutes longer before I stood and bid Tog a polite good-bye. Out on the sidewalk, though, I gave full vent to my annoyance.

"What a hypocrite! Two days ago he could hardly contain his glee when I verified that it was Tiny who'd been squished."

"Maybe it was having me there that made him change his tune," Jake suggested. "He might not have wanted to speak openly about Tiny in front of a stranger."

"But why did he have to lay on the grieving-fellow-citizen act so thick? Did that seem natural to you?"

"I'd never met the man."

I grumbled all the way to the nut shop.

"Back for more fudge?" Dash asked as the bell jangled upon my entrance.

"Mm . . ." Even though I hadn't planned on confessing my Frequent Fudger status to Jake, I was drawn irresistibly to the glass cases of chocolate manna. "Maybe just a square or two of the hazelnut fudge."

Dash tossed a curious glance Jake's way. The detective cut an odd figure in Christmastown. Unlike the color-loving, rosy-cheeked elves, Jake wore all black and had skin so color-less he was one step removed from being snow-colored him-self. His pallor was even more pronounced this morning, and I noticed dark circles under his eyes. Whatever this other job of his was, it didn't allow him much rest.

"So when you were asking me about Tiny the day be-fore yesterday . . ." I began as Dash plopped the wax paper-wrapped fudge on the scale.

"I asked you about Tiny?" His face screwed up in puzzle-ment. "Don't remember that."

"Well, you did."

A smile returned. "Of course, Mrs. Claus. If you say so."

Frustration hummed through me but I tried not to show it. Jake probably thought I was crazy. I was beginning to wonder myself. "You seemed to want to make sure Tiny was dead."

An exaggerated frown played across Dash's face. "You're mistaken. Tiny was a friend of mine. We weren't best friends, but we served on the Christmastown council together for a few years." Catching my incredulous look, he turned and called out for his wife. "Sweetheart—come out here."

Tippi appeared wearing a chocolate-smeared apron and an anxious smile. "Yes?"

He nodded toward me and Jake. "Tell them—wasn't I saying just this morning how broken up I was about Tiny?"

Her head nodded so furiously it seemed in danger of bobbing right off. "Oh, yes. Tiny was a favorite with everyone."

Since when? My anger bumped up a notch. Two days ago they had made it pretty clear that they hoped Tiny was good and dead. Now he was their honored friend.

"Tiny's reputation seems to have undergone an amazing transformation," I told Jake.

"It happens," he said.

Tippi kept up the bobblehead routine. "So often we don't fully appreciate someone until they're gone."

"Or maybe you appreciate them more because you *know* they're gone. Is that it?"

"At the next town council meeting, I was thinking of bringing forth a resolution to honor Tiny in some way," Dash said. "Maybe have a Tiny Sparkletoe Day every year."

"Or an ice sculpture," Tippi suggested. "We could put it in that little park in Sparkletoe Lane."

I grabbed my fudge and gestured for Jake to follow me out the door. "I don't know what's going on around here." I stomped ahead of him toward Gert's. I needed an extra-strength cocoa, stat. "This is some next-level collective gaslighting I'm being subjected to."

When we arrived at Gert's, I ordered a cocoa and Jake asked for a cocoa and a pretzel.

"Did I or did I not ask you two days ago why all these people around here seemed relieved that Tiny was dead?" I asked Gert.

She tilted her head. "You got amnesia or something?"

"I don't, but everybody else seems to."

"Well, you were here and you asked about Tiny." Her words came out slowly, carefully. "Any special reason you feel the need to have that verified?"

"I brought Jake here—" I stopped to introduce the two of them, but they told me they'd already met, so I continued, "to show him how odd people were acting about Tiny."

Gert glanced from me to Jake and back again. "Why?"

I looked around, then lowered my voice. "Jake's a detective."

"Everybody knows that," Gert said.

"He's here to double-check that Tiny's death is just what it appeared to be."

She crossed her arms. "Okay. So?"

"So now everybody's acting as if Tiny was their best friend. Dash practically said as much! And you should have seen the crocodile tears Tog was shedding for Tiny."

"Tiny was a big deal. His death's hitting the town hard."

Oh, no. *Et tu, Gert?* "The last time we spoke you insinuated that most elves in town were glad he was gone."

She blinked slowly. "Did I?"

"Is the whole town in cahoots to make me crazy?" I asked Jake as we walked away.

He chewed on his pretzel. "What, you think there's a conspiracy against you?"

If there was a conspiracy, it had popped up in just a couple of days. What had happened between then and now? I couldn't help feeling a little dispirited. "I thought people around here trusted me."

Jake's expression didn't change, and yet something shifted in his eyes. A sadness? "I expected it to go better with you along, too."

All at once it dawned on me why he'd wanted me along. Not for my phenomenal detecting powers, but because everyone in town knew he was a detective. Jake Frost showed up when bad things happened, serious crimes that needed sorting out by someone more perceptive than Constable Crinkles.

"I get it," I said. "You—and probably Nick, too—assumed

I would be a good buffer while you were trying to get to the bottom of what had happened to Tiny."

"We thought people might be more apt to talk to a Claus than a detective sent here at the behest of snow monsters."

So much for that. The townspeople had seen me with him and clammed up anyway.

"Great. Now I know they don't trust me, either."

He shook his head. "It's not you. These elves around here are wound up tight. There's something going on. We need to talk to someone who'll speak candidly. Someone who won't even pretend to have a fondness for Tiny."

I snapped my gloved fingers. "I know just the elf."

Walnut's Bootie World was as different from Sparkletoe's Bootery as Amazon.com is from a bodega. The plain brick retail fortress stood on its own on the outskirts of Christmastown. Usually it looked a little forlorn compared with the more old-fashioned buildings in the neighborhoods, although at the moment the warehouse was flanked by two giant wavy tube men—a Frankenstein and a vampire.

Inside, the store was a vast wonderland of elf footwear for all ages and tastes. Normally the place was lit up in Christmas colors, but Walnut had gone characteristically overboard in stringing orange and black all over the store. Giant spiders hung from the ceiling, as did Neldors and snow monsters and skeletons. The sound system was playing "Bad Moon Rising" as we walked in, and the elves shopping were bopping and singing along.

I didn't spot Walnut, so I had to ask one of the host of employees dressed in a doublet of orange and black with a Walnut's Bootie World cap. She pointed upward, to the back of the warehouse, past a large net that I assumed, from the stuffed spider hanging on it, was supposed to be a web. Overlooking the retail floor was a glassed-in office that stretched the width of the building. And at the center of it stood Walnut, arms crossed, dressed in a tunic of a blue-and-taupe harlequin pattern. As usual, his hair was swept up in an impressive pouf.

"I'm sure he'll want to see you, Mrs. Claus, and . . ." The clerk looked more dubiously at Jake. "Well, follow me."

Walnut greeted me with a grin, as if getting Mrs. Claus into his store was some kind of retail coup. "Pearly, get the camera," he said to our escort.

"We're just here to talk," I said, interrupting. "This is Jake Frost, a detective from the Farthest Frozen Reaches."

Walnut's brows rose. "A detective! What, am I under arrest?"

"I don't arrest anyone," Jake said. "I'm a private detective."

The shoe seller made a show of wiping his brow. "Phew! That's a relief." He looked up to find the clerk, Pearly, standing at the ready with a camera. He shooed her away. "Never mind that now. Go back to work."

He gestured to us to take a seat on a plush red couch that took up one corner of the vast office. He settled himself in an armchair, crossed his legs, and grinned. "What can I do for you?"

"Jake is looking into Tiny's death, and I thought you might have some insight."

His eyes widened. "Me? I'd think you'd have more answers than anyone around here, Frost. Someone from the Reaches would know more about snow monsters than any of us."

We weren't yet prepared to let it be spread around town that there were serious doubts that a snow monster killed Tiny. "At the orphanage event you and Tiny had words about Pixie."

"You think Pixie stepped on Tiny?" He laughed. "If only!"

"You insinuated that he stole her from you."

"Well . . ." His lips twisted. "He did, but it takes two to

tango. I guess Pixie had her reasons. Two years ago I was just a sleigh wash owner. The concept of Bootie World hadn't yet occurred to me."

"When did it occur to you?"

"Coincidentally, right after Pixie announced her engagement to Tiny Sparkletoe." He grinned.

I looked out the window to the vast showroom below. So all of this sprang from a broken heart? Revenge retail.

"Don't get me wrong," he said. "I'm better off without her. I see that now. Without the adversity of Pixie dumping me like a hot potato I might never have realized I could think bigger. That I could be more than just a sleigh wash owner."

I leaned forward. "How do you see yourself now?"

He straightened, posturing proudly in his fine tunic. "A magnate," he said, as if it should be obvious. "I'm richer than Tiny could dream of being. And look at how he treated Pixie—like a servant. She wouldn't be cleaning people's houses if she'd married me."

"You think Pixie felt she got a raw deal?" Jake asked.

Walnut shrugged. "I wouldn't know. I haven't talked to Pixie since the breakup."

"You haven't contacted her since Tiny died?" I asked. "A condolence call, maybe?"

Walnut's face flushed crimson. "I called her at her sister's house. Pixie refused to come to the phone."

Rosemary must have been apoplectic about that.

"To be honest, I'm too involved in future ventures to bother with romances now, or regrets," Walnut continued. "If you're looking for someone who might've murdered Tiny, don't look at me. You'd just be wasting your time."

"Who would you suggest we look at?"

"How should I know? Tiny pestered everybody. I heard he was going to sue his own sister for a portion of the mercantile's proceeds. He thought he got cheated in his parents' will." He shook his head. "Can't say as I blame him. That dinky old cottage wasn't much to inherit. I certainly wouldn't have made Pixie live in a place like that. I'd have built her a mansion."

As absurd and egotistical as he seemed, I couldn't help feeling a little sorry for Walnut. He was like Gatsby of the Arctic. I wondered if he'd thought his big store and the wavy tube men would capture Pixie's attention and lure her back to him.

But he certainly didn't seem to have her affection now, and that ruled out the shoe coup I'd been imagining on the way over. I'd thought perhaps Walnut and Pixie had conspired to kill Tiny, thus attaining a monopoly on the bootie trade. Walnut would have succeeded in getting Tiny's store, his wife, and his most valuable asset: Louie.

But Walnut's streak of success seemed to have eluded him when it came to winning Pixie's affection. Maybe she wasn't the gold digger people made her out to be.

"Is Tiny's sister the murdering type, do you think?" Jake asked me after we'd left Bootie World.

"Bella doesn't strike me as that way, but who does?"

"I guess I should have a word with her next. And then on to the widow."

We headed back into town, toward Sparkletoe Lane, which was a bit of a hike. The Vigilance Committee had placed another trebuchet at the far edge of town, and it was strange to see it there, a giant wooden insect crouched in the middle of a street of half-timbered shops mixed with cozy cottages. At this time of year, the lights of Christmastown blazed most of the day and night. Someone had even strung a few lights on the long wooden catapult arm of the trebuchet. Every porch had a jack-o'-lantern blazing, too.

I'd discovered a shortcut through an alley once, and I suggested we take it now. On turning into it, we came upon

Quince and Pocket. Quince was leaning against the alley wall, but when he saw Jake, his eyes widened and he took off running.

Wrong move. Running had the same effect on Jake as the call of the horn had on a hunting dog. He bolted after Quince. Alarmed, I called out for them to stop and ran after them. As I was passing Pocket, my coat snagged on something, sending me sprawling onto the slushy ground. I looked up, perplexed. Had I just been kneecapped by a snowman?

Cursing, I scrambled back to my feet and limped up to Jake just after he'd caught Quince. He held him up by the collar so that the elf's feet dangled above the ground.

"Let go of me!" Quince said.

"Why were you running?" Jake asked.

"Why were you chasing me?"

"It's okay," I said to Jake. "You can ease up on the Dirty Harry act. I know Quince."

He glanced over at me doubtfully. "What happened to you?"

I still had dirty alley snow across the front of my coat. "I . . . I think the snowman tripped me."

Quince laughed, which made Jake give him a few shakes. DVDs spilled out of the elf's coat onto the snow. I gasped. *Saw II. Halloween 5. Neldor III: The Icy Vengeance.* "How did you get these? I thought Crinkles confiscated your stash."

Quince smirked. "You think I carry everything on me all the time? Anyway, there's always more on Elfbay."

Seeing the covers of the DVDs made me nostalgic for my own misspent youth. *"Halloween Five?"* I wrinkled my nose. "Not the best."

"I got a deal on a bundle."

"None of these are about Christmas, though," I observed. "Why would the constable take them from you?"

"Selling on the street without a permit," he explained.

Jake let Quince down. "Sorry, kid. It's just that when someone's acting guilty, I get suspicious."

"Who *are* you?" Quince asked Jake.

"This is Jake Frost," I said.

"Like Jack Frost?" he asked.

"Distant cousin," Jake said. "I'm a detective."

"Why are you taking such a chance?" I asked Quince, helping him collect the DVDs off the ground.

"I need money so when I leave the orphan home I don't have to go to the Wrapping Works. Can you imagine me tying bows eight hours a day?"

No, I couldn't.

"You'd think the town would have better things to do than harass me when there are snow monsters on the loose stomping on people," Quince complained.

"You don't have to worry about us," Jake said.

Quince eyed him quizzically. "Where are you from?"

"The Reaches."

"You *live* out there? What's it like?"

He shrugged. "Like most places. Good and bad."

"I've always wanted to see what's on the other side of the border forest," Quince said. "Do they need workers out there?"

Jake's lips twisted. "DVD scalpers? Not really."

"I can do other stuff. I could even be a detective."

"It's not as easy as it looks," I said, remembering the frustration of having shopkeepers lie to me this morning.

Quince shrugged. "Just so long as it's not boring."

"Trouble is, there isn't much work," Jake said. "I'm the only private detective out there—and in Santaland, for that matter. It's not exactly the mean streets around here."

Although it could seem like it. I cast a glance back at Pocket. He moved slowly and hadn't caught up with us during the conversation. As I rubbed my sore wrists I wondered if Pocket weren't a little faster than he let on.

We left the pair in the alley and continued on our way.

At Sparkletoe's Mercantile, we were shown through the storage room back to Bella's office. Bella had a pencil parked behind one of her big ears and appeared to have little patience for talking again about her late brother. She didn't beat around the bush waiting for me to ask about him, either.

"I don't know what about Tiny's death precipitated a visit from Jake Frost, but I can tell you that I won't be able to enlighten you much about anything."

"The last time I spoke to you, you didn't mention that Tiny had threatened to sue you for a share of Sparkletoe's Mercantile."

"You didn't ask." At our impatient expressions, she sighed. "Listen, I wasn't hiding anything—there's nothing to hide. Tiny was full of hot air. A week didn't go by that he wasn't emailing me about suing me or some nonsense like that. I was used to it. To be honest, if it weren't for his grievances, we probably wouldn't have had any relationship at all."

"So you're saying he threatened to take action but never did," Jake said.

"That's right." She shook her head. "I don't know why you're so curious, though. You think I hired a snow monster to step on him?"

Jake and I avoided each other's gazes.

"What do you know about Tiny's home life?" he asked. "Was he happy?"

She let out a grunt. "'Happy' and 'Tiny' don't belong in the same sentence."

"So you don't think his marriage was a success?"

"I wouldn't know the first thing about his marriage. I just meant that it wasn't in Tiny's nature to be content. He was always trying to fix something or to get more. I never knew why he decided Pixie was the girl for him. Everybody else looked on it like a kind of Cinderella story, with poor Pixie as Cinderella and Tiny as the prince."

"But you didn't?" I asked.

"I couldn't imagine what they saw in each other. But I'm not a romantic. I've never been married. The mercantile's my life."

"Were you here the night Tiny died?" Jake asked her.

"That night and every night. I put the store to bed and then I went upstairs and read myself to sleep."

No alibi, then.

"Have you spoken to Pixie?" I asked.

"No, she's still with that crazy sister of hers. I doubt she'll be there long, though."

"Why do you say that?"

"Tiny must've left Pixie pretty well fixed, financially. She's given up her cleaning business."

I remembered Pixie saying she was going to take time off. She didn't mention quitting entirely. "Where did you hear this?"

"Just from everybody who used to be her client," Bella deadpanned. "They're all frantic and seem to think I'd have some influence over Pixie to talk her into staying on with them."

"Do you have any influence over her?"

"Heck no. Pixie wouldn't listen to me. Besides, I can't blame her for not wanting to clean houses anymore. I couldn't see why she kept doing it after she and Tiny got hitched, anyway."

When we were done, Bella walked us out. She seemed to light up when she was on the floor of the mercantile, which was busier than ever. "I hate to say it, but Tiny's death has been good for business. People are stocking up on necessities, and wood to board up windows. I don't know what good they think a boarded-up window will do when a snow monster crushes their house, but far be it from me to argue."

After we left the mercantile, Jake turned to me. "Isn't there a coffee shop around here?"

Fueling up with caffeine before we headed out to Tinkertown to speak to Pixie wasn't a bad idea.

"Night on Bald Mountain" was playing over the speakers of We Three Beans when we walked in, and the few elves scattered at the tables seemed disappointed. It was nothing they could sing along to. Jake and I ordered and claimed our coffees, and I took mine to the station where I could add cream and sugar. While I was there, my phone, sitting on the tabletop, chirped. I caught Jake's eye and pointed at the phone. I meant for him to bring it to me, but instead, he swiped and answered it. Whoever was on the line spoke only a few words with him before he hurriedly handed the phone to me.

I upended the sugar dispenser over my cup. "Hello?"

"Who was *that*?" a familiar voice asked.

"Claire!" I was so happy to hear from her, I felt myself lift onto the balls of my feet. We hadn't communicated at all since she'd sent the email about Nick having a Santa fetish.

"Seriously, who was that man? He has a sexy voice."

"He's not a . . ." I wasn't sure how I could describe Jake to her. She didn't even know I was living among elves, much less odd creatures who weren't elves but weren't quite human, either. I narrowed my gaze on him. *"Sexy?"*

"Oh, God," she said. "You're having an affair."

"What?" I laughed. "No."

"It's okay. I'd completely understand."

I frowned. "There's Nick, remember? You know, that guy I'm married to."

"Yeah, that's what—" Her words died. "Never mind."

Silence stretched over the line.

Nick and Claire hadn't exactly hit it off over the summer as I hoped they would, but it seemed like a big leap from not hitting it off to hoping I'd pulled a Madame Bovary on him.

She lowered her voice. "Is Nick there with you?"

"Not at the moment."

"So you just left him while you went out with Mr. Sexy Voice. Sweet."

"Nick's not here because he's . . ." I couldn't very well tell her he was tending to Santa duties. "It's hard to explain. I'm with Jake, a detective."

"Oh, my God! What's happened?"

"*Nothing.*"

"So what are you doing with a detective?"

"Jake's working on a case, and I'm involved."

She sucked in a ragged breath. "Oh, God. April. You didn't . . ."

"What?"

"Where exactly *is* Nick, April?"

"Why? What are you thinking?"

"What am I supposed to think? You're with a detective. Nick's gone and you can't explain it. But you're *involved* . . ."

"You think I've killed my husband?" I laughed. "You do."

"How am I supposed to know anything, April?" Her irritation came across loud and clear. "You married some guy you barely knew. You never told anyone here where you live or what he does. This summer he just hung out like a beach bum or sat around playing some weird game on his phone. And then I found all that creepy stuff—"

I opened my mouth to respond, but my attention was diverted by something outside. It took me a moment to register that I was looking at Pixie Sparkletoe. She was driving up the street on Tiny's blue snowmobile. She had on mod round sunglasses and was dressed in a bright pink coat with pink faux fur, a pink fur hat, and pink boots with high heels and sharply curling, pointed toes. She didn't look at all like the demure Pixie who'd been huddled on her sister's sofa mere days before. And she certainly didn't look like a grieving widow.

"Claire, I'll have to call you back."

I doubted Jake and I would be headed to Tinkertown today.

Chapter 17

"Where was she going?" Jake asked when we were back out on the street.

Pixie had been heading in the opposite direction of the road to Tinkertown, where her sister lived. On another day, I would have said that her destination could have been any-where in Santaland—her clients lived all over. Yet Bella had just told us Pixie no longer had clients, and she certainly wasn't dressed for housework. That left me with one guess as to her most likely destination.

"The Bootery," I said.

We backtracked to Sparkletoe Lane.

When we walked into the Bootery, Louie and Pixie were talking together by the cash register. The bell above the door jangled, and Louie reflexively stepped back to his workbench.

"Hi, April." He shot a cautious glance at Jake. "Is there anything I can do for you?"

"We came to talk to Pixie," I said.

Pixie's eyes were fixed on Jake. "Who are you?"

"Jake Frost." He moved to her side and leaned against the counter.

"I've heard of you," she said. "You're that detective."

He took off his hat, revealing his head of short black hair. And . . . was that color in his cheeks? "Guilty as charged."

Louie's eyes filled with worry. "Are you investigating something?"

"Nah, just asking questions," he said, as if questions had nothing to do with investigating. "I'm interested in what Pixie has to say about her husband's unfortunate death."

"*I'm* the one who's unfortunate," she said.

Jake tutted sympathetically. "How so?"

"Where am I supposed to go now? Sure, we had the cottage, but I can't live out there after what happened. I never liked the place anyway. It's cramped and dank, and it gives me the willies now. What if the monster comes back there?"

Right, so owning a house she wasn't crazy about was more unfortunate than Tiny's being dead? I folded my arms.

"That's why I'm wearing this outfit," she continued. "I know it might look sort of loud, but it was all that I had at Rosemary's besides my old cleaning clothes. I just couldn't stand to go back to the cottage to get more of my stuff."

"You must have gone back," I said. "You have Tiny's snowmobile." The last time I saw it, it had been parked outside their cottage.

Louie cleared his throat. "She probably meant that she couldn't go *inside*."

Pixie nodded. "That's right."

Jake hadn't taken his smoky grays off Pixie since we'd walked in. "That outfit looks great on you," he practically cooed. "Pink's your color."

Was he serious? "You say you have no place to go," I said. "Can't you stay with your sister?"

"I could, but I don't want to. Rosemary's full of opinions, and she shares them all day long. And my nephews are sweet, but they're so noisy. There's no peace there."

"I can see why you'd want peace and quiet right now," Jake said. "You need it after all you've been through."

"I know, right?" She blinked those long lashes at him. "All I've had to do for the last few days is plan Tiny's funeral, which is one of the things Rosemary was nagging me about. She thought Tiny should be buried right away."

"When will his funeral be?"

"After Halloween, on November first. That was my decision. It'd be awful if everyone's Halloween fun had to be interrupted by a funeral."

"Very civic minded of you," Jake said.

She smiled. "That's not what Rosemary was telling me. She wouldn't stop picking at me—about that, and other things. So I decided I'm just going to stay here."

My bet was that the "other things" Rosemary was nagging her about included not taking Walnut's call. Interesting, too, that Rosemary wanted Tiny's body buried ASAP, while Pixie seemed to be in no hurry.

"You mean you're going to stay here, in the Bootery?" I asked. No wonder Louie looked so uncomfortable. The cobbler was staring down at the booties on his bench, but I could tell from the tense way he held himself that he was paying more attention to Pixie and Jake than to his work. Probably horrified that his workspace was about to be invaded.

"There's a room upstairs," she explained. "Tiny lived there before his folks died. It's perfectly comfortable. I always told him we should have moved back here. Maybe if he'd listened to me, he wouldn't have gotten trampled."

"So you're sure that's what happened?" I asked.

She gaped at me, astonished. So did Louie. "What else *could* have happened to him?" the boot maker asked.

"We were wondering if he might have had any enemies," Jake said.

"Not among snow monsters, if that's what you mean,"

Pixie said. "I can't think of any elves or people who would have hated him that much, either. Maybe not everybody loved Tiny, but he was respected, wasn't he? I mean, he was a big wheel in Christmastown." Her brows knit together. "You think maybe he got on the bad side of someone around here?"

Louie shook his head, continuing her train of thought. "And then what . . . they hired a snow monster to step on Tiny?"

"We were wondering if perhaps snow monsters weren't actually involved. If it was a setup."

"Staged?" She blinked again. "Who would have done that?"

"What about Bella?" I asked. "Do you think she might have hated Tiny enough to want to do him harm?"

Pixie shifted uncertainly. "I don't know. She never liked *me* much."

"We spoke to Walnut Lovejoy this morning," Jake said. "He and Tiny obviously had some animosity."

"Oh, sure," Pixie said. "Walnut was mad when I chose Tiny over him. But what was I supposed to do? *Not* marry Tiny just because Walnut was infatuated with me? That wouldn't have been fair."

I started feeling the same frustration I had the last time I'd talked to Pixie. Her reasoning seemed as jiggly as Jell-O.

"Anyway, that was years ago," she said.

"He's called you since Tiny died," I reminded her.

"So?" Pixie shrugged. "Lots of people have called. Rosemary can deal with them."

"Walnut and Tiny were arguing at an event just last week," I said. "Walnut implied that he was going to start offering handmade booties like the ones created here. It almost sounded like he was trying to hire Louie away from Tiny."

Jake and I both pivoted toward the workbench. "Was he?" Jake asked.

Louie's eyes were owl wide. "He never spoke to me about it. Walnut, that is. I mean, obviously Tiny was angry about Walnut's Bootie World, and our business did fall off a bit."

"Is that why you kept cleaning houses?" I asked Pixie.

She pulled out a package of gum and popped a piece into her mouth. "I didn't mind the job, and Tiny wanted me to keep it."

"You quit it quickly enough after he died, though," I couldn't help pointing out.

"Sure. Tiny left me enough money in the bank that I don't have to worry for a while. What's wrong with taking time off?" She smiled at me. "You don't exactly work your fingers to the bone, do you?"

Was that barb her way of shutting me up?

Louie, ever gallant, half rose to his feet. "I'm sure April does a lot for the community."

No one was listening. Jake was leaning over the counter toward Pixie. "You're the best judge of what you need to be doing right now," he assured her softly.

His fawning over her filled me with disgust. Had he forgotten why we were here?

"Do you think Tiny could have had anything to do with the accident involving the funicular?" I asked Pixie.

Her brow puckered. "I don't think so. Why would he?"

"Like you said the other day, he didn't like me very much."

"Right. He resented it when people had more influence over what was going on in town than he did. He liked to be in control."

That seemed like a truthful answer. So truthful, I was almost disappointed. It would have been so much easier if we'd caught her telling a pack of lies.

After we left the Bootery, I could barely contain my distaste for how Jake had acted. "Never in a million years would I have expected you to turn into a puddle just because a woman batted her eyes at you. What's wrong with you? You stood around making gooey noises and drowning in her gaze, leaving me to ask the questions."

He sent me a wry look. "I believe in the movies it's called good cop/bad cop."

"A likely—" My brain replayed what had just happened. "Oh."

"You did well," he said.

"Well, she lied about going back to the cabin."

"And the cobbler covered for her."

Did he? "Louie would intervene on anyone's behalf. He doesn't like conflict."

"He didn't like me making eyes at the widow, either."

"Pixie's being there seemed to make him uncomfortable."

His lips flattened. "I'm not sure we got much further along to finding who killed Tiny, unfortunately. But eventually, someone will crack."

"Eventually sounds like a long wait."

"No, given all the tension in the town, I'm pretty sure the guilty party will make a mistake. If we keep probing, a clue will surface that'll make it all come clear."

He was right, of course. I couldn't see it then, but that clue had surfaced already. I'd had it for days.

I invited Jake to come back to the castle.

"Thanks, but I've got a room at the Gingerbread House." The Gingerbread House was a small inn near Peppermint Pond. "I want to poke around town this evening, see what I can find out in Christmastown."

That other job, I guessed. I leaned toward him. "Did someone hire you to guard something?"

"I can't say."

"What if this moonlighting job of yours has something to do with Tiny's death?"

"It doesn't."

His terse answers told me that I wasn't going to squeeze any information out of him, so I returned to the castle. Almost as soon as I walked through the door, Jingles buttonholed me. "Thank goodness you're back," he said, taking my coat, gloves, and hat as I shed them. "Waldo's disappeared!"

"Since when?" I'd seen him last night. He'd brought in the lemon while I was talking to Jake.

"He hasn't been here all day, and he was scheduled to work. I told you he wasn't to be trusted."

"Maybe an emergency came up." But even as the words left my lips, doubts arose. What emergency would call him away from the castle without telling anyone? Especially Jingles. "Did you ask Cranberry if she's seen him?"

"First thing I did. She said she has no idea. She didn't seem too worried, either."

"What about Constable Crinkles?"

"I didn't call the constabulary. I thought if you were coming back with Jake Frost . . ."

"The detective is busy." Jake was preoccupied by his mysterious side mission in Christmastown. Fine. I should be able to handle Waldo's disappearance. There was probably a rational explanation for his having gone AWOL.

"Who else in the castle is friends with Waldo?" I asked.

Jingles thought, but looked stumped. "No one."

"But he has a room here?" Many of the elves resided in the castle. Some, like Jingles and Felice, the cook, had large suites to themselves. Most of the other elves had rooms in the elf quarters on the third floor.

"He does, but he spends most of his days off with his grandmother. He's devoted to her—his parents died when he was still a youngster. It was tragic. They were killed by a stampede of reindeer."

"Trampled to death?" Alarms clanged in my head.

Jingles nodded. "I've always thought it accounted a little for his nervous nature."

Poor Waldo. This information about his parents explained a lot. Now that I thought about it, he gave even Quasar a wide berth.

"Send Cranberry to Nick's office," I said.

The mysteries of Christmastown were piling up.

I found Nick at his desk, and from the alacrity with which he shut down his computer screen when I appeared, I didn't have to guess what he was up to.

"Reach the diamond level yet?" I asked.

He smiled sheepishly. "There's an iceberg in my way."

On a credenza near the desk, I noted something that looked like . . . a hand grenade? "What do you intend to lob that at?" I asked. "The snow monster that *didn't* kill Tiny Sparkletoe?"

Nick followed my gaze. "Boots keeps bringing things over—he tends to get a little overzealous when it comes to military hardware. Don't worry, I'll get rid of it."

"Would you mind stowing it now? I hoped to interview Cranberry in here. Waldo's disappeared, and she's our best chance at figuring out what happened to him."

Nick got up and put the grenade away. It made me nervous to be in the same room with it. This country was going bananas.

A few moments later, Cranberry knocked, then entered, followed by Jingles. He didn't seem inclined to be sent away this time, and Nick didn't ask him to leave.

"Have a seat, Cranberry," Nick said in his kindliest Santa tone. He clasped his hands together atop his desk. "We're a little worried about Waldo. He's disappeared."

"I don't know where he went. I already told Jingles that."

"We thought maybe you would have come up with some ideas about what happened to him."

She shrugged. "I haven't given it much thought."

"You don't even care that he's gone?" I asked.

"So you think he really is gone?"

Her hopeful tone reminded me of the shopkeepers who'd wanted to be assured that Tiny was dead.

"We're worried about him," Nick said. "If you have any information—"

She cut him off. "Ask his grandmother, not me."

"You think he would confide in his grandmother before he would in you?" I asked.

"I know he would." She shifted. "So do you think he's gone, as in hiding, or gone, dead?"

I eyed her closely. "Tell the truth, Cranberry. You're not really involved with Waldo, are you?"

Instead of answering my question, she countered with one of her own. "If he comes back, will he still have his job?"

"Should he?" I asked.

Cranberry clammed up.

From the back of the room, Jingles thundered, "Absolutely not! As far as I'm concerned, he should be fired immediately for being so derelict in his duties. Disappearing for an entire day? It's unforgivable!"

He ended his tirade by sending me a meaningful look. Catching on, I edged forward in my chair. "Maybe if we just had one reason more to fire him . . ."

Cranberry bit her lip and then took a deep breath. "All right—here's a reason: We weren't together that day like I said."

"You mean you lied?"

"He made me lie," she said angrily. "I can't stand him. He's a nervous little weasel."

"Where was he that evening?"

"How should I know? He doesn't confide in me." She

shook her head. "I'm sorry I lied, but he told me I'd lose my job if I didn't."

"Why would you lose your job?" Nick asked.

She shifted uncomfortably, then blurted out, "I'm already in trouble, aren't I? So I might as well confess. Waldo . . ." Her gaze slanted sideways.

"Waldo what?" I said.

She bit her lip. "He saw me taking food from the kitchen."

"*Stealing?*" Jingles said, appalled.

Her face reddened, and her fists clenched. "I shouldn't have done it, but there were, um, raspberries in the castle storeroom. My little sister loves raspberries. So I took them, and I'm sorry. But I don't see how something like that should put my job in jeopardy, like Waldo said it did. He used the incident to blackmail me. I can see now that I should have told him to shove his threats right up his . . . chimney."

"I'm sorry that happened to you," Nick said. "You shouldn't have taken the raspberries, at least not without asking. We would have happily spared them for your sister."

She blinked in disbelief. "You would?"

"We would?" Jingles echoed.

Nick nodded. "Thank you for telling us the truth, Cranberry. You've been very helpful."

"And I won't lose my job?"

"No," I said.

After Cranberry was gone, Jingles paced the carpet. "So Waldo's a blackmailer."

Nick looked mournful. "I'm sorry to hear that of him."

He was becoming more Santa-like all the time—offering forgiveness, grieving at naughtiness. I, on the other hand, was just amazed by what we'd heard. "Waldo *was* at the funicular." I'd just about convinced myself that I'd hallucinated seeing him. "He must have sabotaged it. He knew all about my schedule—he'd read it to me that morning."

"After getting rid of me on a false pretext!" Jingles exclaimed.

"I still don't understand why he would have done such a thing," I said. "What would have caused him to want to murder me, not to mention what might have been scores of others if the car had been crowded?"

"A murderer and a blackmailer." Jingles resumed his pacing. "I always thought there was something not right about that elf."

"All we know for sure is that Waldo blackmailed Cranberry," Nick pointed out. "We don't know why, or how much he had to do with the other things that have been going on."

"He must have run off soon after he'd seen Jake and me talking last night." I remembered him dropping a silver tray on the floor. "If he had done something wrong and he recognized Jake as a detective, that would explain why he turned into a quivering wreck."

Nick steepled his fingers, thinking. "If no one's seen him since then, he might have been gone for over twenty-four hours."

That was a long time to have disappeared in a tight-knit place like this. "I'm worried that something's happened to him," I said.

"That evil little blackmailer?" Jingles gaped at me. "He tried to kill you."

Well, yes. There was that. "If Cranberry can be trusted." There was something about that raspberry story that seemed off to me.

"Cranberry wasn't the one who ran away the minute she saw a detective in the house."

True. Everything pointed to Waldo being guilty of the funicular crash. So why did I want to exonerate him?

Nick looked at me sympathetically. "I don't want to believe he's evil, either."

"I'm going to try to find him," I said.

Jingles crossed his arms. "I'm not taking him back. It's difficult enough keeping this castle running smoothly without having murderers working on the staff."

"Aren't elves innocent until proven guilty?" I asked him.

He scowled. "Maybe in a court of law, but not in the court of Jingles."

Chapter 18

The next morning I caught the sleigh bus and took part in an *Addams Family* sing-along all the way into town. I wasn't sure if the elves around me had ever seen the TV show, but they'd certainly embraced its theme song, including finger snapping and other sound effects.

At the Gingerbread House, the concierge told me Jake had already left for the day. I finally hunted him down at the constabulary, scarfing down fresh-baked cinnamon rolls. A string of raffle tickets poked out of his coat pocket.

There was one born every minute.

I had a cinnamon roll, too, and told them all about Waldo's disappearance.

Thirty minutes later, we were knocking at the door of Mrs. Flurrybow, Waldo's widowed grandmother. The house was a modest cottage not far from downtown. The outside had recently been repainted a cheery red with white woodwork and the shutters and door in green. The short walkway leading from the picket fence at the sidewalk up to the front door had been shoveled and salted this morning. The faintest dusting of snow from the current flurries showed our four sets of footprints.

Though Mrs. Flurrybow did her best to disguise the fact,

she obviously couldn't see well. The small, wizened elf woman leaned on a thin carved wooden cane and peered sidewise at the world through what I assumed was her one good eye, which didn't seem to work all that well, either.

"You just brought me my mail, Hap," the tiny elf woman said as she squinted crookedly at Crinkles.

"IT'S CONSTABLE CRINKLES," Crinkles said.

She frowned. "So you are. You don't have to shout at me, though. These old ears of mine work just fine."

Crinkles brought his voice down to normal. "We need to talk to you."

"We?" She squinted around him. "You brought your nephew with you?"

Crinkles cleared his throat. "Yes, and Mrs. Claus is here, too, as well as Jake Frost, from the Farthest Frozen Reaches."

"Oh! I didn't see you. Morning sun's in my eyes."

There was no sun visible behind the clouds releasing light snow flurries, just plenty of streetlamp and colorful decorative lights, but we all went along with the fiction as she bid us come inside. The furniture in the little cottage's parlor she showed us into was obviously old, but the couch had a newer, cheery covering in a pattern with apples on it, which matched the curtains on the front window. I wondered how the nearly blind Mrs. Flurrybow managed to keep the room so tidy, but I wasn't kept in suspense for long.

"I'll get you some tea," she said. "I used to have a girl here to help some mornings, but she quit this week."

My antennae went up. "Pixie?"

She nodded. "A sweet girl, but she's suffered a loss recently. I suppose you've heard all about that."

"Let me help you with the tea things," I offered.

I shot Jake, Crinkles, and Ollie a meaningful look as I ducked through the doorway to the tidy little kitchen. While I kept Mrs. Flurrybow talking in the kitchen, this was their chance to have an informal look around for signs of the fugitive.

Pixie certainly had kept the place spic-and-span. The old tile in the kitchen gleamed like new. Mrs. Flurrybow felt her way to the sink and filled the kettle, and then struck a long match to light the ancient stove. It dropped to the ground. It was a miracle the place hadn't burned down.

"Let me help you."

"Goodness, no. I can manage." She struck a new match. "I wonder why the constable's here."

"It's on account of your grandson."

She turned, the long match burning toward her hand. "Waldo couldn't be in any trouble. He's a good boy. Why, you probably knew him when he started working at the castle when he was just knee high to a snowshoe hare."

Good God, she thought I was Pamela. "I'm *April* Claus. Nick's wife."

"Oh! I don't know you, do I?" The flame on that match was inching its way toward her thumb. She was seconds away from a big ouch.

"Here, let me do that for you," I said, taking the match from her and dropping it down into the iron stove's belly. The waiting kindling, perfectly laid, huffed to life within seconds.

"Have you seen Waldo recently?" I asked.

"Oh, yes. He came by just the night before last, after dinner. I'd already gotten ready for bed."

That had to have been after he'd seen Jake and me talking. "Did he stay long?"

"No, he never likes to stay away from the castle too long. He's so dedicated to his work. But of course you know that."

"Did he mention going on a trip or a vacation?" I asked.

"No . . ." She busied herself pulling out her good china tea service.

I couldn't bring myself to tell her that her grandson and

sole family member was suspected of murder and on the lam. That was better left to the constable, I rationalized. Instead, I brought the subject back around to Pixie.

"You must miss having help around the place."

"Oh, I'll get by just fine," she said, getting ready to reload the sugar bowl from a bag that read *Salt*.

I scooted over and took the bag from her hand. "I think this is the one you were looking for," I said, trading the salt for the sugar bag in the cupboard.

"Thank you!" She chuckled. "That would have made for an unappetizing cup of tea."

"Did Pixie ever speak about her husband?" I asked.

"No . . ." Her wrinkled brow creased even more. "Mind you, Pixie was working for me before she married, ever since she finished school. I looked upon her almost as a daughter. Then there was all that hullabaloo about her marrying Tiny Sparkletoe—people calling it a Cinderella match. I always thought that was hooey. If anyone was lucky in that pair, it was him. But he had money. Or so people thought."

"You think he wasn't well off? Because Pixie kept working for you?"

"That, and . . ." She backtracked. "Well, I think she kept working for me because she enjoyed her job."

I thought of Pixie in her pink outfit and mod shades, zooming down the streets of Christmastown on Tiny's snowmobile. She obviously enjoyed her newfound leisure, too.

Mrs. Flurrybow took the kettle off the stove and poured water into the teapot. "I wish her well, of course. I never bore her any ill will."

A frown tugged at my mouth. Who said anything about ill will?

Before I could pursue the thought, she said brightly, "Let's have some brownies. I made some yesterday."

Sure, why not? After cinnamon rolls, a brownie was just

what I needed. Mrs. Flurrybow got out a decorated tin from the cabinet and opened it.

"Those are your rubber bands," I told her gently. My grandmother had kept tins of everything too—rubber bands, useful-sized pieces of foil, and receipts going back to 1962.

She clucked at herself, pulled another tin out of the cabinet, and opened it up. The chocolaty smell of brownies was like catnip to me. They looked delicious, too, their tops crackling perfectly. Santaland would make a jolly, round Mrs. Claus out of me yet.

We loaded up two trays with the tea things, plates, and brownies. As we headed back to the parlor, I worried we'd catch the others mid-search. Instead, they were seated and had fallen into a heated discussion of the latest reindeer games result, a controversial win by the Rudolph herd.

"The rules clearly say no blinking," the constable said. "You can't blame the Comets for complaining that a competitor's nose distracted them."

Jake shook his head. "It's not a fair rule. They can't help blinking."

"They're athletes—they've been training to control their bodies since they were fawns."

"Blinking's semi-autonomic," Jake said.

At that word, Crinkles and Ollie displayed a good example of semi-autonomic eye blinking.

Mrs. Flurrybow chuckled. "I always thought the reindeer should just take turns winning. That would make it more fair."

At this heresy, the men fell into awkward silence, as if she'd suggested getting rid of competitions altogether. Which I supposed she had.

Mrs. Flurrybow and I handed around cups of tea and the brownies.

The constable took a bite. "This is delicious."

Mrs. Flurrybow smiled. "They're Waldo's favorites."

The name caused a shift in the room. Crinkles set his cup and saucer down on a piecrust table. "Waldo's the reason we've come here, Mrs. Flurrybow. We need to find your grandson. He's missing."

"Oh, dear." Her brow furrowed. "Mrs. Claus asked me if he'd mentioned going on vacation, but I told her in the kitchen that I just saw him night before last. He came to check on me. And then he left."

"Night before last is the last time anyone's seen him, ma'am," the constable said. "We think he might be hiding."

"Why on earth would he hide? Is he in trouble?"

Crinkles hitched his throat. "He seems to be on the lam. We think he might have information about some things that have been happening around Christmastown. Crimes."

"Oh, no, you're wrong about that. Waldo would never get mixed up in anything illegal. He's a good boy. He went to work just after his poor parents died, and has been helping support me ever since. He's a dutiful grandson, and I've never heard any complaints from the castle about his work." She turned toward me, though her eyes were focused more on the fireplace I was sitting next to. "Wouldn't you agree, Mrs. Claus?"

Someone had to tell her the bald truth. "The crimes he's suspected of being involved in are sabotage, attempted murder, blackmail, and murder," I said.

Mrs. Flurrybow let the words sink in and then she drew in a sharp breath. "You're way off the mark if you think my Waldo is involved in anything like that. No, no. You've got the wrong end of the candy cane, Constable."

Jake Frost leaned forward. "There is a witness placing him at the scene of one crime, and an elf at the castle swears she was being blackmailed by him. We're worried Waldo might be in trouble."

"It sounds as if he's in a great deal of trouble," she said, her voice crackling with tension, "but I find it impossible to believe that any of this is true. He never mentioned anything about sabotage or blackmail to me. And the idea that he's 'on the lam,' as you say, is just a load of reindeer poop. Excuse my language, but that's how strongly I feel." She stood, straightening as much as her dowager's hump would allow. Her sweet old lady demeanor hardened. "How dare you come into my house and drink tea and eat my brownies—Waldo's favorite brownies—and tell me that my grandson is a criminal! You should be ashamed of yourselves."

We all stood, too. "We need to find him, Mrs. Flurrybow," Crinkles said.

"Look all you like! Search the house, if you please. You won't find him here."

The constable fidgeted with his cap in his hands. "As a matter of fact, Ollie did take a quick look around the place . . ."

She thumped her cane on the floor. "You should go now. And please don't come back here until you're ready to apologize for this slander against my grandson."

As we turned to obey her order, Ollie reached down to grab another brownie. Quick as an adder, the old elf woman whacked his hand with her cane.

"Ow!" the deputy cried.

Mrs. Flurrybow's cloudy eyes narrowed on him. "I'll save those for Waldo, if you don't mind."

The four of us trooped out of the house and didn't speak until we were through the picket fence gate and back on the sidewalk.

As he put on his gloves, Ollie rubbed his hand where it had been hit. "That old grandma has a killer whack."

"Mother love is fierce," Jake told him. "Grandmother love is even fiercer."

"And blind," Constable Crinkles grumbled. "Once we

find Waldo, we'll have the culprit for the funicular accident, Tiny's death, and who knows what all. She'll be bringing him those brownies to the jail cell."

I couldn't deny that she seemed to love her grandson with every fiber of her being. But more interesting to me was the question of how blind Waldo's grandmother actually was. I'll admit she'd had me going . . . right up to the moment when that cane of hers struck Ollie's hand with pinpoint precision.

"There's something going on here," I said.

"What's going on is that Waldo snapped and is on a crime spree," Crinkles said, ready now to condemn Waldo for every Christmastown crime right down to sleigh parking tickets.

"Why?" I asked. "What motive did he have to commit any crime?"

"Maybe he's a maniac, like in Quince's movies," Ollie said. "There's always a crazy guy. Usually something bad happened in the past. I mean, Jason just lost his mom in *Friday the Thirteenth*, and Waldo lost *both* his folks."

His uncle scowled at him. "I told you not to watch those movies."

"It was just research," Ollie said. "How else am I going to learn about psychos?"

"Right," I deadpanned. "Everyone's so normal here."

Jake almost cracked a smile.

"Tiny Sparkletoe had more of a motive than Waldo for the funicular accident," I continued, "and the greenhouse and library vandalism, as well."

"Tiny's dead," Jake pointed out.

"That's what worries me. He's dead and we don't know why. What if Waldo's in danger?"

"He's in danger of spending a long time in jail if I get a hold of him." Crinkles turned to his nephew. "We haven't sold our quota of tickets today." The lawmen glanced back at Jake and me, but our shaking heads answered Crinkles's next question before he could ask it. "That's right. You two already bought some."

"How about a house-to-house search?" Ollie suggested. "We could ask people if they've seen Waldo and hit them up for raffle tickets at the same time."

"That's using your noggin," his uncle said approvingly. "Let's get going. As long as that elf is at large, no one's safe."

Chapter 19

"Did you get any sleep last night?" I asked Jake after the dynamic duo had set off down the street. The dark circles under his eyes were more pronounced today.

"Working two cases at once is taking it out of me. I could use some food that doesn't have sugar, too. Anything good near here?"

Situated down the street on the corner was Soy to the World, Christmastown's only vegan eatery. Under normal circumstances it might have taken longer to convince Jake to try it, but he seemed inclined to stay close to the Flurrybow cottage, as was I.

We ordered, waited for our drinks—cranberry-hibiscus tea for me, almond milk eggnog for Jake—and then leaned back in the booth by the window. Both of us kept half an eye on the street while pretending not to.

"You should go back to the inn and catch a few z's," I said. "You won't miss much. It's not like Crinkles and Ollie will make much progress in their search for the fugitive today."

"Or ever."

His response was all the confirmation I needed that we shared a strong hunch: Waldo was still in his grandmother's house.

"How did you figure it out?" I asked.

"The same way you did. Something in that place seemed off from the moment we walked up that perfectly shoveled walkway."

I'd noticed the walkway but I hadn't recognized it as a clue. "You think Waldo did that?"

He shook his head. "No—she wouldn't risk having Waldo outside, even in the dark. The old lady did it herself, or had it done so that no one would notice a certain pair of bootie tracks in the snow."

I nodded. "When she lit the fire for the kettle, the kindling in the stove had been perfectly laid, just like elves at the castle prepare fires. Waldo must have done it for her."

"That batch of brownies, too," he pointed out. "Why would she have made a fresh batch if he weren't around?"

"Where do you think he was while Ollie searched?"

"Anywhere. Ollie was far from thorough. The attic, maybe? Heck, he could've been hiding in a kitchen cupboard."

"You didn't tell Crinkles."

"Neither did you." He shrugged. "I figured your silence had to mean something."

He'd taken a cue from *me*? I sat up straighter. "It's not that I think he's completely innocent. I don't think even his grandmother believes that."

"All that insistence on what a good boy her grandson is." He shook his head. "If ever a lady protested too much . . ."

"The weird thing is that I still don't think Waldo's a bad elf. Mrs. Flurrybow might not be as helpless as she seems, but she needs some looking after, and Pixie doesn't work for free. Waldo has been supporting her, and even buying her things like new curtains and slipcovers. He *is* a good grandson. There's a piece here we're missing."

"What do you think it is?"

"Something about Pixie," I guessed. "Mrs. Flurrybow told me she thought of Pixie almost like family, yet Pixie dropped Mrs. Flurrybow just like the rest of her clients. Mrs. Flurrybow didn't seem too broken up about it, either."

"It'd be understandable if Pixie isn't her foremost concern at the moment."

The waitress arrived with our food. Jake picked up his mock-ox seitan burger, frowned at the contents, then took a tentative bite. It took a full minute of chewing before he worked up the courage to swallow. He waited a moment, as if half expecting to keel over, but in the end he nodded and took another bite.

My quinoa salad came dotted with sugared cranberries, which I pushed to the side before digging in. I'd been consuming so many baked goods lately, my molars were shocked by any food with a consistency crunchier than memory foam. "I never thought I'd be so happy to eat something not made of dough."

Jake smiled faintly, clearly distracted by something else. "You don't seem too sympathetic to Pixie."

"Every time I see her it's like meeting a different person. Maybe she did kill Tiny or hired someone—or some monster—to do it. But I get the sense there's something we're not seeing."

Jake put his half-eaten burger down and pushed the plate away. "It wouldn't have to be a snow monster. It was snowing that night. Pixie could've bashed Tiny on the head, positioned him facedown in the snow, and then smashed the snow he fell on in a footprint pattern good enough to fool Crinkles after the night of snow had fallen."

I nodded. "But why? Why go to such bizarre lengths?"

He nodded to the street outside. Every doorway had a jack-o'-lantern in front as a talisman to ward off the monsters. If I peered down to the corner, I could see a trebuchet with gravelly snowballs piled in a pyramid beside it. Windows were boarded up, a vigilance committee had been formed. Santa Claus was dressed in camouflage and packing heat. All because of a single footprint.

"Whoever made that print was counting on the ensuing chaos to distract the constable from looking further for a culprit," Jake said.

They didn't foresee that the snow monsters would send an emissary to investigate on their behalf.

I put down my fork. "What's next?"

Jake looked uneasy. "I have a bit of split focus today. What worries me now is what Waldo will do next. If he leaves that house, we need to know."

"I could watch the house," I said. Then I remembered I couldn't. "At least until my band rehearsal this afternoon."

He looked at my outfit, a red wool suit lined with white braided trim. "Even a half-blind old grandma might notice Mrs. Claus standing across the street."

I had another idea.

"I know someone who could watch Waldo for us. He could park himself outside the house and stare right into the windows and no one would think twice."

Jake's dark brows quirked upward. "Is he invisible?"

"No, he's a snowman."

Quince and Pocket weren't hard to locate. We came across them two alleys away, selling bootlegs of *Silent Night, Deadly Night* and *Christmas Evil*. Quince picked up his stash and started to run, but then he saw it was just Jake and me.

I shook my head at the titles. "No Halloween stuff?"

"They get snapped up right away," Quince said.

"Too bad. I'm curious about those Neldor movies."

Jake cleared his throat. "We have a job for you and Pocket."

Quince looked wary. "Doing what?"

"Surveillance."

"Why should we do that?"

I started to give a lecture on altruism and good citizenship, but Jake interrupted me. "You'll get paid by the hour."

At his readiness to hand out money, my gaze snapped toward him. "You've never offered to pay *me*."

He glanced back at Quince and aimed a sharp jerk of the head at me. "Listen to her. Miss Altruism."

Some haggling ensued, but soon the two had received their orders and set off for the Flurrybow cottage. "What are you going to do for the rest of the afternoon?" I asked Jake.

"I have that other thing."

"Your mysterious moonlighting job." It was beginning to irritate me. Not knowing something is like having an unreachable back itch. "What kind of client is this?"

"The kind that likes to keep his business confidential."

His business. I'd learned it was a he, at least. "You're sure it has nothing to do with the death of Tiny Sparkletoe?"

"Or the funicular or Pumpkin Slayer."

I kept forgetting about Pumpkin Slayer, who seemed to have gone silent for the present. Or had he gone silent forever when Tiny was killed?

I flipped my phone's cover open, making a show of checking the time. "I need to get some things done before this afternoon's rehearsal," I said. "I'll let you know if I discover anything new."

Quince had promised to call us both if Waldo was on the move. Pocket was going to be the eyes of the surveillance team, but Quince would station himself nearby and sound the alarm if anything happened.

I had my own plan now, just for a lark. There was no time to go back to the castle before rehearsal, so I ducked into Festive Fashions down the street and found an off-white puffer coat that was as close to generic North Pole outerwear as it came. I eyeballed the coatrack for my size, pulled one out, tried it on right there in the aisle, and told the astonished elf saleslady I would pay for it and wear it out of the store.

"Sure you don't want to accessorize your new coat?" she asked. "A sparkly scarf would really make it pop."

"No, thanks. Popping is the last thing I want at the moment." I did grab an elf hat in the largest size they carried. It was mostly green, but with a muted cream-colored crown. The top, which drooped slightly, had a matching green pom-pom.

She rang me up and I was in and out of the store in less than five minutes—the speediest shopping I'd ever done. I wadded up my green coat, a Madame Neige original, in the Festive Fashions shopping bag the saleslady had provided me, and then put the hat on. It was warm, at least.

I set off to find Jake.

When tailing someone, losing sight of him for ten minutes can mean losing him forever. I had a hunch Jake was going to return to the Gingerbread House, though, probably to phone his secret client in privacy. I hoped he didn't plan on taking my advice and dozing the afternoon away.

I waited outside the Gingerbread House for ten minutes, trying not to stomp my feet or flap my arms too much, even though it was flippin' cold outside.

When Jake emerged from the inn's front door, I wheeled toward the store window I stood next to, feigning rapt interest in the offerings on display, which belonged to Naughty or Nice Lingerie. I pinned my gaze on a sexy snow monster outfit while surreptitiously watching Jake's movements reflected in the glass. After leaving the inn, he turned left and walked toward the west side of town. I counted to ten and followed him. His hands were buried in his pockets, his head was down, and his legs ate up the sidewalk with a purposeful stride. He'd been given a mission, obviously. My curiosity ramped up a notch.

Who was Jake's client? I knew he'd spoken with Nick in private the night before last, before Nick had brought him in to talk to me. Maybe Nick was more worried about that funicular accident than he was letting on and had hired Jake to investigate it on the q.t.

I hung back half a block as we made our way across town. A tense moment occurred when Jake passed We Three Beans, then doubled back and went inside. I pivoted quickly to keep from being spotted. Five minutes later he came out with a cardboard tray holding two coffees in insulated sleeves.

Two coffees? He either expected company or was settling in for a long stakeout.

He took a right turn and continued in the direction of the library. He stopped across the street from that building's fanciful edifice and found shelter under the awning of a sporting goods store.

He was watching the library.

Blood drained from my face. All at once, I knew who'd hired him. *I'm always curious about what she's up to,* Chip had told me. *I guess that shows how in love with her I am.*

Anger pounded through my veins. I marched toward Jake.

I wasn't three feet away when he plucked the second coffee off the tray and held it out to me.

The fact that I was the company he'd been expecting only incensed me more. I planted my gloved fists on my puffy hips. "Really? You're spying on librarians?"

"I'm a detective. I don't choose whom I watch, the client does."

"Let me guess—your client's name is Chip Pepperbough, and he's paranoid that his girlfriend might have a life."

"He was burned once before."

"Who hasn't been? Juniper's my friend."

"That's why I wanted to keep you out of it."

"That's why you should have involved me. Chip is paying

you to do his stalking for him! That doesn't make you feel icky?"

"You saw me paying a teenager to watch the house of a little old lady, and you never once used the word *icky*."

"Waldo's grandmother is harboring a suspect who may be a murderer. I know Juniper. She's honest. The person who needs watching in this scenario is crazy Chip."

"He's not crazy. I checked him out."

"Not well enough. He might not have a criminal record— yet—but I've spoken to him and he's definitely developed a paranoia bordering on psychosis."

"Sounds like something you should warn your friend about."

"I did."

"And what did she say?"

I shifted uncomfortably. "She said she didn't want to speak to me anymore." Jake gave his head a shake, and I added, "But that was because I said I thought he was a murderer. I'll admit that maybe I went a little overboard with that accusation."

"Yeah, people are apt to be touchy about things like that."

"I was worried about her. Now I'm even more worried." I eyed the coffee. "Did you really buy that for me?"

"Milk, one sugar."

I opened the lid and leaned my back against the wall so we were both facing the library's open plaza. "How long have you been watching her?"

"Since I got to town."

"That's why you said you'd rather stay at the Gingerbread House than the castle."

"The inn suits me fine." He glanced over at me. "No offense—it's a little nuts where you live."

I couldn't argue. Sometimes I dreamed of living in a place without all my in-laws plus a reindeer with a malfunctioning nose wandering around it. That's why I clung to my inn in Cloudberry Bay. Nick and I had decided to summer there every year and recharge our batteries. It made Pamela and the reindeer musk easier to bear the rest of the year. Plus my friend Claire was there . . .

I drew in a sharp breath. I'd almost forgotten about Claire's call. It had come in the middle of a strange week—and the things she was insinuating were so bizarre. Now I felt bad for not getting back to her. Somehow in one week I'd managed to accuse one friend's boyfriend of being a murderer, while my best friend in Oregon thought, however briefly, that *I'd* killed my husband. A husband she assumed, best case, was a creeper with a Santa fetish. At some point I was going to have to straighten everything out again.

"You know I'm going to talk to Juniper about this," I warned Jake.

"You said she wasn't speaking to you anymore."

Right. That would be an obstacle. Also, even if she did agree to speak to me, the last thing she probably wanted to hear was more warnings about Chip. How could I persuade her to listen?

"Okay," I said, thinking on the fly, "whatever Chip's paying you, I'll double it for you to stop spying and tell Juniper what Chip hired you to do."

"I can't turn on a client like that. It wouldn't be ethical."

"Ethical? Spying is unethical."

He eyed me. "I'm not breaking into her apartment or reading her mail. I'm following her movements."

"On behalf of a controlling creep."

He leveled a wry look on me. "Do I tell you how to be Mrs. Claus?"

A frustrated sigh huffed out of me. "If Juniper *ever* appears to be in danger, you'd better tell me."

"I'd tell Constable Crinkles." The declaration hung in the air a moment before its feebleness made him add, "And then I'd call you."

We lapsed into silence, our gazes pinned on the library's front door. Elves came and went.

I took another sip of coffee, brooding. "Be honest. How soon did you spot me?"

"The moment I walked out of the Gingerbread House."

I laughed in disbelief. "Sure you did."

He slanted an arch look my way. "For the record, that sexy snow monster outfit wouldn't suit you. I always figured you for the Lusty Lucasta type."

Damn. He really had spotted me. "I changed my coat and everything."

"You're a tall woman in a townful of elves, and you've got auburn hair sticking out of that ridiculous hat, and that coat makes you look like a giant, half-toasted marshmallow."

Oh, well. At least it was warm.

I had to leave Jake to get to band rehearsal. It was only when I arrived at the Community Center and saw Juniper's empty seat that I remembered she should have left the library around the same time I had. As I was setting up my percussion equipment, my gaze darted toward the door every time a new person entered the hall. No Juniper.

Had Chip won?

It was hard to say who looked more depressed at our lack of a euphonium player—me, Smudge, or Luther, our conductor, who was always concerned about the lack of low brass. "I hope Juniper's not sick," he said, eyeing me questioningly.

I lifted my shoulders. I just hoped she was safe.

The band played through our Halloween program, and then Luther went over the plans for tomorrow night. It was hard to believe Halloween was upon us. Much as I hated to admit it, I'd be relieved to finally have it over with. With all that had happened in the past week, I couldn't help wondering if the doomsayers like Lucia and even Tiny had been right all along. It seemed as if I'd unleashed something dark and dangerous on Christmastown.

Juniper's absence from band rehearsal continued to worry me. Had Chip convinced her to drop it or was she skipping it to avoid me? Even if she thought I was a pest, a terrible friend, or even an awful person, I needed to warn her that her dream elf was spying on her. I spent most of the evening angsting over how and when to contact her.

After dinner, I called her number but was quickly sent to voice mail. I hung up and sent a text instead. **Missed you at rehearsal. Call me. I have something important to tell you.**

For good measure I added a smiling snowman emoji and then read the text over. I didn't mention Chip. Doing so would have made her ignore me forever. But the snowman made it look like I was trying too hard to make her not ignore me. I deleted the emoji and hit SEND.

Juniper didn't answer my text or my phone message for the rest of the evening, so maybe she did plan to avoid all communication with me. I didn't hear from anyone else, either. Jake was probably staking out Juniper's place, and presumably Pocket was still stationed in front of Mrs. Flurrybow's and would let Quince know if Waldo emerged from his hiding place. Where would Waldo go, though?

Before bed, I texted Juniper again. **Chip is having you watched. If you don't believe me, peek out your window. If there's a man in black posted there, you'll know I'm telling the truth.**

Restlessness overcame me as soon as my head touched the pillow. Worries crowded my mind. Snow monsters, band concerts . . . a missing elf . . . a dead elf.

Tomorrow was Halloween. It would be a long day. I needed to sleep. I tossed and turned for a long time, long after Nick was snoring softly away into dreamland. I watched him enviously. *Why can't I do that?* Maybe I needed a new hobby—hunting for murderers wasn't a soothing pastime. I could try knitting, like Pamela. Or follow Ollie's example and take up baking.

Something gnawed at my memory. Something to do with Pamela. Or baking. Or Pamela and baking . . .

I gasped and sat up. *Cookies!*

Specifically, fifteen dozen reindeer cookies, which I'd promised Pamela I'd have ready for the bake sale tomorrow morning. Fifteen dozen cookies I'd completely forgotten to make.

Chapter 20

Confession time: I've never liked making cookies. They're so time consuming, and all for a snack that people gobble down with barely a thought. Pies make an impression. Cakes elicit compliments on their appearance and the artistry that goes into them. A cake or pie is an event, to be displayed and then served on attractive plates. Cookies are a grab-and-go food.

But I'd promised to make reindeer cookies, so I had to get on with it. Fast. On my way down to the kitchen, I did a quick Internet search on my phone. Reindeer cookies didn't strike me as Halloween-like, but mine was not to question why. Anyway, it was just like Pamela to insist on Christmas cookies no matter what the holiday.

The reindeer cookies I found were either the silhouettes of leaping reindeer or cutesy reindeer heads with either red hots or gumdrops for noses. The thought of gumdrops soothed me. I couldn't be sure of what ingredients would be available in the kitchen, but if there was one thing Castle Kringle was well stocked with, it was gumdrops.

In the kitchen, I flipped on the lights and began assembling what I'd need: the mixer and bowls, cookie sheets, and ingredients. The butter would need to be softened. Instead of a freezer, the pantry next to the kitchen simply had an open window, rendering the whole room icy cold. I retrieved several slabs of butter from there and set them by the stove, which I lit. Then I tried to figure out what kind of cookie I could make.

There were no leaping deer cookie cutters among Felice's utensils, but I did find a gingerbread man. One of the iced cookie recipes I'd looked at online used a gingerbread man turned upside down as the reindeer: the legs had icing squiggled on them to look like antlers, the outstretched arms were the ears, and the head was its chin. *I can do this.* I just needed to make a ton of dough and icing, and pull an all-nighter getting them baked and decorated.

I was tired, but there was no way I could sleep now with this project hanging over my head. Even if I managed to roust myself in the morning in time to bake fifteen dozen cookies, Felice would take a dim view of my being underfoot in her kitchen the next day. She had a job to do, and it wasn't her fault that I'd forgotten my promise to Pamela to bake these infernal cookies.

First things first: I needed to stop thinking of them as infernal cookies. They were going to be tasty morsels of happiness. I hunted for a sugar cookie recipe that looked fast and foolproof. None of this chilling-the-dough nonsense.

Unfortunately, it turned out that most recipes for the cookie-cutter-type cookies called for chilling the dough. But the night was young(ish) and I was resilient.

Three hours later, I was lugging a vat of frozen dough in from the cold room. I'd made the mistake of taking a little nap, and the egg timer I'd set to wake me after an hour hadn't done the trick. I'd awoken with a start when Lynxie, during his middle-of-the-night prowling, had let out a shriek somewhere just outside the kitchen. It was the first time I'd been thankful for that cat.

While the dough unfroze enough to make it pliable, I got

to work on the icing. *I can do this*, I repeated. Falling asleep was just a minor setback. Wasn't I better off for having had a nap? Yes. Although I was still exhausted, so much so that the words of the icing recipe swam fuzzily on my phone screen. When I was able to focus on it, the ingredients seemed too bland. The sugar cookies were already plain enough, so I decided to punch up the icing. I went back to the salon with the liquor cabinet and grabbed a bottle of rum, which I used as the liquid to add to the powdered sugar to make the icing. Then I divided the icing into multiple bowls to create different colors. I'd never done cookies like this and actually had fun messing with food coloring and cinnamon to create the various colors for my reindeer. It reminded me of the time when I was eleven and got a chemistry set for Christmas.

Except I'd ended up burning a hole through my parents' dining room table that day, so maybe that wasn't a good thing to think about at this particular moment.

Another gripe about cookies: you have to watch them. These were supposed to bake for ten minutes. Nine minutes in, the first batch looked scorched. Of course, they'd be iced, so hopefully nobody would notice. But I started giving them eight minutes after that. Eight minutes doesn't give you time to do much. I could only slather brown icing on the burnt cookies and maybe do an antler or two before the next sheet had to come out. Then I had to roll more dough and cut more cookies. Then back to the icing and—

Shock made me cry out. The adorable reindeer face I had intended had transmogrified into a nightmare cookie—the icing had melted and dripped toward the edge, giving the reindeer a horror look.

Well, it *was* Halloween.

The door behind me opened, and I whirled on my slippered feet, a surprised cry on my lips. What was I expecting? Not Nick, certainly.

But there he was in his large red robe, which matched my own. "What on earth are you doing?" he asked, surveying the mess I'd made. Every surface was covered in cookie detritus— cookie sheets, mounds of chilled dough, flour everywhere, powdered sugar. The white tile floors, which had been spotless when I started, bore splatters of colored icing, along with my footprints in the dusting of flour.

"I'm making cookies," I said.

"At four in the morning?"

Oh, no. "Is it that late?"

Warily, Nick came closer to inspect my operation. Just then, the oven timer buzzed. I jumped for the pot holders and lunged to rescue the latest cookies from burning.

When I turned back around, he was casting a critical eye at my first icing attempt. "What is this supposed to be?"

"A reindeer?"

Ever the diplomat, he refrained from commenting.

"I'm still working out a few kinks," I explained. "And I don't have much time. You see, I promised Pamela I'd make fifteen dozen cookies by tomorrow, and then I forgot until I went to bed tonight, and now I've only got a few hours before the kitchen elves get up, and they'd probably appreciate not having to stumble over me and my mess as they prepare breakfast."

I felt foolish babbling about my cookie conundrum, but he listened not just sympathetically but intently. "Maybe we can streamline this," he suggested. "Show me how to roll out dough, and I can cut out cookies and pop them in the oven. That way you can concentrate on the decorating."

I could have wept in gratitude. Just having someone else there made me feel less alone. I should have known that a man who delivers toys all over the globe in a single night would have thoughts on efficiency.

"You also might want to give the cookies a few minutes

in the cold room to cool them down before you ice them."
He nodded to my demented reindeer. "Unless the crazy-eyed
look is intentional."

Why hadn't I thought of that?

*Because you were dead on your feet and working in a frenzy
of panic.* Nick's presence made the project seem more do-
able and helped me think more clearly. He was right. I just
needed to take this step by step. With someone helping, we'd
have plenty of time to get the cookies finished and clean the
kitchen before the Patton of the Pantry reported for duty. Best
of all, Pamela need never know I'd almost royally screwed up.

After an hour, Nick and I had the routine down to a sci-
ence, like an assembly line. We were the Ford Motors of
cookie production. After two hours, we were almost done.
Nick stopped and took a bite out of a cookie that had been
broken by mistake.

He frowned.

Oh, God. That was not a good sign. "What's wrong with
it?" I asked, not sure I wanted to know.

"Nothing—they're tasty. Just unexpectedly potent."

I reached for the other broken half and took a nibble.
Wow. "I put rum in the icing."

"That would explain it. It's like happy hour in a cookie."

Great. My cookies needed to come with a surgeon general's warning. Feeling defeated, I grabbed another cookie.

"What are you doing?"

"Drowning my sorrows," I said, taking a bite.

"It's not a big deal, April. It's just cookies."

I sank down on one of the stools the kitchen elves used
to reach high shelves. Days of turmoil boiled up inside me.
"This week has been disturbing."

"Of course. Someone tried to kill you."

"It's not that," I said. "Although that wasn't great. There's
also all this controversy around Halloween, which was sup-

posed to be a fun thing, but instead it seems to have unleashed bad feelings. Maybe even a murder. Now jack-o'-lanterns are being used to ward off snow monsters, and Christmastown looks like it's expecting a war. And I'm wondering why I ever suggested celebrating this stupid holiday. Maybe doing so has ruined Santaland forever." I looked him in the eye. "What if I'm like one of those time travelers who goes back and inadvertently changes one thing so that Hitler ends up winning World War Two?"

"That's ridiculous."

"Is it? I feel like I've failed everyone."

"You haven't failed me."

Was he serious? "You most of all. I thought our marriage would bring you peace and happiness, and instead Santaland is on the verge of chaos. And then there's Juniper. I've lost her friendship because I accused her stupid boyfriend of being a murderer—and now I'm less sure that he's a murderer but more certain than ever that he's a psychopath. Your mother thinks I'm a flake, Lucia thinks I'm encouraging reindeer abuse, and apparently I can't even make a batch of cookies without screwing it up. What kind of Mrs. Claus can't make cookies?"

Nick dragged another stool over next to me. "You *have* made me happy. I'd go crazy here if it weren't for you. I certainly didn't marry you so you could be a model Mrs. Claus and bring peace and happiness here. I don't even know if any one person could achieve that feat. Santaland's just like any other place."

I laughed.

"I mean we have our share of problems," he corrected. "As for the other things . . . I don't know what's going on with Juniper, but I'm confident you'll patch things up eventually."

He had more confidence in that than I did.

"And trust me, your cookies will be a hit. If I know those Ladies' Guild women, they'll be all over your alcoholic cookies."

His positive words melted my despair like rum icing on a hot reindeer cookie. Maybe things weren't a disaster, after all. I leaned into him. "It's a lucky thing you woke up and came down."

He kissed me, a kiss that tasted of rum and optimism. Troubles fell away, and we were just Mr. and Mrs. Claus, in our nightclothes and flour-dusted robes, making out in the kitchen in the middle of the night.

"Let's clean this place up and try to catch a snooze before the rest of the castle wakes up," Nick said. "Today's a big day, and we'll both have a lot to do."

"I know I'll be busy," I said. "What are you going to be doing?"

"The Vigilance Committee is taking a field trip to Wonderland Valley tomorrow morning and afternoon to do team building and training exercises."

Poor Nick. In just a few hours, he would be running around playing war games with armed elves. And I was whining about my problems.

"But first . . ." He reached over, grabbed the remainder of the cookie I'd broken in half earlier, halved it again, and handed a part to me. "Care for a nightcap?"

We clicked cookies. "Skoll," I said.

"To Halloween. I predict this will be one of the most memorable days Santaland's ever seen."

He might have been drunk on cookies, but he wasn't wrong.

Chapter 21

Nick's optimism stayed with me while I slept and carried me through the morning. Before going to bed, we boxed up our cookies and added them to Pamela's stack to be taken to the Community Center. I was on the roster to work at the bake sale, but not till a later shift. I was exhausted, yes, but I also brimmed with a sense of accomplishment. Looking at my fifteen dozen cookies, I couldn't help feeling I snatched victory from the jaws of defeat.

Nick had obviously told Jingles that I intended to sleep in, because I was already dressed by the time he tapped at my door. When he appeared, we both let out appreciative gasps.

Jingles was in a red devil's suit, including a cap with horns and a satin cape.

I'd already put on my Madame Neige creation—a witchy Mrs. Claus dress in a forest-green velvet so deep it was almost black. Jet-black velvet lined the long dress's hem, the sleeve cuffs, and the collar. A matching hat had been expertly wired to give its pointy crown and wide brim a jaunty tilt. I couldn't bring myself to walk around in green makeup all day, but I did some gothic work on my eyes and lips and added a large false wart to my nose. I looked like the Wicked Witch of the West's couture cousin.

I gulped down some coffee, gave myself a final mirror check, and said, "I guess I need to go down and greet the others."

"No point," Jingles said. "You overslept breakfast. The dowager Mrs. Claus ordered it cleared before she left for the bake sale."

Hm. "What about Lucia?"

"She's gone to check on the reindeer herds. She's worried they'll be spooked by the noise and lights."

I might have a problem. "I suppose Tiffany's long gone?"

Jingles nodded.

Of course she was. She had the tearoom to open and an ice show to get ready for.

"And Nick's gone," I said, thinking aloud. The Vigilance Committee would already be headed to Wonderland Valley.

I drummed my nails, painted black for the occasion. "I guess it's the sleigh bus into town for me."

"I'll take you."

"Really?" Jingles wasn't usually wild for people to ride his snowmobile, a fancy model that was his pride and joy.

"Of course," he said, as if he offered me rides all the time, instead of once in a blue moon. He was so paranoid about getting so much as a scratch on his snowmobile that he barely rode it himself.

When, a half hour later, he pulled up in front of the castle to pick me up, the reason behind his eagerness became clear. He hadn't just fashioned a costume for himself, he'd dressed up his snowmobile like a demon. It was sporting a red nose cone with a shark grin and crazed eyes painted on. Horns stuck out just in front of the windshield. He nodded to the seat in back. "Climb on, and hang on to your witch hat."

Over my costume dress I was wearing a warm black woolen cape. As we whizzed by, Salty and his assistant groundskeeper, out clearing pathways, stopped to stare at us. I could just imagine the sight we made: a demon and a witch, capes flapping, on Jingles's newly decorated demonmobile.

The snowmobile made short work of the way into town. We were headed for the Community Center when something I glimpsed through a window caught my eye.

"Stop!"

Jingles might be high strung, but he was a careful driver. Despite my agitation, he continued halfway down the block until he could find a place to sensibly pull over.

"What's wrong?" he asked.

I hopped off. "I think I saw something back there at Merry Muffins. I need to check it out."

"Maybe I should go," he suggested.

"Why you?"

"Because you're conspicuous."

I gave his outfit a pointed look. "You're an elfman in a red devil suit."

"And you're Mrs. Claus, no matter what you're wearing."

He was right. Even in my witch costume, it wasn't as if I could run around incognito in this town. I was Mrs. Claus in Santaland. "There's an elf couple sitting at the table by the window inside Merry Muffins. I need you to go in there and confirm who they are."

"I don't know every elf in Santaland," he said.

"You'll know these two. Watch them for a little while and tell me how they're acting. And maybe eavesdrop, if you can."

"You want me to go in and sit down?"

"Just order something to go. Be surreptitious."

"You'll look after the demonmobile?" he asked.

"Of course."

He hesitated, casting a wary glance around the bright, picturesque half-timbered buildings of the neighborhood as if surveying an urban hellscape.

"It's Christmastown, Jingles. No one's going to trash your vehicle while you're in Merry Muffins."

While he was gone I checked my messages. Nothing from Juniper, nothing from Claire. I tried not to feel discouraged. Nick was right—all friendships had their ups and downs.

Though mine seemed to be extraordinarily down at the moment.

A clopping sound made me look up. A reindeer careered down the street, its gait unsteady. It saw me and gave a few fitful hops and bucks, and to my horror kept coming straight toward me.

A pair of reindeer at the head of a sleigh parked next to me yelled a warning. "Watch out!"

I couldn't tell if they were talking to me or the crazy animal careening in my direction.

Do reindeer go rabid? This one wasn't foaming at the mouth, but he was acting deranged in every other way. He lowered his antlered head and snorted and puffed as if he would charge right at me. There was no time to run. All I could do was dive headlong under the neighboring sleigh. The other reindeer continued to shout warnings at their fellow ruminant, to no avail.

I peeked out from between the treads of the sleigh I was hiding beneath. My heart was in my throat as the reindeer bolted and hopped straight toward the demonmobile. Jingles's pride and joy. I braced myself for the impact of antlers against metal.

Then something strange happened. There was no crash at all. I poked my head out farther and looked up at the reindeer flying unsteadily through the air. He cleared half a block before coming back down on the snowy pavement and galloping on. The harnessed reindeer called after him.

"What's the matter with you!"

"You want to get yourself killed?"

I couldn't understand it myself. I'd never witnessed a reindeer acting that strangely. And I lived with Quasar, the oddest reindeer there was.

I crawled out from my hiding place and was just twitching the snow off my witch dress and cloak when the distant whine of a motor came nearer. Constable Crinkles's snowmobile turned onto the street, and a siren was added to the noise. The constabulary vehicle barely slowed down as it passed.

"Did a crazy reindeer pass this way?" Crinkles called out.

I pointed down the street, and he buzzed off in frantic pursuit.

Jingles bolted out of Merry Muffins, red cape flying, a large white box in his hands and a terrified look on his face. "What happened? Is the demonmobile okay?"

"It's fine."

He shoved the box into my hands and practically collapsed with relief upon his beloved. "Through the window it looked as if that crazy beast was charging right at you."

"I'm all right."

"Not you," he said dismissively. He ran his red satin gloved hand over the sleek surface of the snowmobile.

"Is it common for reindeer to act like that?"

"How would I know—do I look like Lucia?" He shook his head. "I had a premonition that something bad would happen."

"Nothing bad happened," I reminded him. "Everything's okay." I looked in the box, which was filled with muffins. "What's all this for?"

"I bought those as cover," he said. "Carrot, orange cranberry, and white chocolate hazelnut. The white chocolate hazelnut are their specialty. You should have one. You look peaky."

I hadn't eaten anything yet. I picked one up and took a

nibble. It was heavenly—dense as a brick, but moist. There must have been two dozen muffins there. "That's a lot of muffins."

"Having the clerk box them up bought me time to run surveillance."

The backfire of a snowmobile engine grabbed my attention. I looked down the street, expecting to see Cringles and the crazy reindeer racing back in our direction. Instead, I caught a glimpse of Louie driving away with Pixie sitting behind him. We'd been so focused on the demonmobile that I hadn't noticed the pair leave Merry Muffins.

"There they go," Jingles said. "Before all heck broke loose, I watched them sitting at a table together. She was eating a lemon poppy seed, and he was having a peppermint iced chocolate cupcake—which are disgusting, in my opinion. I hope that's not his entire lunch."

"I didn't send you in there to tell me about their dietary errors," I said. "What were they saying?"

"Nothing. They were eating."

"Just eating?"

He nodded. Noting my disappointment, he added, "But underneath the table, they were touching booties."

"Not accidentally?" The bistro tables at Merry Muffins didn't offer much legroom.

"Not a chance. Their feet would touch, and then they would look at each other and smile. Like you and Nick do at dinner sometimes when you think no one is watching."

Lesson learned: Someone is always watching. Especially if Jingles is in the vicinity.

"Louie and Pixie," I said. "Interesting."

"Have I cracked the case?" he asked excitedly. "I'll lay odds that the lovey-doveyness between those two predates Tiny's demise."

Was it possible that Tiny's death and Pixie's moving to

town had thrown the two together, and that this relationship between them had just recently sprung up?

But a mere three days had passed since Tiny was killed. *Mrs. Sparkletoe and I don't talk much,* Louie had assured me a few days ago. What a load of marshmallows. But I'd swallowed it, because Louie seemed like a nice guy and we played in band together.

Something else was bothering me. I pictured the two of them on that snowmobile. It hadn't been the fancy blue one—Tiny's—that I'd seen Pixie on yesterday. This vehicle was old, and not in the greatest shape, if that backfire was any indication. It had to be Louie's.

"Louie did it," Jingles said with finality. "He killed Tiny and made it look like a snow monster, and now he's got the widow *and* the store."

The shoe coup scenario, minus Walnut.

But what about the funicular accident? Louie wouldn't have tried to kill me, would he? Also, there was Waldo's involvement. If Louie was the culprit, why had Waldo disappeared?

"I'm not sure what it means," I said, "but I need to tell Jake about it." *If he can spare the time from spying on my friend.*

I sent Jake a text telling him briefly what Jingles and I had observed.

During the ride over to the bake sale, I sifted through this new information. Pixie and Louie, if truly in love, would have had every reason to separate themselves from Tiny, but killing him seemed extreme. Pixie might have been desperate to hang on to Tiny's money . . . but someone who continued to be a housekeeper after her marriage didn't strike me as a gold digger, no matter what Walnut had said about her. And everyone knew Louie could have found work with Walnut or even set up his own shoe store. Maybe Tiny had threatened him, though.

"Should I go tell Constable Crinkles what I've discovered?" Jingles asked when he dropped me off in front of the Community Center, where tents and heat lamps had been set up for the bake sale.

I tried to imagine Jingles walking into the constabulary in his red devil suit and spouting his theory about Pixie and Louie's playing footsies in the muffin shop. I doubted Crinkles would take him seriously. Besides, the constable had decided Waldo was the culprit. He wasn't going to hound Tiny's widow with questions as long as his prime suspect remained at large.

"Crinkles is off chasing that reindeer," I told Jingles. "I'm going to try to talk to Jake Frost first and see if he's found anything else." At Jingles's crestfallen look, I added, "But you made an amazing discovery."

This appeased him somewhat. "Back to the castle for me, then. Let me know if you need anything."

He buzzed away, and I was off to sell baked goods.

I walked up to the long bake sale booth where a Raggedy Ann stood sentry next to a woman in an elaborate, sparkly dress of pink satin and tulle with puffy sleeves and a bell skirt. She wore a silver crown and carried a wand. And when she turned—

I almost fainted. *"Pamela?"*

My mother-in-law executed a Glinda the Good Witch smile, raising her hands and the wand in greeting. "April, you made it. And how nice you look. What a lovely . . . wart."

I lifted my hand to my nose. The wart was still there.

"That's an amazing outfit," I told her.

"Glinda was always a hero of mine," Pamela said. "Always a solution, always a smile."

"She wasn't the one getting terrorized by winged monkeys, though," I pointed out.

"Well!" Pamela chirped. "Wasn't that the whole point of

the movie? Dorothy wouldn't have had to deal with all that unpleasantness, either, if she'd just had the presence of mind to tap her heels together."

"I don't . . ." I was going to argue with her, but she was smiling at me so determinedly, the words vaporized in my brain.

She clamped onto my arm and pulled me aside. *Uh-oh*, I thought, wondering what bit of North Pole propriety I'd breached now.

When we were out of earshot of the booth, she lowered her voice. "I didn't want to speak in front of Mildred. Poor thing, her boo bars haven't sold at all." Then her face broke out in a disarming, genuine smile and she tapped with her wand like a queen knighting a subject. "Whereas *your* cookies sold like hotcakes. Well done!"

I looked over at the long table of baked goods. My cookies had been set up on a card table slightly apart from the rest, with a large *Reindeer Cookies* sign on it. Someone had added *Sold Out* with a marker pen. All that was left was a plate holding a few crumbs.

"Out of fifteen dozen, there's nothing left?" I asked, astonished.

"I was surprised, too. They didn't look like any reindeer cookies I'd ever seen. The reindeer seemed doubtful at first, too, but once a few had sold, oh, my goodness! There was practically a stampede on the things."

"Reindeer?"

"We never made so much money so fast," Pamela enthused. "I thought we'd have a riot on our hands when the animals learned we were sold out."

Blood drained from my face. "I didn't realize reindeer came to the bake sales."

"Of course they do. We're careful not to discriminate—

and they've become some of our most reliable customers from year to year. That's why I asked you to make so many."

So many reindeer cookies.

Cookies *for* reindeer.

Oh, crap.

"Tell me . . ." I tried to keep my voice casual. "What do most people put in their reindeer cookies?"

"Oats, lichen, and nuts," she said, as if this were common knowledge.

I thought back to the reindeer incident in front of Merry Muffins. Had that reindeer been to the bake sale? Sure, Nick and I had joked about my alcoholic cookies—but I'd assumed they were for people.

Why hadn't Nick warned me about reindeer cookies? Surely he noticed that these didn't have oats and lichen in them.

I thought back. I'd never told Nick what kind of cookies I'd been asked to make. He must have thought I'd picked the reindeer design on my own. I groaned.

"What's wrong?" Pamela asked.

"Could you excuse me for a moment? I think I have a phone call."

I didn't, but I opened my phone and tapped *Reindeer-alcohol-sugar ill effects* into the search engine. No results. This bake sale might be the world's first test case.

With any luck, the crazed reindeer outside Merry Muffins was an outlier. Otherwise, there would be more than a hundred geeked-up reindeer on the loose.

"Have there been any . . . incidents?" I asked when I turned back to Pamela.

She blinked at me. "What kind of incidents?"

"Uh . . ." I considered fessing up to not knowing what a reindeer cookie actually was. But perhaps it was better to button my lip while I still found myself accidentally in my mother-in-law's good graces. "Never mind."

She squeezed my shoulder. "I'll be off, then," she trilled. "I'm leaving the bake sale in your and Mildred's competent hands."

Mildred Claus was a distant cousin of Nick and Lucia. She was always perfectly polite to me, although I'd never warmed up to her. She wasn't much older than me but she was so awkward. Talking with her could be like pulling teeth. But that's why costumes were so great. I took in her Raggedy Ann outfit—a gingham dress and red yarn wig. Fake freckles dotted her cheeks.

"Excellent costume, Mildred."

"You look nice, too," she said, giving me a shy up-and-down glance. "Madame Neige?" she asked, nodding at my outfit.

"Yes."

"She did mine, too."

Madame Neige must never have warmed up to Mildred, either. Otherwise she would never have put her in that gingham sack.

I took my place behind the table, sold a half-frozen lemon bar to a passing elf, and tossed the money in the tin change box.

"Has it been this uneventful all morning?"

She lifted her arms and let them drop—almost like a rag doll. "I arrived after the reindeer rush. Since then it's just been a trickle. Thank goodness for the heaters."

Amen to that.

Another five minutes went by with no one approaching our table. And when someone did, my stomach clenched: Chip. His face was florid, his eyes were bloodshot with an expression that made me wonder if he was going to start flipping over tables. His demeanor wasn't very different from that of the demented reindeer, to be honest.

Mildred forced a smile. "Hello, Mr. Pepperbough. Can we help you?"

He stopped, his lips turning into a sneer. It was the first time I'd seen him be openly unpleasant to anyone. For a moment I wondered if *he'd* gotten hold of a reindeer cookie. Something had brought out his inner Mr. Hyde.

"You!" he shouted at me.

It was tempting to look over my shoulder in hopes that what was happening wasn't really happening. "Hey, Chip. Would you like to buy a boo bar? Screamsicle cupcake?"

"I'd like you to leave me alone, you—you—witch!"

I laughed. "That's original."

"Do you know who you're talking to?" Mildred asked Chip. "You should watch your language!"

I came around from behind the table. I didn't want him to start shouting about Juniper in front of Mildred and whoever else happened to pass by. "It's okay, Mildred, I'll handle this."

I jerked my head toward a spot farther away from the sale table. "What's wrong with you?" I asked when we were out of Mildred's earshot.

"You told Juniper I was a murderer!"

"Not true." I crossed my arms. "I said you *might* be."

"You've never liked me, so you set out to turn her against me."

"You hired someone to have her followed. Why are you with her at all if you don't trust her?"

"I was trying to protect her! And I'm not with her at all now, thanks to you. You planted suspicions in her head and made her look at every action of mine in the worst light, just like you do."

She'd dumped him? It seemed too good to be true.

"You say you want to protect her," I pointed out, "but you really want to make sure she's not seeing anyone else. You didn't want her to have a life. You're a control freak."

For a moment he looked so explosive I thought he might spontaneously combust. Then there was a rumbling underneath us. Like an earthquake. I panicked for a moment before remembering I'd felt this sensation before: a reindeer race.

I frowned. Lucia usually warned us when they were having reindeer games in town.

The next second, a horde of reindeer charged down the street full tilt, sending pedestrians jumping like fleas out of their path. Chip and I ducked into a doorway just in time to avoid getting crushed.

"What's happening?" he asked, bewildered.

Mildred cried out. Looking back at the bake sale table, I saw her, yarn wig askew, holding on to one of the tent support poles while two reindeer fought over the crumbs on the plate. They started to lock horns.

I picked up my phone and speed-dialed the constabulary. "We have a reindeer situation at the Community Center," I said as soon as someone picked up.

It was Ollie who replied. "Not another one! It's happening all over town. What's going on?"

"No idea," I said, hanging up quickly. *Coward.*

I stood, but Chip practically yanked me down again. "Where are you going?"

He was trembling like a wet Chihuahua. Pathetic.

"Where do you think?" I said. "I'm going to rescue Mildred from the drunken reindeer."

Second lesson learned: Be very careful what you put in your reindeer cookies.

Chapter 22

You can call off your stakeout. Your client is in full freak-out mode because Juniper broke up with him.

Typing that last sentence into a text gave me less pleasure than I would have expected. I was glad Juniper had finally discovered how toxic Chip was, but whatever she was going through, she still wasn't in a mood to confide to me. I contemplated the real possibility that my meddling had caused a permanent rift between us.

As I made my way to the band shell by Peppermint Pond, the path was blocked by a reindeer lying in the snow. I dropped to my knees, leaning in to him to see if he was breathing. He was, and I assumed his temperature was close to normal for someone of the caribou persuasion. He appeared to have passed out, though. Those infernal cookies.

"Are you all right?" I asked. "Can you talk?"

His eyelids fluttered, but before he could respond, Lucia buzzed up the path on a snowmobile. She stopped, hopped off, and ran toward me. "Is that Quasar?"

"No . . ." Oh, no. My gut twisted. "Is Quasar missing?"

Her worried look told me all I needed to know. "I think he cadged some of your poisonous cookies from the kitchen this morning."

Word of my mistake was evidently out. I felt even worse. "I didn't know what I was doing."

"Obviously. Reindeer aren't used to sugar and alcohol. They can't metabolize it."

"I'm so sorry."

I'm not sure she heard my apology or cared. She examined the reindeer and stood up. "I'll call Constable Crinkles to come pick this one up." She pulled out her phone and started scrolling through her contacts.

"Is there anything I can do?"

"Sure. You can say no the next time someone asks you to bake anything." Her attention turned abruptly to the phone at her ear. "Hey, we've got a cookie casualty near the band shell. No, not Quasar. Vixen herd. Uh-huh . . ."

Speaking of the band shell, I needed to get over there. Lucia was still on the phone, so I pointed in that direction. She dismissed me with a wave.

I'd held out hope that Juniper would show up for the band concert, but she wasn't in the greenroom where we players put on our uniform jackets and hats and warmed up our instruments. I took off my cloak and shrugged on my jacket over my dress. The uniform jacket was black with orange braiding, to which I'd sewn many pockets in the lining to make it handy to reach the little noisemakers I used in songs like *The Addams Family* theme—bike horn, slide whistle, and ratchet. Wearing it, I felt like a one-woman percussion band. The matching hat was typical marching-band headgear—it looked like something a Napoleonic soldier would wear, only with an orange plume coming out the top. Escaping the cacophony of forty horns playing different warm-up notes, I wandered out to the bandstand to help Smudge set up the percussion equipment.

"Have you seen Juniper?" I asked.

He shook his head. "Maybe she's got too much going on at the library. I hear they're having a costume contest."

Of course. I sighed and made sure my cymbals were on the table in back of the glockenspiel. I considered telling Smudge the news about Chip but decided against it. I'd already butted in to Juniper's love life and I doubted she appreciated my interference even if she had broken off with Chip. Sending Smudge her way might not be met with gratitude.

A text came in on my phone. Jake's belated reply. **Waldo left his grandmother's and gave us the slip. Quince and I are searching.**

Waldo was on the move? Why now? I looked around at the crowd that had gathered on the rows of bench seats skirting out in front of the band shell. Spillover spectators stood at the edge of Peppermint Pond. Most people were just in caps and coats, although I spotted a few costumes here and there. Even a Frankenstein monster in the back row. A very short one—this Frankenstein was an elf. The green makeup and square head was very well done, though. And he wore a dull black boxy suit with a black knit shirt underneath, much like the one Boris Karloff wore in the movie.

Another text from Jake popped up: **If you see him, stop him.**

I'm on the bandstand, I replied. I snapped the phone's cover closed, annoyed. I should be out searching for Waldo, too.

"What's wrong?" Smudge said, alarmed. "Is it Juniper?"

I glanced at him uncomprehendingly as I tucked the phone back in my pocket. "No."

"That's good. Because you looked like someone was in danger."

Who was most endangered by a fugitive Waldo? Me, maybe. "I just heard something about Waldo, an elf who works at the castle."

His brows drew together. "Waldo Flurrybow? Old lady Flurrybow's grandson?"

I nodded.

"What's he done?" he asked.

"Nothing . . ." Nothing that I could talk about. "Do you know the family?"

He grinned. "Lots of people knew the Flurrybow house for a while, back when the old lady was selling her brownies. Gooood stuff!"

I'd had one of her brownies. It was good but it didn't seem *that* remarkable.

"She lives down the street from my boardinghouse. It's the kind of neighborhood where you sort of know everybody, but you really don't, if you catch my drift."

"Not exactly."

He shrugged. "Everybody goes to the same stores, schools, churches. The same lady who cleans for Mrs. Flurrybow cleans for my landlady. The kids all got jobs at the castle."

"Wait," I said. "Your landlady's kid works at the castle?"

"Yeah. You must know her. Cranberry."

Smudge knew Cranberry. Small world.

Of course it was a small world. It was Santaland.

"She was the one who told me her parents were renting out the room," he said.

"So . . . Pixie cleans house for Cranberry's family?"

"Not anymore. She quit."

"Did she do a good job?"

He looked confused for a moment. "I don't know. I guess. She just cleaned the common areas, not my room." His forehead puckered into a frown. "In fact, Cranberry's mom told me to keep my room locked on days when Pixie came around. I got the impression that she didn't trust her."

Did she think Pixie was a thief? "Yet she kept employing her?" That was weird.

Smudge shrugged. "Good help is hard to find. They're still scrambling to get someone new."

Luther's baton rapped against the conductor's stand to

bring us to attention, but my brain felt muzzy. I struggled through "In the Hall of the Mountain King," which sounded different. Puny, almost. I looked over to the low brass section. Juniper's chair was empty, but so was a chair in the middle of the trombones. Louie wasn't there. What did that mean?

His absence made me uneasy. I needed to alert Jake. But Jake was already chasing Waldo. And I was in the middle of a concert, even though I could hardly concentrate on music as details swam through my mind. Pixie. Cranberry. Waldo. Pixie and Louie.

A funicular accident . . . Tiny's death . . . Snow monsters. Nothing seemed to add up.

To applause, Tiffany took to the ice in her pumpkin outfit, and the band broke into "The Mephisto Waltz" by Franz Liszt. This number was light on percussion—Smudge was on timpani—so I allowed myself to be mesmerized by my sister-in-law's skill as she flashed across the ice. She'd lost nothing of the razzle-dazzle that had won her trophies as a competitive ice skater in her youth. Even in a pumpkin outfit, she could spin, twirl, and jump as if she were nothing but sinew and springs. But even as I admired all the spins and salchows, my mind felt preoccupied.

Was Pixie a kleptomaniac? That had to be why Cranberry's mother didn't trust her.

But why keep on a cleaner you didn't trust?

At the end of her routine, Tiffany pulled off a dangerous-looking back flip that brought the audience to its feet. She took off her pumpkin head for a bow and introduced her class of Tiny Gliders, which for this evening were called the Ghoulish Gliders. They came out wearing adorable little outfits that made them look like marionettes. That was our cue for the Alfred Hitchcock theme, "Funeral March of a Marionette."

Even when the distant whoops of drunken reindeer vied to distract the crowd, it was impossible not to watch the tiny elves snaking around the ice in figure eights. One pint-sized marionette seemed prone to skate in the wrong direction, but the audience was rapt.

A movement in the audience caught my eye. A parent late for the show, I assumed. When I looked out, though, I saw Quince, all in black, scanning the crowd. Looking for Waldo.

I gazed around the audience, but the individuals were a blur. The only standouts were the ones in costume. A Neldor, two snow monsters, the Frankenstein in the back row. I almost didn't see Frankenstein because he'd sunk low on the bench, his green face barely visible. Almost as if he were trying to hide . . .

I tried to zero in on that face. It wasn't the features beneath the makeup that gave him away, though. It was the quick glance he flicked at Quince before angling his body away.

I could see from the tension in Quince's stance that he hadn't yet spotted Waldo-Frankenstein. I wanted to wave my arms and point, but Quince wasn't looking at me, either. He turned to leave the area.

In frustration, I banged my triangle. My musical cue went unheeded by Quince.

Smudge glared at me. The conductor wasn't pleased, either.

"What's wrong with you?" Smudge hissed.

Quince was leaving. Waldo would get away.

If you see him, stop him, Jake had said.

I felt like a person seeing an accident in progress who's unable to do anything to stop it. I was on stage. Trapped. A performer had to remain on even when the scenery was falling down around her ears. That's what my high school drama teacher Ms. Wilkins taught us when we put on *Bye Bye Birdie* my junior year. What was true for high school dramatics surely went double for performing in a band, amateur or not.

I watched Quince head off in the direction of Walnut's Bootie World.

Raucous applause broke out at the end of the number when the tiny marionettes took their bows. It was time for "Danse Macabre." I reached for my eighteen-inch cymbals, looping the leather handle straps around my wrist. Smudge always warned that this wasn't the proper way to hold them— he also told me I was a wimp for not using his twenty-inch ones—but cymbals were heavy and I was always worried about dropping them.

While I took my place, I kept one eye on the audience. Waldostein was edging his way out of the back row, preparing to duck out and run in the opposite direction Quince had headed, no doubt. He would get away, right under my nose.

Luther raised his baton.

I glimpsed Waldostein headed in the direction of the buildings of downtown.

The show must go on, I told myself.

It must go on without me.

"Cover for me," I whispered to Smudge as the first notes of the piece began. I was trying to put down the cymbals, but the straps were tight around my wrists.

His face collapsed in disbelief. "What are you doing?"

"Catching a killer, I hope."

I gave up on the cymbals. If I put them down now it would be more distracting, anyway, so I just hurried off the bandstand with them. No telling what Luther—or the audience— thought when the second percussionist exited stage right at a gallop. I skirted my way around the crowd in the direction Waldo had taken. I wished I could text Jake, or Quince, but it was hard to run and text at the same time. Especially with seven pounds of copper alloy on each wrist.

My feet pumped to the rhythm of "Danse Macabre." My legs were longer than an elf's, but I wasn't as adept as the locals at running on perpetually slushy sidewalks. Even on wide, well-traveled Festival Boulevard, my heels skidded across a film of icy slurry. My gait was something like an accelerated mince, while Waldo was moving with surprising speed.

Where was he going? For a moment I was torn. Catch him or just follow him? *If you see him, stop him.* That's what Jake's text had advised. Who was I to argue with a professional?

Waldo zigged onto Sparkletoe Lane. I followed suit, but as I rounded the corner, the cymbal in my right hand hit the side of a stone building. The crash sounded deafening to my ears, and the vibration jolted my arm as if it were a tuning fork attached to my shoulder. Ahead, Waldo turned, eyes bugging in his green face.

After that, he stepped on the gas, short legs pumping like pistons. Slush or not, the bloodhound in me kicked in and I flat-out ran after him. Sparkletoe Lane was not as crowded as it would have been if there hadn't been a crowd down at Peppermint Pond, but we still had to be careful of ice patches, jack-o'-lanterns, and other decorations.

Ahead of me, Waldo jinked around jack-o'-lanterns and displays of scarecrows spilling out from Sparkletoe's Mercantile. I followed suit, irritated by his agility. What had happened to the nervous bumbler I'd known at the castle? Still, my longer legs served me well. I'd nearly caught up to him.

"Waldo, stop!" I yelled.

He didn't stop, but a floating ghost hanging from an awning let out a mechanized howl as he passed. Spooked, he turned, slipped, and crashed his skull right into my cymbal in my left hand. Another clang rang out, followed by a prolonged, reverberating *bong* when we both spilled to the ground.

Chapter 23

"I didn't mean to kill anybody."

Waldo trembled in his chair in the constabulary office. A bandage was wound around his head where his skull had hit the cymbal, and most of the green makeup had been wiped off his face. Doc Honeytree had sworn he was well enough to be interrogated.

Of course, an interrogation at the Christmastown Constabulary was not exactly an undertaking designed to make a suspect sweat, except from the heat created by Ollie's carrot cake baking in the oven. Instead of intimidating glare lights, there was a welcoming fire in the hearth. We all sat around a table draped with a clean cloth with a poinsettia design. Before each of us was a cup filled with our choice of tea, eggnog, or cocoa.

Yet the intensity in Jake's eyes was enough to jangle Waldo's nerves. "You didn't mean to. So you *did* kill Tiny," the detective said.

Waldo's denial was vehement. "Of course not. I never would have, no matter how much I—"

Reddening, he reached for his cocoa. He had to hold the mug in both trembling hands to bring it to his lips.

Guilt was written all over him. "But you tried to kill *me*," I said.

He ducked his head. "No."

"Cranberry retracted her statement backing you up. You no longer have an alibi."

His face sank into a dumbfounded expression. "She couldn't have."

"Why, because you were blackmailing her?" I asked. "She told us about the raspberries, too."

"Raspberries?" Waldo clearly had no idea what I was talking about.

I'd thought Cranberry's stolen fruit story had a made-up quality.

"What hold did you have over her?"

"That's not my secret to tell."

"Just to twist someone's arm with," Jake said.

Waldo's mouth remained stubbornly closed.

"Son," Crinkles said kindly, "this is a murder inquiry. At some point you need to start coughing up what you know."

"I shouldn't have known anything about Cranberry." Clearly anguished, he buried his head in his hands. "I wish I never had known anything."

Frustration roiled through me. "Known what?"

"You might as well spit it out," Crinkles said. "The truth's going to come out eventually, but this unpleasantness can end now."

Hardened criminals would have laughed at the mild unpleasantness, but Waldo looked into all our faces and took the constable's words to heart. "I knew about Cranberry's family. Her brothers are longtime employees at the Candy Cane Factory. For all I know, they're good workers! But I learned that for a while they were stealing candy canes from the strategic reserve and selling them."

I was shocked, not by the severity of the crime so much as the weirdness of it. "There's a black market for candy canes?"

They all gaped at me. "For the best candy canes in the whole world?" Crinkles asked. "You bet."

"They don't do it anymore," Waldo said, "but Tiny said it didn't matter because they'd get in trouble just the same."

Tiny.

"So it was Tiny who was blackmailing Cranberry?"

Waldo looked deflated. "No, it was me. Tiny told me to do it. He made me do all of it."

"All of what?" I asked.

His lip quivered. "I sawed into the cable on the funicular. Tiny told me how much to cut so that the car would make it partway up the mountain, and exactly when to do it so no one would see me. But I didn't know why! I thought maybe he just wanted to embarrass the city government—make it seem inefficient so he could complain about it. He was always going on about how incompetent people were. And he was so mad about all the Halloween preparations—he believed they were a waste of money, on top of all the other reasons he hated the new holiday. I just assumed that messing with the funicular and creating chaos would give him ammunition. I had no idea what he intended, I swear."

"But you saw me walking toward the funicular that evening. You must have known that I was about to get on it."

He rubbed reddened eyes. "I know I should have warned you, but I panicked. I ran to tell Tiny, but he just laughed. Laughed! After the funicular disaster, I told him I wouldn't have anything more to do with his evil schemes. I meant it, too."

"Why did you have anything to do with them to begin with?" I asked.

He stared in stubborn silence at the carrot cake Ollie had put on the table.

I tried to piece it together. Tiny had found out something about Cranberry's family and had used it to give Waldo, his creature, an alibi. He must have known something about Waldo. Or . . .

"It was about your grandmother," I guessed. "He found out about her."

Shock flashed in Waldo's eyes. "You knew already? You mean I could have spared myself all this?"

The others were staring at me as they expected me to announce what Mrs. Flurrybow's blackmail-worthy misdeeds were, when in truth I'd just been taking a shot in the dark. Since it was a successful shot, though, I hesitated to let on that I had no idea what I was talking about. "You can tell them, Waldo. I'm sure your grandmother was just trying to get by. It was probably mostly for you that she did it."

When he nodded, tears spilled down his cheeks. "I told her she was taking a big risk, but she wanted me to have the place at the castle, and I needed enough money to pay for my livery. That's the *only* time Granny did it—and it was only for a month. Maybe two."

The slack-jawed stares of the others made it clear that they were imagining all sorts of vice. But, remembering what Smudge had told me, I said, "The best brownies in Santaland." Mrs. Flurrybow must have been lacing them with happy juice.

Waldo shuddered in shame. "I told her to stop, and she did. And that was the end of it, I swear. No harm was done! But of course Tiny knew. When he asked me to spy on what was going on in the castle, that's how he made me do it."

"Did he make you pose as Pumpkin Slayer?" I asked

He blinked. "What?"

"On Elfbook," I prompted him. "The threatening messages and the library break-in."

"That wasn't me."

Given that he'd just confessed to what amounted to attempted murder—of me—I was inclined to believe him when he denied mere vandalism.

Tiny must have been Pumpkin Slayer all on his own. Which made sense, since the Pumpkin Slayer messages ended when Tiny died.

"I don't know if you realize this," Jake told Waldo, "but you're making a good case for why you would have wanted to kill Tiny."

"I didn't! I would never hurt anyone!" Waldo sent me an apologetic glance. "Purposefully, I mean."

"I know," I said.

Waldo's faults were weakness and fear. But he wasn't vicious.

"*I* don't." Crinkles puffed up. "I'm hearing about all sorts of terrible things, and we only have his word for it that it was Tiny pulling all the strings. Very convenient to have the man you murdered to blame your crimes on."

"I didn't murder him! It was a snow monster!" Waldo's face fell. "Wasn't it?"

"How did Tiny find out secrets about your grandmother and Cranberry's family?" Jake wondered aloud.

"I don't know." Waldo sagged in exhaustion. "I just don't know."

"I do," I said.

I remembered how people in town had seemed relieved Tiny was gone. I'd thought it was strange and callous of them at the time, but now it made sense . . . if he'd been blackmailing them all. And how could he have done that? Because he had the perfect way to get into their houses and learn their secrets, through his wife. Smudge had told me his landlady, Cranberry's mother, hadn't trusted Pixie but had kept her on as a housecleaner. That made sense to me now, too. She hadn't dared fire her.

"Pixie cleaned the houses of half the elves in town," I

explained, "and she kept her ears and eyes open. Tiny found out everyone's secrets through her. Then he leveraged those secrets for money and favors."

No telling what she and Tiny had found out about everyone. Maybe dozens of stories, no doubt many of them more sordid than the tale of Mrs. Flurrybow's brief career as a magic brownie dealer.

"A blackmail ring!" Crinkles said. "That's monstrous."

Jake also looked horrified, but for a different reason. "It also means half the elves in town probably wanted him dead." His investigation had just ballooned from a few suspects to an entire town.

"You don't need to question them all, though," I said, "or even more than one if you start with Pixie."

"How could that little mite of a thing kill Tiny?" Crinkles said.

"Never mind fool us all into thinking it was a snow monster!" Ollie added.

The set of Jake's lips told me all I needed to know of his opinion of how hard it was to fool the Christmastown Constabulary.

I thought of all the years Louie had spent hunched over his bench, taking orders from Tiny. Probably resenting Tiny more with each passing day. "She had the help of someone who knew more about making footprint patterns than anyone in town—Louie."

When that sank in, Crinkles was more dubious than before. "The cobbler? He wouldn't swat a fly. He certainly wouldn't have the nerve to kill anyone."

I leaned back in my chair. "He had nerve enough to carry on a clandestine affair with his boss's wife." The lawmen looked astounded at this news. "He and Pixie were seen together just this morning, playing footsie under the table at Merry Muffins."

"Maybe their legs just bumped," Ollie said. "Those tables in there are awfully small."

Crinkles scratched his chin. "It doesn't mean they were having an affair before what happened to Tiny. Maybe it only just got started?"

I'd wondered that, too, but now I remembered one detail that damned them both. "Pixie's alibi for the night Tiny was killed was that she had stayed at her sister Rosemary's. But when I was talking to Rosemary, she said she hadn't been able to sleep because a vehicle with a backfire had driven down her street several times during the night. Louie's snowmobile has a backfiring tailpipe. I heard it just a few hours ago."

"He could have picked Pixie up while the rest of the house was asleep," Jake said.

"And brought her back after they'd killed Tiny." Which meant Pixie had given an Oscar-worthy portrayal of shock and grief the next day. She'd even thought to point the finger at me—it hadn't stuck, but it had seemed so like something a hysterical person would be inclined to do that I hadn't thought to wonder if she was lying.

For the first time since being taken into custody, Waldo brightened. "Then you don't think I did it? I'm a free elf?"

"Not so fast," Crinkles said. "You admitted to sabotaging the funicular. You're going to sit tight right here until we get this all untangled." He glanced at his watch. "Which we need to do soon. I'm due at Peppermint Pond for the raffle draw and announcement at six o'clock."

"Too bad for you we don't have the new wallpaper yet," Ollie told Waldo as he led him away to the constabulary's cell.

The rest of us made our way over to Sparkletoe's Bootery. In front of stoops and doorways, the jack-o'-lanterns were all lit, and displays of ghosts, witches, and reindeer with deformed horns took up part of the sidewalks. Smoke was in the air, which alarmed me until Jake pointed out the bonfire that

had been lit close to the pond, where the band was now playing "The Sorcerer's Apprentice."

We stopped our vehicles not far from the Bootery, and as
we walked past the plate-glass window I caught a glimpse of
Louie and Pixie together on his workbench. They'd separated
by the time we were inside the store, though. His head was
bent over his work and she was leaning against the counter near
the old manual cash register with an exaggerated casualness.

"How can we help you?" Pixie asked, as if she weren't
at all worried to see the constable, a private investigator,
and Mrs. Claus in a worse-for-wear band uniform coming
through her door.

I did catch a hint of alarm in Louie's eyes before he flicked
his glance away from us, though.

"We've come to talk to you about Tiny's death," Crinkles
said. "We know who did it."

Her slow blink betrayed nothing. "Do you have the au-
thority to arrest snow monsters, Constable?"

"No snow monster killed Tiny," I said. "You know that
better than anyone."

She stiffened. "What are you talking about?"

"The oldest story in the book, ma'am," Jake said, not un-
kindly. "A woman and a man fall in love and want to be
together. Only trouble is, one of them's already married. So
someone has to be gotten rid of."

"A monster killed Tiny," she insisted. "There was a footprint."

"That was maybe your biggest mistake," Jake said. "Hard
for a snow monster to walk across a property and only leave a
single print, however much snow falls afterward. It alerted me
right away that something was amiss."

"Why would I want to kill my husband?" she asked. "I
was lucky to have been his wife. It was a Cinderella story,
remember?"

"But you were a Cinderella whose prince kept her working at the scullery," I said. "Tiny was using you, wasn't he? You found out things about people through your work, and then he blackmailed them."

Her eyes hardened, and I could see the struggle between wanting to acknowledge what a vile jerk her husband was and not wanting to admit her own guilt.

"I would have hated him, too," I said.

"You don't know anything about me," she snapped. "Mrs. La-Dee-Da Claus living up in your castle. What do *you* know about drudgery? Or about finding out that your dream marriage is nothing but a mirage? That instead of landing on Easy Street, you'd become just another way for Tiny Sparkletoe to line his pockets. *Everything* was business to him, including me."

"Many people seemed happy that he was gone," I said.

"Then why didn't *they* kill him?" she said in frustration. "Why did they leave it to m—?"

"Don't listen to her!" Louie jumped up from his bench. "She didn't kill Tiny. I did."

He had our attention now.

"How?" Jake asked.

Louie's Adam's apple bobbed in his throat. "I clunked him on the head with a length of pipe. And then I used a big piece of cardboard to tamp down the earth underneath and around him. I knew a snow monster print would cause a lot of talk and take the pressure off a search for the real culprit." His shoulders sagged. "But I guess I also knew that the law would catch up to me eventually."

Crinkles rocked back on his heels. "We always do."

"There's only one problem," Pixie said. "Louie's lying. He's just repeating what I told him about how I did it."

"Sweetie, please," Louie said. "Let me do this."

"No, you let *me*." Her eyes shone with tears. "I'm not going to see you exiled to the Farthest Frozen Reaches."

He stood and crossed to her, taking her hand. "I don't care if they send me to the Farthest Frozen Reaches for the rest of my life, as long as I know you love me."

"I won't let them take you from me. Not now that we finally have each other. They'll have to exile both of us."

I glanced at Crinkles, whose eyes were filling up. He'd become so mesmerized by the Romeo and Juliet scene playing out before him that he'd forgotten he was here as a lawman.

Jake cleared his throat to goose him back to reality. "Constable?"

"Right!" Crinkles wiped his eyes, chins jiggling. "Pixie Sparkletoe, Louie Terntree, I arr—"

CRACK!

A sound as loud and bone-jarring as a sequoia snapping in two made us all jump. We traded alarmed stares, until screams brought us to the door. Out in the street, a wave of elves was running up Sparkletoe Lane from Festival Boulevard. The ones whose faces I could make out had terror in their eyes.

"What's happening?" Crinkles called after them as they stampeded past.

One of the elves skidded to a stop just long enough to catch his breath and point behind him, practically hopping in fear. "Ermlau the Abominable is here! He knocked over the sled slide by the orphanage, and now he's going to squish us all!" The elf grabbed his hat and fled after the others.

"Holy doodle!" Crinkles exclaimed, poised to plunge into the panicked swarm.

Jake grabbed him by the collar.

I was in shock. "Why is Ermlau the Abominable attacking Christmastown?"

"The bonfire probably set them off." Jake shook his head. "The noise probably didn't help, either. Most likely they assumed Santaland was working itself up for an invasion to avenge Tiny's death."

"But we've found out who really killed Tiny."

"The snow monsters don't know that."

"How could this have happened?" Crinkles wondered aloud. "What happened to our safeguards? Where's the Vigilance Committee?"

I knew where they were, and my heart sank at the thought. "They're doing training maneuvers in Wonderland Valley."

And the reindeer who would naturally be alert to the presence of the monsters were distracted because so many in their herds were geeked up on my cookies.

I was unable to keep the rising panic out of my voice. "We have to let Ermlau know it's been a big misunderstanding. Quick, before he flattens the entire town."

Jake looked as cool as ever, though one of his eyebrows arched. "Have you ever tried to reason with an angry snow monster?"

I swallowed past the dry lump in my throat. "Difficult?"

"Like teaching civics to Godzilla," he said.

Chapter 24

They say heroes are people who run toward danger when everyone else is running away. I would add that sometimes people running into danger are simply too harebrained to know better. That was certainly the case as I fought my way to Festival Boulevard against the fleeing horde. If I'd truly known what I was running toward, I might have turned tail and joined the stampede.

The town that had struck me as festive and friendly a half hour before had now taken on a nightmarish aspect. The mad dash of terrified elves fleeing for their lives was a large part of that. Lights within the jack-o'-lanterns flickered uneasily as everyone raced past. Trebuchet arms jutted above the buildings. Even the piles of snow cannonballs brought hysterical laughter to my gorge. *Snowballs? Seriously?* It was like arming yourself with peashooters to fight off a polar bear.

If a creature could smash the giant slide I'd sledded down with Quince, it would be able to snap our trebuchets like toothpicks.

We jumped on Jake's snowmobile and rode toward a sound that was like the angry bellow of a raspy elephant. It was followed by another terrifying crunch. I winced, wondering what had been destroyed this time.

While Jake drove, I texted Nick. **Town under attack by snow monster. On my way to talk to Ermlau the Abominable.**

Usually Nick was too busy to answer my texts right away, but this one produced an immediate reply. **Please tell me you're joking.**

Not joking. Any advice?

Run.

That last message jangled my nerves. **I love you**, I texted back, adding a heart emoji. Then another one for good measure. Then I snapped closed my phone.

Within seconds it vibrated in my pocket. I opened it, expecting Nick to tell me not to be foolhardy. Or just to say that he loved me, too, but this message wasn't from Nick at all. It was from Juniper. **I'm trapped, hiding inside the library. Help!**

Poor Juniper. Maybe she didn't know everyone was in the same boat. I messaged back. **Hunker down. We're on it.**

I was so distracted by my phone, I didn't see what was ahead until Jake braked suddenly, slamming me forward. I managed not to hit the windscreen by bracing my hands forward. When the snowmobile bucked to a stop, I looked up.

And up.

Imagine a great ape about the size of a two-story building, with gray-tipped white fur all over except for its chest and leathery face, which seemed, from my angle, to consist of sharp, pointy teeth. Its mouth was incredibly wide, and it gaped open in a terrifying rictus grin even when it was glaring down at us and letting out huffing grumbles. His King Kong paws—big enough to squish a person like Play-Doh in his fist—swiped at the bothersome lights that were swagged between lampposts across the boulevard.

"Let me handle this," Jake said.

I gulped and nodded, not about to argue. I was too terrified to speak.

He hopped off the snowmobile and approached the monster, waving his arms. Jake was taller than me, but next to Ermlau he still came only midway up the giant's furry calf.

"Ermlau!" he called up to the beast. "Stop! The guilty one has been found."

Ermlau's fist, which had been about to take a swipe at the Cornucopia's chimney, froze. He blinked down at Jake and then let out a roar that was accompanied by a hurricane-force blast of halitosis. I tried not to gag—I didn't want to be rude to a creature who could crush me like a bug—but I'm not sure how successful I was in hiding my reaction.

"Does Ermlau speak English?" I asked.

"I'm not sure," he said. "Some do, but when we talked before, we had an interpreter."

Just our luck that the snow monsters sent a non-bilingual abominable to attack us.

"Ermlau!" Jake repeated. "The murderer has been found! Christmastown holds no grudge against the snow monsters."

I was so busy trying to read Ermlau's inscrutable expression that I didn't see at first what was going on behind him. When I did, my heart sank. Ollie and Crinkles had taken control of a trebuchet and were wheeling it into position. It took two of them to load a snowball cannon into the arm of the giant slingshot, and then both of them pulled back the arm, which began to creak from the building tension.

Ermlau the Abominable heard the sound and let out a roar. I braced for the fetid gust. It would take a container ship of Tic Tacs to mask that breath.

Jake peered around the snow monster's furry legs to see what Crinkles and Ollie were up to. "No! Don't!" he called out.

And small wonder. The trebuchet was going to sling a giant snowball at the back of Ermlau's head. I doubted that would go over well.

I also started yelling at them to hold fire. Unfortunately,

our actions only served to agitate Ermlau, who seemed to think we were egging on the constable. The snow monster hopped to one side as the trebuchet flung its ammunition, which sailed through the air past Ermlau and hit the street next to Jake. The pebbles inside the giant snowball unleashed a pellet spray in all directions. I dived under the snowmobile for cover, but Jake, caught in the barrage, was thrown to the ground. I scuttled toward him on my hands and knees. He was out cold, but still breathing.

The snow-covered pavement was shaking from Ermlau's angry stomping. In obvious retaliation against the snowball attack, he leaned down and scooped up a handful of pumpkins from the display in front of the grocery. They looked laughably small in his hands, like orange marbles. But when, one by one, he started hurling them, they proved to be effective weapons. Ollie and Crinkles dived to hide beneath the beams of the trebuchet just as pumpkins hit the ground and splattered around them. If you think a pumpkin is a laughable tool of war, wait till one is lobbed at you like a missile. It's terrifying. Soon the street was littered in pumpkin flesh and seeds. I dragged Jake back toward the sled, dodging a fusillade of exploding gourd.

I should have listened to Nick. In retrospect, running really had been the best option. Even Jake had warned that reasoning with snow monsters wouldn't work, though he'd given it a try. Now it was my turn to try to calm him down. Who else was there? I didn't kid myself that my attempt at a parlay would be any more successful than Jake's had been. But how else could we get through to Ermlau before he destroyed the entire town?

What soothed the savage beast? There was a quote about that. Or maybe it was something that soothed the savage *breast.* Something like . . .

Music!

Of course. If I'd had a boom box, that would have been dandy. Maybe a little Mozart could have calmed Ermlau down. I was still wearing my band jacket over my witch dress, but the only instrument I had on me that was capable of playing melody was my slide whistle. I might not have resorted to using it had I not seen Ermlau pick up the trebuchet by the arm and break it like a twig. He raised it above his head like a club and was about to bring it crashing down on Ollie and Crinkles.

"Ermlau!" I shouted. I ran forward, pulling out my slide whistle.

The giant beast pivoted toward me, club lifted to swing. I raised the slide whistle to my lips with shaking hands. I barely had the presence of mind to take a breath, never mind to give any thought about what to play. I just tried the first thing that came to mind: the *Addams Family* theme.

The tune came out shakily from the cheap slide whistle and my finger snaps were muted by my gloves, but the distraction was enough to stay Ermlau's hand. Grumbling, he tilted his head and looked down at me as if I were a performing flea. Tog poked his head out of the Cornucopia's front entrance. I did a double take. I'd never seen an elf dressed as Dracula before. He must have been dressed for Bella Sparkletoe's party.

"What are you doing?" he asked in an urgent voice.

I took the whistle away from my lips only long enough to reply in a stage whisper, "Soothing him! Sing!"

With frightened eyes, the grocer croaked out an unsteady chorus. Thank goodness for *Spooktacular Hits*. The people huddled in doorways of nearby buildings knew the words better than I did. Ollie and Crinkles even joined in, along with a few other merchants. I could even hear Gert's throaty croak.

I braced my nerves and looked up to see what kind of reaction we were getting. Ermlau still had the trebuchet arm lifted, but his head was cocked curiously. His big eyes blinked in confusion. In the next moment, though, a strange kind of grunting emanated from him. Was he singing?

I motioned Ollie, Crinkles, and the others to repeat, and they got louder.

Just as I was wondering how long we could keep this up, the sound of jingle bells reached me. Not the song "Jingle Bells," but the real thing. Their familiar timbre made my heart race. A sleigh pulled by eight reindeer circled overhead. To Ermlau's astonishment, the sleigh skimmed just past him and landed on the street. I felt like crying when I saw the whites of the reindeer's eyes. They were frightened but remained steady and stopped on Nick's command.

Still in his Santa camouflage, Nick stepped down from the sleigh. He looked over at me, his eyes narrowing in concern when he noticed Jake lying on the ground. I sent him an encouraging smile, although I didn't know what he would be able to do that Jake couldn't. I almost wished he hadn't come. The monster could kill us all.

And then I remembered that hand grenade I'd seen in Nick's office, and I was seized by a moment of panic. Nick wasn't carrying a rifle or a crossbow, but did he have some hidden weapon that he was going to use? I would rather sit here slide-whistling all day than have all-out war.

Nick stopped just a few feet from me and looked directly up at Ermlau. Then he opened his mouth and said something utterly incomprehensible. It was a hideous sound—loud and guttural. My jaw dropped. Was he possessed or was he purposefully provoking the beast towering over us?

When Ermlau blasted right back at him, I understood what was happening. Nick did have a secret weapon: He knew Ermlau's language. Their incomprehensible dialogue astonished me. Though Nick's voice lacked the belching pachyderm quality of Ermlau's, he clearly was able to communicate.

Damn. You think you know someone, and then they start speaking snow monster.

Maybe we wouldn't die, after all.

"Tell him that we realize that no snow monsters were involved in Tiny's murder," I prompted. "Tell him that we've already caught the killers."

Nick's brows went up. "Who?"

I'd forgotten this would be news to him. "Pixie and Louie."

His face looked pained for a moment, but he nodded and proceeded to grunt and growl up at Ermlau, who rasped and huffed something in return.

"What's he saying?" Crinkles called out.

Nick said, "He wants to know if the snow monsters could roast the guilty party over a spit at their next solstice celebration."

I shuddered. "I hope you're going to tell him no."

"You don't say no to an abominable," Nick said. "You negotiate."

He and Ermlau continued to speak for longer than I would have thought possible. The snow monster kept gesticulating at the ground around us, and at one point lifted his furry, sharp clawed fingers to his mouth and sucked on them. I feared the negotiations weren't going well for Pixie and Louie.

"What's going on?" I asked.

Nick shushed me with an impatient wave of his hand. I tried not to take offense. It couldn't be easy talking to a creature ten times your size, especially not one with breath strong enough to peel paint. Especially not when you were the only thing standing between the monster and the total annihilation of your town.

The next ten minutes felt like ten years, but finally Ermlau grunted and turned to leave. Ollie and Crinkles scrambled out of their hiding place beneath the trebuchet, which was in the monster's path. But Ermlau sidestepped it and moved northward on Festival Boulevard with a heavy, shuffling gait. Each footfall shook the earth and my nerves.

We watched until the monster was out of sight. Slowly, the residents who'd been cowering in nearby buildings emerged from their hiding places, too spent from nerves to rejoice that the danger was past. The ground around us was thick with broken strings of lights, snowball cannon pellets, and pumpkin detritus.

"Is it really okay?" I asked Nick. Would Pixie and Louie avoid being roasted, I meant. God knows they deserved some kind of punishment, but becoming snow monster dinner fit the bill of cruel and unusual in my book.

Nick looked almost satisfied with himself. "We're getting off easy."

"What do the snow monsters want?" I asked.

"Our pumpkins."

At first I wasn't sure I'd understood. "Pumpkins?"

"Ermlau got a taste of them after he threw a few around. We have to deliver all our pumpkins, even the shells of the ones used as jack-o'-lanterns, to the Farthest Frozen Reaches after Halloween is over."

Tears of relief welled in my eyes. I put my arms around Nick and felt his welcome warmth against me. "You're a hero."

He smiled down at me. "Nice wart, by the way."

I laughed.

A groan nearby distracted me. "Jake!" I'd almost forgotten him. Leaving Nick to speak to a group of merchant elves, I hurried over to check on the detective. "Are you okay?"

He lifted himself up to sitting, rubbing his head. "I feel like someone clunked me on the skull with a rock. What happened?"

"You were struck by snow cannon shrapnel." I indicated

the other end of the street, where the remnants of the trebuchet stood. "Friendly fire from Crinkles and Ollie."

He nodded, then winced at the pain that movement
caused. "I remember now. Is everything okay?"

"Nick negotiated a settlement with Ermlau. I didn't even
know he spoke snow monster." I told him about the pumpkin
agreement. "Isn't that wonderful?"

"Great." He sounded less than enthusiastic, but there was
respect in his eyes as he watched Nick speaking to the town
elves who had gathered around. A bonus was that the snow
monsters were going to save the town from having to figure
out what to do with hundreds of rotting pumpkins.

While Nick finished talking to the townspeople and Jake
tried out his legs, I sidled over to Constable Crinkles. "Are
you going to announce that you've discovered Tiny's killer?"

His eyes bugged. "Golly wiggles! I forgot about those
two." He nudged his nephew toward their snowmobiles. "We
better go find them. Not that it gives me any pleasure arrest-
ing them. Louie was always a nice fellow."

"He killed his boss," I reminded him.

"It's too bad," Crinkles grumbled as he and his deputy
walked away. "All we have left now is Walnut's Bootie World.
They're just not the same quality."

"I guess my work here is done," Jake said as we watched
them go. "Not sure I accomplished much."

"*Au contraire.* We found out who killed Tiny. You realized
your second client was demented. And if you'll think about it,
you also found a solution to your own problem."

"I wasn't aware I had a problem."

"Of course you do. You're overworked. You should definitely have an assistant."

"Don't tell me you want to be a detective."

"Not me—Quince." I overrode his objections before he
could voice them. "Just give him a chance. He'll be a natural,

and think what a wonderful thing you'll be doing. You'll be keeping him out of the constabulary's visiting quarters. Besides, you've just had a bump on the head. You'll need to take it easy for a few days."

"That kid won't go anywhere without that snowman," he grumbled.

"So you'll get two assistants for the price of one." I was racking my brains to think of all the useful tasks Pocket could perform for him when my phone pinged. It was Juniper.

He's pounding on the door now.

I frowned. **Who?** I thought she'd been hiding from Ermlau the Abominable.

Chip!

"Oh, no." I turned to look at Nick, who was still answering the questions of the Christmastowners. "I've got to get to the library," I told Jake. "Juniper's barricaded herself in against Chip."

"I'll take you." After two steps toward the snowmobile, though, he staggered to a stop, clearly dizzy.

"You need to see Doc Honeytree."

"I'm fine," he insisted, but after two more steps he handed me his keys. "Take my snowmobile. And be careful."

"I just need to pick up Juniper. I'll be right back."

Famous last words.

Chapter 25

The gothic outlines of the library looked sinister silhouetted against the night sky. I'd stared at the library plaza for nearly an hour the day before, but it hadn't struck me until now how isolated it was from all the other buildings around it. Of course, I'd never approached the library knowing that my friend was trapped inside.

Juniper had turned off all the inside lights, but with all the streetlights blazing, it was impossible to miss Chip standing in front of the building.

"I know you're in there!" he hollered up at a second-story window. I couldn't spy Juniper there, but his gravelly voice made me suspect he'd been standing here all night yelling at each individual window.

I'd intended to sneak around back, but Chip spotted me driving by. If Nick could stand up to a snow monster, I decided, I could confront Chip Pepperbough.

"What are *you* doing here?" he asked as I walked up.

"I'm here to pick up Juniper. You need to leave."

He tossed his head back in indignation as he glared up at me. "This is public property. I have a right to be here."

"If Juniper wanted to speak to you, she wouldn't have locked herself in the library."

"You turned her against me."

"You did that by spying on her." How often would he have to hear that before it sank into his thick skull?

"I was just trying to look after her."

I rolled my eyes.

"The library was getting threats," he said, getting in my face. "You saw them yourself."

"Please, everyone knows who those threats were from." All right, *everyone* was exaggerating a wee bit, but I didn't want him to know that so far only I had figured this out. "Tiny might have written the original message on the Elf-book page, but *you* were the one who broke into the library, weren't you?"

His jaw dropped. "Me?"

"Pumpkin Slayer gave you the idea. The next threat the library received was anonymous, and then someone broke in and tore up construction-paper pumpkins. That was you."

"Very inventive," he sneered. "I only read stories, you make them up!"

"No. Tiny was Pumpkin Slayer, Chip. But when the library was broken into, Tiny was already lying dead in the snow. *You* broke into the library."

His mouth opened, then closed.

"You broke in to make Juniper feel her safety was threatened—and there you were, her protector. Like the arsonist who shows up to put out the fire."

"You can't prove that," he said.

"I don't need to. What you're doing right now is proof enough that you've crossed a line. You need to leave now before you bring serious trouble down on yourself."

"You're not the law! Clauses don't control everything in this country. Only Constable Crinkles has the right to arrest people."

"Fine. Juniper's not going to come out while you're standing here, so you might as well leave before we do call Constable Crinkles."

"I know how to make her come out."

I give Chip credit for one thing—he was quick as a snake. The jerk grabbed my wrist with one hand, stepped behind me, and twisted my arm between us. In the next moment, metal flashed and something poked into my side approximately where my appendix had once been. My mouth went dry. Thank goodness Chip was too short to slash my throat, but I assumed there were other things in the vicinity of my missing appendix that I didn't want sliced open.

"Come out, Juniper!" Chip yelled. "I have your friend!"

Did I mention that the library was isolated? I looked around for help, but there were mostly businesses surrounding the plaza. Most residents nearby had probably gone to the festival—and then scattered to the winds when Ermlau began his rampage.

Above, in the library's second story, a window slid open. I could just make out my friend's features. "Chip? Are you crazy? What are you doing?"

"If you don't come down and talk to me, I will slide this knife into your friend."

Much as I wanted rescue, I didn't like the odds for either of us if Juniper followed Chip's instructions. "Call Constable Crinkles!" I yelled. "Better yet, call Nick!"

The grip around my wrist tightened. "Do either and I will kill her."

Juniper's shaky voice answered, "It's all right, Chip. I'm coming down. Stay calm."

Stay calm? The man had gone feral. But I supposed "Don't get any crazier" wouldn't have been a helpful thing to say at this juncture.

Juniper shut the window, and time slowed to a crawl. I had to do something, or my friend might soon be in the same position that I was in now . . . assuming that Chip was actually going to let me go. For all I knew, once Juniper came out that door, he'd plunge the knife in me anyway. The thought made me woozy. Sliced up by a demented elf was not the way I wanted to go. My ears started ringing.

Or maybe I *heard* ringing.

I did.

I looked off in the distance. "What's that?"

Behind me, Chip tensed. "What?"

"I hear bells. It's probably Nick."

He listened for a moment—the ringing had faded—then let out a disgusted breath. "Nice try. Do you think I'm some stupid kid that you can distract so easily?" He jabbed the knife into my side so that I felt the sharp point through my band jacket, which I was still wearing. Maybe if I was lucky, Chip would only stab me in the kazoo. At the thought, a nervous laugh bubbled out of me.

"You think this is funny?" Chip asked.

I tried to swallow. "No." Nervous sweat made me feel clammy. And colder.

But I kept hearing those bells. Faint, then closer, then farther away again. Maybe it was just wishful thinking on my part, but . . .

I tilted my head. "You don't hear that?"

"No."

"Hear what?" Juniper asked from the library door. In spite of everything, the sight of her made me smile. She was in some sort of costume. Her hair had been braided into one long plait that went over her shoulder. A tiara perched on her head, and she wore a medieval-looking dress belted with a rope. It wasn't until she turned slightly that I noticed a hump. She was Lucasta, the hunchback princess.

Her eyes were huge as she took in the glint of the knife poking into my side. She didn't seem in any hurry to get closer to Chip, and I didn't blame her.

I shook my head at her, trying to convey a silent message. *Stay where you are,* I mouthed.

"You really don't hear bells?" I asked.

"What bells?" Juniper said.

Chip clucked in annoyance. "There are *no bells.* April's just trying to fake me out. It's the oldest trick in the book."

"I'm not a liar," I said.

"She's not, Chip."

"Don't defend her! She's not your friend. She broke us up!"

I couldn't help snorting. "Right. Why would I ever have done that?"

"Shut up!"

Juniper gasped. "Watch your tone. That's Mrs. Claus you're talking about."

"So what! I'm sick of bowing down to Clauses. They're not so special."

Maybe we weren't special, but I was beginning to wonder if I possessed extra-sensitive auditory perception. "You seriously don't hear anything?" I asked them both.

"No!" Chip yelled.

"I do." Juniper peered up at the sky. "It's coming from above us."

A bell. A sleigh bell? My heart jumped. Nick! Could he really be coming to rescue us? But his sleigh was drawn by eight reindeer, and they made much more noise than the anemic tinkling I was hearing now.

"Look!" Juniper pointed over the buildings opposite.

Chip tightened his grip. "Now it's both of you. I'm not falling for it."

Juniper wasn't bluffing, though. It took me a moment to make out what was up in the sky until it grew larger. An irregularly blinking red light swooped and swayed in the air just over the buildings opposite—and then began to dive right toward us. "Oh, crap!"

Juniper gasped. "April, duck!"

At the urgency in her voice, Chip was finally distracted enough to let up on his grip for a split second. It was all I needed. I hit the ground and rolled as far away as I could. Chip, taken by surprise, was too stunned to react in time.

Quasar, who'd been veering unsteadily up in the clouds on a cookie high, chose the expansive library plaza as a landing strip. In his inebriated state, he didn't see Chip until it was too late. At the last second he swerved, but he still managed to wing the elf during his landing. Chip went flying, and so did the knife. I grabbed the weapon. Juniper and I then ran to make sure Quasar was okay.

He was standing on his own four hooves but weaving unsteadily. He must have had a whole cache of those cookies.

"Is this the c-castle?" he asked.

"No, it's the library."

He looked depressed. "I-I keep trying to get home. Lucia'll be worried."

She would be apoplectic, and if I knew Lucia, she would have been tracking Quasar through the sky.

Sure enough, within moments I heard a snowmobile buzzing up the street. She got out and dashed toward us. "What's going on?"

"Quasar saved my life." I hugged him around his neck. I'd never loved this fizzle-nosed, slightly malodorous animal as much as I did at that moment.

"Maybe both our lives," Juniper said.

Quasar's nose blazed uncertainly. "I did?"

Juniper gestured over to Chip's prone form. "He was trying to kill April."

Both Quasar and Lucia looked astounded and confused in equal measure.

"Is that Chip Pepperbough, the optician?" she asked. "What happened to him?"

"Quasar landed on him."

"I didn't mean to," the reindeer said.

"You're a hero," I told him.

As Juniper and I tried to explain it all to them more slowly, Nick's sleigh pulled up in front of the library. He jumped out and ran to me. "Are you all right?"

Now that it was all over, I felt shaky, but I was so happy to see him, I practically jumped into his arms. "Everything's okay now. How did you know I was here?"

"Juniper called me," he said, as if he'd assumed I knew that.

"You didn't think I'd come out of the library without calling for help, did you?" Juniper said. "I might show bad judgment in the elves I date, but I don't have a death wish."

"Thank you." I left Nick's embrace to give her a hug. "I was so worried you'd be mad at me forever."

"I misjudged everything," she admitted. "But when I found out Chip was having me spied on, I knew you were right about him." She shuddered. "I never dreamed he would lash out like that. He was always so careful to hide anything negative."

I'd seen signs—passive-aggressive digs, mostly. Tonight he'd surprised me, too. "He was a powder keg."

"I should have seen it." She looked up, her face darkening. "And I'm sorry. I shouldn't have called you rhythm-challenged."

I laughed. "You might have been right about that, actually." I took a moment to admire her Lucasta outfit. "Nice costume, by the way."

She turned, showing off her hump. "Thanks. I made it myself."

I was a little disappointed in my own costume now. The band jacket and plumed hat detracted from my witchiness. I still needed to go back to the band shell to retrieve my witch hat and cape.

Crinkles finally arrived, followed by the Christmastown ambulance service. Two elves hoisted Chip onto a gurney to cart him off for Doc Honeytree to look at. When Crinkles wandered back over to us, I asked him, "Did you find Pixie and Louie?"

"Not yet. They escaped during the snow monster attack."

"Escaped where?"

"Someone saw them on a snowmobile, heading north."

Toward the Farthest Frozen Reaches, I had no doubt. They'd said they wouldn't care if they were exiled, as long as they could be together. Fugitives could spend their entire lives hiding out in that wilderness. They could also lose their lives in a hundred unpleasant ways.

"They exiled themselves rather than wait for the law to do it," I said.

"I sent Ollie after them, but I doubt he'll be able to catch up." Crinkles took out his pocket watch. "He's due back any minute. I told him to meet me at the band shell soon."

"What for?" I asked.

The constable looked at me as if I'd lost my wits. "The raffle draw."

Unbelievable. The entire town had descended into pandemonium, but Crinkles hadn't lost his focus on that raffle.

"That's still on?"

"Of course." He seemed astonished that I would suggest otherwise. Even after a night of snow monsters, drunken reindeer mayhem, and a crazed, knife-wielding elf optician, the show must go on.

Nick stepped forward. "It wouldn't be a bad idea for the town to gather together after all we've been through. We can reassure everyone that the danger is past—all of it. Plus we can make plans for cleaning up, repairing the damage from Ermlau, and begin gathering all the pumpkins."

Lucia added, "We also need to advise the reindeer to destroy all uneaten cookies."

Crinkles bobbed on his heels. "That's right. Like a real community meeting. *And* have the raffle drawing."

Which gave me an idea. I looked at Juniper. "Maybe some of the band will still be around."

She smiled. "We could at least be there to do a fanfare for the raffle draw."

"And a drumroll." I could handle that.

"Hop in the sleigh," Nick said. "I'll give you both a ride."

The raffle would probably be a good thing, after all. Pixie and Louie might have escaped being the jail's next residents, but there was Chip to consider now. If he survived his collision with Quasar, he would surely do time for attacking me.

"Chip likes nice things," Juniper said wryly on the drive to Peppermint Pond. "He'll appreciate the jail's new wallpaper."

I hoped he'd be able to appreciate the jail's new wallpaper for a very long time.

Chapter 26

The night after Halloween, once everything had settled down, Jingles brought a special nightcap up for Nick and me. "It's my newest creation," he said as he put down the tray on the table by the sofa in our bedroom. "I thought you might want a little something to celebrate a job well done."

It was hard to look at the results of the past week as a raging success. There was still snow monster damage to fix, two fugitives to find, two formerly upstanding elves in jail, a best friend with a battered heart, and a hundred eighty hungover reindeer.

But I couldn't deny a nightcap sounded soothing. I picked up a glass, lifted my glass to Nick and Jingles, and took a sip.

Fired burned down my throat. Fire and pumpkin spice.

I coughed. "What is it?"

"I call it a Pumpkin Slammer." Jingles looked pleased. "I was going to call it a Pumpkin Slayer Slammer, but then I thought—with Tiny's memorial service tomorrow—maybe that was too soon."

"If Tiny was Pumpkin Slayer," Nick said.

"Of course he was. Who else could it have been?" I took another sip. The kick wasn't so bad when you were ready for it. "Crinkles and I finally looked over the shoe-size list Louie had drawn up. Who wore a four and a quarter? Tiny Sparkle-toe. Ollie's going through Tiny's computer now to see what else he can find."

"Why bother?" Jingles asked. "The case has been solved."

Nothing would convince Jingles that he hadn't cracked the whole Tiny Sparkletoe murder case practically single-handedly. And I wasn't about to try.

When the door closed behind Jingles, Nick and I sank down to sit on the rug, our backs against the sofa. A warm fire glowed in the bedroom hearth. I set a handled plastic pumpkin bucket full of treats next to each of us. "Now for the fun part," I said.

He peered into his pumpkin. "I don't understand."

"It's a sacred childhood ritual. It's called haggling over the Halloween spoils." I held up a white chocolate–covered marshmallow snow monster. "I'll trade you this for a caramel Neldor."

Nick moved his pumpkin out of reach. "No way."

I laughed. "So you *do* understand. What if I threw in two peppermint devils?"

His jaw worked. "Well . . ."

Peppermint devils were his weakness. I dangled two foil-wrapped devils, tempting him.

Caving in, he swiped them from me, plus the nasty snow monster. I grabbed my Neldor in triumph and unwrapped it before he could change his mind.

We hadn't gone trick-or-treating, but I'd bought the pumpkins off Elfbay and had gathered the goodies from the sale bins at the Cornucopia and from Dash's Candy and Nut Shoppe. We'd had plenty of frights; I wanted Nick to have at least a little taste of the fun part of Halloween.

He bit into a mint devil. "These pumpkins might be the only ones left in Santaland now." The rest had been collected and sent across the forest to the Farthest Frozen Reaches. One of the delivery sleighs had been driven by Quince and Pocket, off on their first adventure.

The thought of Quince made me glance around the room.

"What is it?" Nick asked.

"Quince gave me a farewell gift. He told me to open it in private."

"Would you like me to leave?" Nick joked.

"He just meant to wait until I got back to the castle." He'd been too embarrassed for me to open it in front of the crowd around us at the time, which had included Jake, Crinkles, and Ollie. I tried to remember where I'd put the gift.

My phone was ringing. I didn't know where that was, either.

Nick, who possessed a better radar for tracking my purse than I did, pointed to a nearby chair. I lunged for it and was able to retrieve the phone and swipe before the call went to messages.

"Claire!" I exclaimed. "How are you?"

"I'm three-glasses-of-wine regretful," she said. "I'm calling to grovel."

"What for?"

"For even insinuating you'd want to kill your husband."

I looked over at Nick, whose hand was moving surreptitiously toward my pile of caramel Neldors. "It's okay. I do occasionally have homicidal impulses." I glared at him, and he retracted his hand.

"Also," Claire said, "I shouldn't have sent you the Santa stuff I found at the inn. You must think I'm turning into a nosy busybody like Damaris Sproat."

"Never."

"Believe me," she assured me, "there are worse kinks than a Santa fetish. Did I ever tell you about the guy I dated who was seriously into Smurfs cosplay?"

"Uh, no, you didn't, and don't feel obliged to, either."

"I won't go into detail. Suffice it to say I've still got a tub of blue body makeup somewhere."

I laughed.

"Anyway," she continued, "if you ever find yourself in a Mrs. Claus outfit—"

I couldn't let her go on. "I shouldn't have been so secretive, Claire. I've been meaning to tell you more about life up here. It's pretty amazing. I'd like you to come visit and see it all for yourself."

I looked meaningfully at Nick, and he gave a thumbs-up.

"I'd love to," Claire said. "When?"

I considered putting her off until next year, but why? "What would you think about a white Christmas?"

"Oh." Never had one syllable carried so much reluctance.

"What's the matter?" I asked.

I could hear her take a gulp of wine. "It's just that I'm more of a Christmas person than you are."

"I wouldn't be too sure of that." I smiled at Nick. "We celebrate the holiday pretty big up here. I don't think you'll be disappointed."

"Well . . . I'll think about it."

"Do," I said. "I believe we can even provide free transportation. Nick's going to be flying down your way on Christmas Eve."

After I hung up, Nick leveled an amused look at me. "You might have warned her about the flying sleigh."

"I'll call her back in a few days and tell her to stock up on Dramamine." Putting the phone back in the purse, my hand found the gift Quince had given me. I pulled it out and gasped as I unwrapped it.

"What is it?" Nick asked.

I held up the DVD. *"Neldor Three: The Icy Vengeance."*

A forbidden video. Nick and I both eyed the entertainment cabinet in the corner, then shared a conspiratorial glance. "Shall we?" he asked.

We locked the doors, gathered our candy, and settled in for the night.

Acknowledgments

A book is written solo, but it takes a lot of people to usher it into the world. I'm so grateful to John Scognamiglio, Carly Sommerstein, Larissa Ackerman, and all the other wonderful people at Kensington Books who are responsible for making the Mrs. Claus series a reality.

Mrs. Claus and the Halloween Homicide was written during the 2020 pandemic. I'm incredibly lucky to belong to wonderful groups of authors who made the months of isolation and canceled conferences bearable. My fellow writers at Sisters in Crime-Canada West and Crime Writers of Canada always do a great job reaching out and providing online activities. Special thank-yous to Winona Kent and Charlotte Morganti, who have worked overtime to keep mystery writers in British Columbia connected.

As always, I owe endless thanks to my sister, Suzanne Bass, for being my first reader, and to Joe Newman, for everything.

Connect with Us

Visit us online at
KensingtonBooks.com
to read more from your favorite authors, see books
by series, view reading group guides, and more.

Join us on social media

for sneak peeks, chances to win books and prize packs,
and to share your thoughts with other readers.

**facebook.com/kensingtonpublishing
twitter.com/kensingtonbooks**

Tell us what you think!

To share your thoughts, submit a review,
or sign up for our eNewsletters, please visit:
KensingtonBooks.com/TellUs.